DEATH COMES TO LONDON

Center Point
Large Print

Also by Catherine Lloyd and available from Center Point Large Print:

Death Comes to the Village

**This Large Print Book carries the
Seal of Approval of N.A.V.H.**

DEATH COMES TO LONDON

CATHERINE LLOYD

CENTER POINT LARGE PRINT
THORNDIKE, MAINE

This Center Point Large Print edition
is published in the year 2015 by arrangement with
Kensington Publishing Corp.

The text of this Large Print edition is unabridged.
In other aspects, this book may vary
from the original edition.
Printed in the United States of America
on permanent paper.
Set in 16-point Times New Roman type.

ISBN: 978-1-62899-442-1

Library of Congress Cataloging-in-Publication Data

Lloyd, Catherine, 1963–
Death comes to London / Catherine Lloyd. — Center Point
Large Print edition.
    pages ; cm
    Summary: "A season in London promises a welcome change of pace
for two friends from the village of Kurland St. Mary—until murder
makes a debut"—Provided by publisher.
    ISBN 978-1-62899-442-1 (library binding : alk. paper)
    1. Great Britain—History—Regency, 1811–1820—Fiction.
    2. Large type books. I. Title.
PS3612.L557D426 2014
823´.92—dc23
                                                        2014044231

This one is for Dermot, my husband.
Trust me, he deserves a dedication in every book
I write, because he's absolutely wonderful.

Acknowledgments

I'd like to thank Steven Broomfield, the honorary archivist from Horse Power, the Museum of The King's Royal Hussars, in Winchester, England (www.horsepowermuseum.co.uk) for his help in dressing my hero appropriately in his uniform.

I also appreciate the experts of the Beau Monde special interest chapter of the RWA for answering questions about every aspect of Regency life.

Several people read through this manuscript prior to release, including Amanda Brice, Ruth Long, Sabrina Darby, Dayna Hart, and Sadie Haller. I'd like to thank them for their wisdom and patience in helping me move that dead body closer to the start of the book!

Finally, I'd like to mention that the Marsh test for detecting arsenic in a human body came slightly later than the date of this novel—in the 1830s—but Orfila, who is considered "the Father of Toxicology," had his book published in 1813, which meant it was available in 1817 for Lucy to read.

DEATH
COMES TO
LONDON

Chapter 1

Kurland St. Mary, England
March 1817

It was a beautiful spring morning and Major Robert Kurland intended to enjoy it to the fullest. After breakfast he planned to take a turn around the home park with Simmons, his head gardener. It would be his first opportunity to discuss his plans without the loving interference of his aunt Rose, who had very particular ideas about what should be planted where, and often forgot whom the garden actually belonged to. Then in the afternoon, he was going to the home farm to discuss the more agricultural aspects of the Kurland estate with Mr. Pethridge.

For the first time in more than two years, Robert was almost content.

"Here's the post for you, sir."

"Thank you." He glanced up as Foley, his butler, placed a silver tray with a pile of letters on it by his elbow. "Is there more coffee and some fresh toast?"

"Of course, Major. It's good to see you eating so heartily again." Foley offered him a fond smile. "Oh, and, sir, don't forget that you have Mr. Thomas Fairfax coming for his interview at three o'clock this afternoon."

Robert paused, the letter knife in his hand. "I had forgotten it was today."

"I thought you might have, sir. I only remembered because as Mr. Fairfax was traveling down from the north, we offered him a room for the night. Mrs. Bloomfield was asking me which bedroom you wanted to put him in."

"How would I know? One that's clean, dry, and doesn't have leaks in the ceiling will suffice."

Foley looked pained. "All the bedrooms at the manor are up to the highest standard now, sir. It's more a question of where will he *suit*. As your potential land agent, he might well be a gentleman, so it wouldn't do to offer him a bed in the attics, now would it?"

Robert groaned. "Foley, put him wherever you like, but please try not to mention the subject to me again, would you?"

"As you wish, sir. You know you can trust my impeccable judgment in these matters."

Foley left and Robert looked through his correspondence, which consisted of his usual monthly letter from Aunt Rose, and four or five bills from tradesmen pertaining to his spate of renovations to the manor house. He'd keep his aunt's letter to read later, and pass the rest over to Miss Harrington to deal with in her usual efficient manner. Stacking the post in a neat pile, he hesitated. Miss Harrington wouldn't be here for much longer to deal with anything. She'd gotten some foolish notion in her head about rushing off to London for the Season in search of a husband.

He snorted. She had no idea what she was letting herself in for. In his opinion London society could go hang. If he never had to return to the city he'd consider himself a lucky man. And what was wrong with Kurland St. Mary? It was a quiet, peaceful place where very little happened to disturb the rural way of life that had contented his ancestors for centuries.

He finished his coffee. Perhaps after the shocks of the previous year, Miss Harrington had a valid reason not to feel safe in her current environment. A few months in the chaos and filth of London would surely change her mind and bring her home. He would be willing to wager a large sum on it.

A buzz of noise made him lower his morning newspaper and turn toward the open door of the breakfast room. Foley was talking to someone female and excitable, which was never a good combination at this hour in the morning. After perusing the paper, he'd planned to walk along the terrace to ease the ache in his thigh and smoke one of the cigarillos Foley refused to allow him to enjoy in his own house.

He half-rose from his chair and grabbed his cane, but it was far too late to flee. He remained standing instead and tried to look agreeable.

"Miss Harrington and Miss Anna Harrington to

see you, sir." Foley bowed low. "I have your fresh coffee and toast. Shall I fetch some more cups?"

"Oh, yes, *please,* Foley," Miss Anna said. "I'm quite thirsty after that walk." She twirled around to face Robert, her beautiful face aglow. "I do hope you don't mind us arriving while you are still at breakfast, Major, but we wanted to see you before we left."

Robert nodded at Miss Anna and waited until she took a seat at the table before addressing her quieter companion.

"Good morning, Miss Harrington."

"Major Kurland."

When Miss Lucy Harrington turned toward him he suffered a small shock. She looked quite unlike herself in a new traveling outfit and a blue bonnet that he'd never seen before. He held out a chair for her. "Please be seated. I apologize for still being at the breakfast table."

"We're the ones who should be apologizing for calling so early." Miss Harrington shot a fond glance at Anna, who was chatting to Foley. "But my sister could not be dissuaded from her plan."

"I'm glad you both came. When are you leaving?"

"As soon as Sophia and Mrs. Hathaway arrive to collect us. We're expecting them at noon." Miss Harrington lowered her voice. "Are you sure you are going to be all right?"

"Whatever do you mean, Miss Harrington?"

14

"There's no need to stiffen up, I wasn't trying to imply anything, just that you still need a secretary, a valet, *and* a land agent, so you will be managing everything by yourself."

"Despite your fears, I am quite capable. In fact, I have an interview today with a potential land agent."

Her brow cleared. "Oh, yes, that's right. Mr. Fairfax. He sounded quite satisfactory in his correspondence. I *do* hope you can get along with him." She sighed. "I almost wish I could be here."

"To interview him in my place?"

"You are rather impolite, Major."

"I prefer to consider myself *direct*. In my opinion, if the man can't stand up to me in an interview, he won't be worth employing anyway."

"You may have a point. He does have to work for you, after all." She removed her gloves. "Betty, our housemaid, has an uncle who is looking for a position as a valet. Would you like me to ask for his references?"

"You might as well." He sighed. "I'm finding it rather more difficult than I anticipated to replace my valet."

"I'm sure Betty's uncle will be perfectly suited to the task."

"I'll need to meet the man first."

"Naturally. I'll get his direction from Betty and write to him when I am settled in London."

His good humor dissipated. "I wish you'd reconsider leaving Kurland St. Mary."

"Why?"

"Because I"—he scowled down at his plate—"I've become used to the way you manage things around here."

"You mean you appreciate having an unpaid drudge to do your bidding."

"I don't think of you as a drudge. You are far more useful than that."

"I only offered to help you on a temporary basis until you hired a secretary of your own. As an unmarried woman, my presence in your house at all hours of the day and night is not acceptable."

He frowned. "No one has said anything untoward to me about your being here."

"Well, they wouldn't, would they? Everyone is too in awe of you to dare to criticize a war hero."

"You have been criticized?"

She looked away from him. "Yes, the majority opinion being that I have set my cap at you and am determined to be the new lady of the manor."

"But that's ridiculous."

"Thank you." She folded her gloves and placed them on the table. "That's one of the reasons why I decided to go to London and seek my own husband."

"Which means you might not come back at all."

"I'm sorry, Major, but I cannot live my life for the benefit of every male of my acquaintance. The twins are settled at school, and Anthony is with your old regiment. If I don't leave my father now, I am quite certain that I will never have the opportunity again."

"So you'd rather be subject to the will of one man, your husband? I think you'll find that harder than you imagine, Miss Harrington."

"Not if I choose carefully."

"By finding a spouse who is willing to let you have your way in everything?" He inclined his head an inch. "Good luck with that."

"You—" She blinked hard at him. "You have no right to judge me. My choices are my own. I do not have to explain myself to anyone."

Robert opened his mouth to argue and then closed it again. "I apologize, Miss Harrington. What I meant to say is that I will miss your company. I wish you a safe journey and a successful outcome to your husband-hunting."

"Thank you." She turned her attention to her coffee cup.

Robert looked across the table at Anna Harrington, who was also dressed in brand-new clothes and was a vision of soft gold curls and sparkling blue eyes. Robert doubted she would have a problem acquiring a husband in London at all.

"Are you looking forward to going to Town, Miss Anna?"

Anna smiled and clasped her hands to her bosom. "Oh, *yes.* . . ."

Several hours later, Robert sat in his study awaiting the arrival of Mr. Thomas Fairfax. From all reports, the Hathaways and the Harringtons had departed Kurland St. Mary at noon, and would be conveyed to London in easy stages in the Hathaway family coach. Miss Harrington hadn't quite forgiven him for his petulant outburst over her leaving, and had departed without giving him her usual smile.

He felt bad about that. He of all people knew how restricted her life had become since the death of her mother and how she longed to escape the rectory. She deserved to be happy. If it hadn't have been for her, he would still be cowering in bed unable to walk and unwilling to accept his place in the world. She'd put up with his ill humor, bullied and cajoled him first into a wheelchair, and then outside to reestablish his connection with the lands his family had owned and farmed for centuries.

Who was he to begrudge her the same freedoms he had always taken for granted? He doubted she'd find a spouse who was willing to put up with her rather managing ways, but she deserved the opportunity to find that out for herself. She was no fool. If such a paragon existed amongst the vapid fops of a London Season, he was certain she would discover him.

He imagined her face as she stepped out of the Hathaway carriage and got her first sight of the teeming, bustling city of London. Would she let it overawe her and behave like a subdued country mouse? Somehow he doubted it. She'd probably treat society with the same lack of respect as she did him. Such boldness in the notoriously fickle world of the upper ten thousand could be a blessing or a curse.

Lucy gently wiggled her nose, which had been pressed up against the grimy window of the coach for what seemed like hours. The road had widened again, and the carriage slowed to a crawl to avoid the river of people streaming through the streets. She had never seen so many people before in her life, and had never imagined that so many would choose to live in such squalor and close proximity.

Mrs. Hathaway patted her arm.

"Are you all right, my dear? We'll take Anna to Clavelly House first and then proceed to Dalton Street. I *do* hope the house Perry has chosen for us is acceptable."

"I'm sure it will be, Mrs. Hathaway. It is a shame that he has been called away to the embassy in France and that we will not see him."

Lucy stared up at the tall white town houses of the square they were turning into. "Is this truly where my uncle and aunt live? Uncle David and my father do not like each other at all, and we have never visited before."

"If we have the correct address." Mrs. Hathaway looked worried. "It is rather grand, isn't it?"

Anna positively bounced in her seat. "Uncle David is an *earl*. He is supposed to live like this."

"I often forget how high and mighty your family are, dear Lucy," Mrs. Hathaway murmured. "I can only hope that they will treat us with kindness."

Lucy was about to say something encouraging when the carriage drew to a swaying halt and a footman leaped forward to open the door. Anna and Sophia were the quickest to alight, leaving Lucy to assist Mrs. Hathaway down the small steps. She kept her on her arm as they ascended into the mansion and were greeted in the hall by a tall man who bore a distinct resemblance to their father.

"Good evening." He bowed to Mrs. Hathaway. "Ma'am, may I take you up to my wife? She is so looking forward to meeting you." He smiled at the sisters. "I do hope we can put our family grievances behind us and enjoy this reconciliation."

Lucy curtsied. "We are very willing to do that, sir, and very grateful to you for offering Anna a chance to enjoy a Season."

She relinquished Mrs. Hathaway to the earl and

followed meekly behind him as he took them up the stairs and into a large drawing room on the first floor. The house was decorated in the latest classical style and in the most expensive taste. Lucy found herself cataloguing how much it would cost to make such luxurious curtains and chair coverings, and then reminded herself that it was none of her concern.

Anna squeezed her hand, even her natural confidence awed by the grandeur around them. When they entered the drawing room, the countess had already risen from her seat and was welcoming Mrs. Hathaway and Sophia. Lucy hung back a little as the countess moved toward them, her pleasant face all smiles.

"And you must be Ambrose's girls." She offered them each a hand and they curtsied. "You are Anna, I think? Your father said you were blond and very pretty."

Anna blushed charmingly. "It is a pleasure to meet you, my lady. I am so grateful that you offered to bring me out."

"Please call me Aunt Jane. I was already set to bring my daughter, Julia, out and, as I said to your father, if I was forced to scale the social world once more, another young lady to chaperone would not make any difference."

She turned to Lucy. "And you must be Lucy."

"Yes, my lady."

"I understand that you are staying with the

Hathaways, but you must not hesitate to consider this your home as well. I consider you both as in my charge."

"That's very kind of you," Lucy said. "But I want this to be Anna's moment, not mine."

The countess drew them over to a sofa and sat down between them. "You don't wish to be married, Lucy?"

"Oh, I do, Aunt, but my expectations are far more modest than Anna's." She glanced over at the Hathaways, who were conversing with the earl. "My friend Sophia is a widow. She and her mother will be able to chaperone me quite adequately."

"But if they are unavailable, you will come to me." Aunt Jane held Lucy's gaze. "And when we have our ball here, you will be part of the receiving line."

"If you wish, my lady." Lucy was reluctant to start arguing with her aunt on their very first meeting. "But my father—"

"Your father is a man who has no understanding of such things. If I choose to aid you in your search for a husband, then he has nothing further to say in the matter." She looked Lucy over. "I think you will do very well, indeed."

Lucy held her tongue as the countess beckoned to her husband. "Will you ring the bell, dear, and ask Julia and Max to come down?"

She had a sense that she'd met her match in her

aunt, who appeared to be just as managing as everyone insisted Lucy was. It was also comforting to know that the countess didn't share her father's opinion that she was too old and too plain to find a husband. She glanced over at Anna, who was smiling again, and felt far happier about leaving her with her uncle and aunt than she had earlier.

When the door opened to admit the butler and her two cousins she rose to her feet and was introduced to them. Julia was of a similar age to Anna and the two girls were soon talking as if they'd known each other for years. The eldest son, Max, was a little more reticent than his sister, but perfectly amiable and more than willing to meet his new relatives.

She'd never met her cousins before. After the death of their father, the rector and his brother had fallen out and visits between the two families had ceased. Lucy had never been given the exact details, only that it had to do with her father's portion of the unentailed part of the estate. Communication was reestablished when the dowager countess died and Lucy insisted on writing a letter of condolence. That led to an exchange of letters resulting in the invitation for Anna to join the family and be chaperoned by the current countess.

Eventually, Mrs. Hathaway caught Lucy's eye and reluctantly stood up.

"We will have to be going. We've left the horses standing for far too long as it is." She turned to Anna. "Come and give me a hug, my dear."

Anna obliged and then made her way to Lucy. It was the first time in their lives that they would be apart.

"Oh, Lucy . . ."

She hugged Anna hard and then stood back with a decisive nod. "I will send you a note first thing tomorrow so that we can make plans. I'm quite certain you will be happy here."

Anna nodded, her eyes bright and her mouth trembling at the corners. "I wish—"

"You will be fine." Lucy blew her a kiss and started for the door before her sister noticed how close she was to tears herself. That would never do. Aunt Jane followed her out, tucking her hand into the crook of Lucy's elbow.

"We will take good care of her, I promise."

Lucy nodded and kept her gaze fixed on the stairs, which seemed to be blurring in front of her eyes.

"And I meant it about you considering this your home, too."

"Thank you."

They reached the grand entranceway and Lucy followed Sophia out into the carriage and sat down, her face averted. As the horses moved off, a lace-edged handkerchief appeared under her nose. She took it gratefully and blew her nose.

By the time they reached the far more modest street where the Hathaways had rented their town house, Lucy was able to tuck the handkerchief into her reticule and step out of the carriage with her usual air of assurance. She couldn't forget that she'd come to London with a *purpose.* Now all she had to do was ensure that she was suc-cessful.

Chapter 2

M ajor Kurland!"
Foley burst into Robert's study without knocking, startling his employer, who was reading through one of the accounts books.

"What?" Robert demanded. "This had better be important, Foley; you just made me forget the sheep tally in my head."

Foley proffered a silver salver on which lay a single letter with an elaborate seal. Robert picked up the letter and frowned. "Who's it from?"

"The Prince Regent!"

"That's extremely unlikely. Why would the prince be writing to a nonentity like me?" He perused the envelope, noting the Carlton House address and the scrawl of a regal signature franking the corner of the letter. Taking out his knife, he carefully slit the seal and smoothed out the single page concealed within. Eventually he raised his head to find Foley almost dancing with impatience in front of him.

"I'll be damned. It *is* from the Prince Regent—well, from his personal secretary, which is almost the same thing. Apparently the prince has heard of my heroism during the Battle of Waterloo and wishes to reward me for my service. Good Lord, I'm to be made a baronet."

"Oh, sir!" Foley clasped his hands together. "I'm so delighted for you. A hereditary title that can be passed down to your children!"

"If I ever have any children." Robert read the letter again. "I wonder if it's possible to refuse such a thing?"

"Major, you *wouldn't,* you . . ."

He sighed. "I don't think it's possible to say no. It seems as if I'm to proceed to London with all haste to meet the Prince Regent and receive his thanks in person. Devil take it, I *hate* London."

"I'll need to press your new dress uniform and make sure that your weapons are polished and . . ." Foley paused. "What about your lack of a valet? Perhaps I should accompany you to London myself. We can't have you meeting the Prince Regent without looking your best."

"Foley . . ."

His butler was already heading for the door muttering to himself, so Robert let him go. He returned his attention to the letter. How on earth had the Prince Regent got to hear about him? He flipped the letter over and noticed that directly underneath his name was printed in smaller letters *L. Harrington, secretary.*

His frown deepened. Had Miss Harrington taken it upon herself to write to the Prince Regent and draw his attention to Robert's so-called heroics? Why would she do such a thing? If he had to go to London, he would make sure to find his meddling neighbor and ask her what the devil she'd been thinking.

London was far more tiring and intimidating than Lucy had expected. As the Hathaways had engaged an extremely competent staff, she also had very little to do, which was disconcerting in itself. Apparently, living like a young lady at home was remarkably boring. They'd shopped for new clothes, found an excellent dressmaker to bring them up to scratch and a milliner whose new style bonnets were reasonably priced. She yawned discreetly behind her hand as Sophia started talking about which of the events they should attend.

"Lucy! Pay attention!"

She jumped and returned her gaze to her friend, who was waving an invitation card practically under her nose.

"I'm happy to do whatever you want, Sophia."

"Thanks to you, Lucy, we'll meet all the right people at the Clavelly ball tonight." Sophia clutched the invitation to her bosom. "Do you think the countess will be able to get us admitted to *Almack's?*"

Lucy raised an eyebrow. "Is it really that important? I've heard the refreshments are indifferent and the company insufferable."

"Who told you that?"

"Major Kurland."

Sophia dismissed him with an airy wave of her hand. "Major Kurland is never pleased with anything. They don't call it the Marriage Mart for nothing, Lucy. All the most eligible gentlemen attend their balls."

"So it's rather like the county fair at Saffron Walden?"

Sophia mock-frowned at her. "If we are granted vouchers for Almack's, I would be in *heaven.*"

"Then I'll write to my aunt immediately and ask her if it is possible." She walked over to the small desk at the end of the drawing room. "Have you met any man you particularly like yet?"

Sophia sighed. "Not really. They are all very nice, but none of them can hold a candle to my Charlie. I know I said I wished to remarry and have children, but I don't intend to just pick anyone. Charlie would only want the best for me."

"Well, he was an exceptional man." Lucy drew out a fresh sheet of paper. "I doubt it will be easy to replace him." She looked up as the butler appeared, and took the two letters he offered her from the tray. "Thank you."

As Sophia and Mrs. Hathaway discussed what they would wear to the Clavelly ball, Lucy wrote to her aunt and then turned her attention to the letters she'd received. After a week away, news from home was definitely welcome. She was surprised how much she missed the irascible Major Kurland and Kurland St. Mary.

"Oh dear."

"What is it, Lucy?" Sophia came over to her.

"Nicholas Jenkins is coming to London expressly to see Anna."

"Well, that isn't a surprise, is it? Everyone knows he's in love with her. He was threatening to follow her here months ago."

"But I didn't think he'd actually do it." Lucy passed the letter to Sophia. "I can't wait to tell Anna this news."

"Foley, stop fussing." Robert stood patiently as his butler brushed down the dark blue coat of his uniform for the third time. "I'll be fine. I'm not seeing the Prince Regent this morning. I'm just going to my regimental headquarters."

"And you still need to look your best."

Foley tweaked the ornate gold braiding cascading down from Robert's shoulder before finally handing him his tall hat.

"You look very smart, Major."

"Thank you."

In truth, after almost two years without active military service, Robert felt quite uncomfortable in his uniform. After he'd been cut out of his last set of clothing after Waterloo, Bookman, his former valet, had ordered him a whole new kit from his military tailor. The heavy fabrics were rigid and the gold braid that covered most of the front of his coat was so stiff it wouldn't lie down properly. He'd heard the Prince Regent had a hand in the design of the 10th Hussars uniform, and that wouldn't surprise him. It was rather too ornate for his taste and hopelessly impractical in battle. But that was true of most uniforms. At least the majority of his regiment wore blue, unlike the poor redcoats who stood out like a sore thumb in every battle scenario imaginable. He'd been told that red had been chosen so that blood didn't show and strike fear into the hearts of the enemy.

Somehow he doubted that worked.

He tucked his scarlet peaked shako under his arm, avoiding the feathers, and assessed his appearance in the mirror. He looked quite impressive. His fingers traced his clean-shaven upper lip where once, like most of his military associates, he'd sported a fine moustache. He hadn't the heart to grow it back. Foley had made his boots shine and polished all the metal buttons and facings on his coat until he could see his reflection in them.

"Your sword, Major?"

"Ah, yes, thank you." Robert threw the gray fur-lined pelisse back over his shoulder and buckled on his sword. "I think I'll do. Can you go down and find a hackney cab for me?"

Foley paused at the door. "You don't wish to drive yourself, or ride, sir? I believe your phaeton is available, as are several of your horses."

"Not today."

He might look the part of a dashing Hussar officer, but the thought of actually getting back on a horse still terrified him. Of all the scars left from his horrific injuries at Waterloo, that ridiculous fear was the hardest to bear. He'd managed to force himself to sit in a horse-drawn vehicle, but even that brought him out in a sweat. The thought of navigating through the streets of London on the back of a nervous steed was too much for him to deal with.

He'd become what the professional soldiers jokingly referred to as a Hyde Park soldier, one who never saw active service, but always looked impeccably dressed and was seen in all the right social quarters. His mouth twisted and he turned away from his resplendent image. Better to get this over with. If there was a way to slide out of accepting the baronetcy, his commander in chief would surely know of it.

Robert went down to the hotel entrance and got into the hackney cab Foley had called for him. If his visit with his commanding officer went well, he might be more inclined to seek out the Harrington sisters and see how they were faring in the bustling metropolis. Foley had managed to find both addresses, and it would be uncivil of him not to acknowledge the ladies.

He put on his gloves and settled back in the seat. And if Miss Harrington was responsible for bringing him to the attention of his regiment's fond patron, the Prince Regent, he might have a few specific things to say for her ears alone.

When the hackney pulled up, Robert alighted with as much speed as he could manage and, using his walking stick to balance on the uneven cobbled street, paid off the driver. Just as he approached the daunting array of steps, a man coming down them hailed him.

"Major Kurland? Is that you? By all that's holy!"

He looked up into the familiar face of one of his fellow officers.

"Lieutenant Broughton. What a pleasure to see you." Robert transferred his stick into his left hand and shook Broughton's hand. "What brings you here today?"

"I'm selling my commission." Broughton made a face. "There's no point in remaining in the service if the regiment is bound for the Americas or India, and I don't want to sit around on half pay." His gaze swept over Robert, lingering on his walking stick. "I heard you were badly injured at Waterloo."

"As you see, I'm probably going to be selling out myself."

Broughton glanced up the steps. "Do you have an appointment?"

"Yes."

"Then I won't keep you." He paused. "Would you consider meeting me at my club when you're done? It's Fletchers on Portland Square, a new meeting place for those of a scientific bent."

"I would be delighted." Robert had always liked Broughton's no-nonsense approach to life, although some of the other officers had thought him lacking in social graces. Lacking them himself, Robert had never taken offense at the man's blunt manners. "I shouldn't be too long."

"Where are you putting up?"

"Fenton's."

Broughton tipped his hat. "I look forward to seeing you again very shortly."

Robert laboriously made his way up the steps and inside the dark paneled entrance hall with its massive portrait of the Prince Regent dressed in an even more glorified version of the uniform of the Royal 10th Hussars. A man rose to greet him from behind a desk.

"How may I help you, Major?"

Robert saluted. "I have an appointment with

Lieutenant Colonel Sir George Quentin. I'm Major Robert Kurland."

"Yes, sir, I'll show you right up."

Robert followed the man into the shadowy depths of the house and into another anteroom, where the lieutenant colonel's aide guarded his master's door.

"Major Kurland." The aide snapped to attention. "The lieutenant colonel will see you now."

Robert saluted again and was taken through into the lair of the lieutenant colonel. He was an interesting man of Germanic origins who had been famously court-martialed for excessive brutality to his men in 1814 and had survived to continue his career. Privately, Robert thought him something of a tyrant, but also understood that when dealing with common men, especially soldiers after a battle, displaying superior strength was as necessary as breathing.

"Major Kurland."

Robert saluted and stood to attention. "Sir."

"Please sit down." His commanding officer grimaced. "I see we both still bear the scars of our victory at Waterloo."

"I'm recovering, sir, but I doubt I'll ever return to the regiment."

"That's a shame, Kurland. You were an excellent officer."

"Thank you." Robert wasn't sure if he was relieved or terrified by the thought of the permanent end of his army career. "I intend to sell my commission."

"I don't think you'll have any problem finding a purchaser. Due to our royal patron, this regiment is still considered a prime place to advance a military career." The lieutenant colonel looked down at some papers on his desk. "Now, as to that other matter—"

"May I ask how the Prince Regent heard about my so-called heroic exploits?" Robert interrupted him. "I did nothing more than any other commissioned officer during that battle."

"I beg to disagree, Major. You led the charge that took out that French gun position that had half a brigade pinned down in the ruins."

"I hardly remember, sir. It still doesn't explain how I came to the prince's notice."

"Ah, that would be because your secretary replied to a dinner invitation directly to the Prince Regent's private secretary rather than to our office here. The Regent happened to take a personal interest in who was attending the reception. Sir John McMahon showed him the letter sending your regrets and mentioning your injuries. The prince tends toward the sentimental, as we know, and ordered Sir John to find out about you. I was able to provide additional information, and the Regent decided to honor you with the baronetcy."

Robert shifted uncomfortably in his chair.

"With all due respect, sir, is there any way to decline such an honor? I hardly feel I deserve it."

"I fear it is unavoidable, Major. The prince needs the popular vote too much to resist ennobling a hero. I would prepare yourself to be lionized."

"Damn," Robert said feelingly. "I can't think of anything worse."

"Well, it is too late to do anything about it now. Steps have already been taken to start the process. I've been ordered to bring you to a private audience with the prince in the next week or so."

"I suppose that means I'll have to stay in London? What was my 'secretary' thinking?"

"It's an honor, and one that is well deserved. Let my aide know where you are staying."

"Thank you, sir."

Robert saluted, turned as smartly on his heel as he could, and left the room. So he did have Miss Harrington to thank for the unexpected and unwanted honor. His scowl deepened as he made his way carefully down the steps and looked about for a hackney. After his meeting with Broughton he'd find out the truth from the lady herself.

Luckily, the driver knew exactly which building in Portland Square housed Fletchers and set Robert down right outside it. The interior looked much like any other gentlemen's club he'd ever frequented, but rather less intimidating than

Whites or Boodles. The members appeared a lot younger and rather less blue-blooded, which in his opinion was a blessing. Having served alongside a lot of bumbling aristocratic offspring in the army, he'd never had much patience for the arrogance of the nobility.

And now he was to become one of them. . . .

A footman had him sign the guestbook and wait until Lord Broughton came and claimed him. He followed his old acquaintance through into a paneled room with a roaring fire and several seating areas where a man could choose to read the paper, converse with his friends, or play a hand of cards. Broughton sat in a large wing chair and Robert took the one opposite him. A waiter immediately appeared and they ordered their drinks and were assured that if they wished to eat, the club's dining room was still open.

Robert toasted the other man and then drank his brandy, which was excellent.

"How did your meeting go?" Broughton asked.

"Well enough. I told the Lieutenant Colonel I was going to leave the regiment, and he took it in good part. Do you know who is the agent for selling commissions at the moment?"

"Yes, it's Dagliesh. I'll get his information for you."

"Thank you. And how about yourself? What do you intend to do if you're no longer in the army?"

"Take up my duties as my father's heir."

Broughton's mouth twisted. "Not that I see the old man much. He's stationed in India at present as an ambassador to one of the minor royal courts. My mother's been nagging me for months to settle down and secure the succession."

"All worthy objectives," Robert said diplomatically.

"And all fairly pointless." Broughton sighed. "My *real* objective is to establish my reputation as a man of science."

"And what exactly does that entail?"

"Using my mind instead of blindly following my family's dictates for one. Learning about the new science and sharing my knowledge with the pioneers in their fields."

"It sounds rather like going back to school to me." Robert shuddered. "I intend to concentrate on managing my estate and making it profitable."

Broughton grinned. "Well, to each his own. How long do you intend to stay in London?"

"I'll be here for at least the next couple of weeks."

"If you plan to settle down in the countryside, you can accompany me on my search for a suitable wife, and perhaps find one for yourself."

"I'd rather not contemplate matrimony at this point."

"Then perhaps you might just keep me company? I'd appreciate having a second opinion about my selection."

"I'll certainly do that, but I must warn you that my opinions are rather too forthright for most people." Robert hesitated. Broughton's matter-of-fact manner made him sound rather like he was about to pick a new horse at Tattersalls rather than a bride. "I have little to no understanding of the *ton* and the ramifications of choosing one young lady over another."

"Which is exactly what I need. I'd rather have a military man by my side than anyone else."

Robert put down his brandy glass. "Then if you insist, I'll accompany you. I can hardly leave a fellow officer out in the open without adequate cover."

He suspected he had weeks of dawdling his heels while he waited for his audience with the Prince Regent. Staying in Town would also give him the opportunity to see how the Harrington ladies and Sophia Giffin were dealing with London and perhaps reconnect with some of his old acquaintances.

"There is one young lady I rather like. She is remarkably forthright."

He realized Broughton was still talking. "And who might that be?"

"Miss Chingford. Do you know of her?"

Robert took a deep breath. "Miss *Penelope* Chingford?"

"Yes."

"Then I know her quite well. We were betrothed,

but we mutually decided we wouldn't suit."

"Oh good Lord! What a remarkable coincidence!" Broughton's smile faded. "She hasn't mentioned you by name, but she did indicate that she'd been horribly let down by someone."

"That would be me," Robert said drily. "I had the temerity to be wounded and was no longer the fine physical specimen she required to appear at her side."

"That's hardly fair."

"She had a point. I have no desire to continue my career in the military, or become a leading light of the *ton*, so we definitely would not have suited. It was brave of her to see that." He paused. "I'm sure she would be far happier with a man such as you."

Broughton didn't look convinced as he finished his brandy and then rose to his feet. "Shall we eat here? We can further discuss our plans. I have to escort my family to Almack's this week."

"I understand that it is still considered the best place to find an eligible mate."

"Which is why the female members of my family insist I accompany them. At least if you come with me I can look forward to some decent conversation and maybe a hand of cards."

Robert rose, too, and picked up his cane. "As long as you don't require me to *dance*, Broughton, I am completely at your service."

Chapter 3

Lucy tried not to stare too much at the other guests arriving at the ball, but it was rather difficult. She smoothed down the skirt of her amber silk gown and checked the neckline of her bodice. It was a new dress and she'd felt rather fashionable and daring until she'd seen what the other ladies were wearing.

"Come on, Lucy!"

Sophia and Mrs. Hathaway were already ahead of her, and she hurried to catch up. She spotted her uncle David and then her aunt, and headed toward them. It was hard to see Anna or Julia, who appeared to be surrounded by a crowd of young men.

Sophia elbowed her. "I knew Anna would cause a stir. I'll wager she's filled her dance card twice over."

Lucy hoped so. Anna deserved every opportunity to marry successfully and well, not just because she was beautiful, but because of her sweet, loving nature.

"Ah, there you are, Lucy." Her aunt smiled and beckoned her forward. "Anna was asking where you were. She and Julia have been very popular this evening."

"Lucy!" Anna turned away from her group of

admirers and came over to grasp her sister's hands. "I was wondering what had become of you."

"Sophia's little dog, Hunter, was unwell, so we had to ensure he was settled before we were able to leave."

"Oh dear, is he all right now?"

"He's fine. We discovered he'd found Sophia's box of toffees and had helped himself." Lucy studied Anna's flushed face. "You look happy and that gown is most becoming."

Anna wore a white lace overdress with a pale pink satin slip underneath. The delicate lace also trimmed the bodice and the tiny puffed sleeves.

"Thank you." Anna mock-curtsied and touched her throat. "Father lent me Mother's pearls. Aren't they beautiful?"

"Indeed." Lucy surveyed the packed ballroom and struggled to overcome a pang of jealousy. As far as she was aware, as the oldest daughter, the pearls had been left to her. She assumed her father had thought Anna would make better use of them.

Sophia had already attracted her own share of eager gentlemen around her while Mrs. Hathaway had taken a seat by the countess and was deep in conversation. Lucy smiled politely at a couple of the young men who were waiting for Anna to notice them, and then stiffened.

"Oh, good gracious, not *her.*"

"Who?" Anna asked.

It was too late to hide. Lucy braced herself as Miss Penelope Chingford, who was dressed in vibrant daffodil yellow silk, marched up to them.

"Miss *Harrington?* Miss Anna Harrington?"

"Miss Chingford. I hope you are well." Lucy curtsied.

"As well as a woman who has been forced to return to the marriage mart by an uncaring man can be."

"But I thought you broke off the betrothal, Miss Chingford? Doesn't that make Major Kurland the injured party?"

"Not in the eyes of the *ton.*" Miss Chingford's icy gaze swept over Anna and then returned to Lucy. "Excuse my bluntness, but how exactly did you get invited here? I didn't realize that a country parson's daughters were now considered eligible to receive vouchers for Almack's."

"But then you probably haven't been introduced to our aunt and uncle, the Earl and Countess of Clavelly. Let me remedy that *immediately.* Aunt?"

She performed the necessary introductions, aware that Miss Chingford was silently seething, and enjoying it far more than was proper. When she'd finished, Miss Chingford stalked off to speak to Julia, who was apparently an acquaintance of hers.

Lucy let her gaze wander again as the musicians began to tune their instruments. Two soldiers dressed in dark blue had just arrived and stood in the doorway talking to the hostess. What was it about a man in uniform that set a young lady's heart fluttering? She was no longer young or particularly romantic, but even she was entranced by a well-turned-out military man.

The taller of the two men began to descend the stairs at a slow pace, one gloved hand wrapped around a walking stick.

"Oh my goodness," Lucy whispered.

Across the dance floor, Major Kurland's direct blue gaze met hers. The look on his face was one she was remarkably familiar with, and didn't usually bode well. She unconsciously patted her hair. Did she look out of place? Was he going to tell her she should go home, accept her fate as an old maid, and be useful to him until he married some young chit and no longer needed her?

What on earth was wrong with her? He was hardly likely to berate her in the middle of a ballroom, or indeed care about any of the matters she had so foolishly imagined. He eventually reached her through the throng and bowed.

"Miss Harrington."

Her awestruck gaze took in the gold braid cascading down the front of his uniform, the fur pelisse that swung from one shoulder, and the dark blue coat that matched his eyes.

"Major Kurland, you look *magnificent,*" she breathed.

He scowled at her. "Good Lord, don't tell me you are one of those women who swoon at the sight of a uniform?"

Lucy hastily recollected herself. "Of course not, Major. One word out of your mouth would crush any illusions that I might have about you being some romantical hero."

"I'm glad to hear it, because this is all your fault."

"How so?"

He raised his eyebrows. "Don't you know?"

"If I did I wouldn't be asking you, would I?"

"Lucy, are you all right?" Aunt Jane was now beside her and staring at Robert with considerable interest. "Do you know this gentleman?"

"Yes," Lucy said. "Major, this is my aunt, the Countess of Clavelly."

He saluted. "My apologies, my lady, for not introducing myself to you immediately. I'm Major Robert Kurland."

"Kurland?" Aunt Jane turned to Lucy. "This is the wounded soldier Anna told me you nursed back to health?"

Lucy's cheeks heated. "Hardly that, Aunt. Anna exaggerates somewhat."

"Actually, Miss Anna speaks the truth," Robert said. "Miss Harrington was essential to my recovery. I will always be in her debt."

"I'm glad to hear that she was a comfort to you, Major."

A *compliment* from Major Kurland? Lucy stood back and let her aunt make small talk while she attempted to gather her scattered senses. It was quite overwhelming to see the major in a London ballroom dressed in full uniform. And it was interesting to note that he could be quite charming when he wanted to be—at least to her aunt.

"What brings you to London, Major?" Aunt Jane finally asked the question that had been hovering on Lucy's lips.

"Business with my regiment, my lady." The major gestured at his cane. "As you see, I'm no longer fighting fit and have decided to resign my commission."

"You came all the way to London just to do that?" Lucy interrupted.

The major's enigmatic dark blue gaze rested on hers. "And other matters." The musicians struck up the first chord of a dance and he looked around. "Am I detaining you? If you have a partner waiting I'll come back after I've introduced myself to my friend Broughton's family."

"She does." Aunt Jane turned to her husband. "David? Lucy is ready for you." She smiled at the major. "Why don't you come back and share supper with us? You can converse with dear Lucy during the preceding supper dance. She

46

hasn't been given permission to waltz by the patronesses yet, so she would have to sit it out anyway."

"I'll do that." Major Kurland saluted.

The earl came forward, spent a moment being introduced, and then led Lucy inexorably away onto the dance floor. She tried to see what the major was doing, but it proved impossible to see him and concentrate on the intricacies of the dance.

"You didn't tell us you already had an admirer, Lucy."

She blinked at her uncle. "You mean Major Kurland? Oh no, he's nothing of the sort. He's simply a close neighbor and a good friend of the family."

"He seemed rather keen to speak to you, my dear. That denotes an interest you cannot deny."

"I've been helping him with his household while he was injured. He probably has some questions as to that. I knew he'd never manage everything on his own."

He squeezed her hand. "Mayhap he missed your help more than he thought he would, eh? They do say absence makes the heart grow fonder."

"Not in this case, sir," Lucy said firmly. "If he wishes to speak to me it's more likely that he considers me at fault for something. He is quite tenacious when riled."

The music ended and she sank into a deep

curtsy and allowed her uncle to lead her back to their seats. It would be at least an hour or so before the supper dance. She proposed to put Major Kurland out of her mind until she actually had to face him. To her surprise, one of the older men clustered around Anna turned and smiled.

"Miss Harrington? May I have the pleasure of the next dance?"

She remembered her aunt introducing the man and curtsied. He was a widower with two young children on the lookout for a new wife. "Yes, Mr. Stanford. That would be delightful."

Avoiding the dancers as best he could, Robert made his slow way over to Broughton's side of the ballroom. Lucy danced by with her uncle and he found himself stopping to study her oblivious face. She looked remarkably happy, and quite unlike herself in the fashionable ball gown with its puffed sleeves and low-cut bodice. Not that she looked any different from the other young ladies. It was just that he wasn't used to seeing her so *uncovered.*

"Kurland."

Broughton was waving at him. His friend stood with a group of people who all bore a striking resemblance to him.

"May I introduce my grandmother, the Dowager Countess of Broughton, my mother, the current countess, and my younger brother, Oliver?"

Robert saluted. "Major Robert Kurland at your service. It is a pleasure to meet you all."

The countess smiled and held out her hand to be kissed. She was a handsome woman with the same dark coloring as her oldest son. "Major, a pleasure. James has told us so much about you."

Robert kissed her fingers and then turned to the dowager, who was regarding him with all the warmth of a French soldier at the end of a bayonet. Her hair was white and the family nose was the most prominent feature on her angular, sunken face. She pointed at his cane.

"Are you permanently lame, Major?"

"It's highly likely, my lady. It's been almost two years since my accident. I've yet to recover full use of my leg and I'm about to sell my commission."

"So, I believe, is my grandson, although he has much less of a reason for doing so."

Broughton's smile was tight. "We've already discussed this, Grandmother. I wish to be closer to home."

She snorted. "Like a crow hanging around waiting to pick the carrion from this family's bones."

The countess cleared her throat. "Are you staying in London for long, Major?"

"I'll be here for a few weeks. I haven't been up to Town for years, and there are several business matters awaiting my attention."

The countess glanced up at her eldest son. "Perhaps you would like to invite the major to share our accommodation at the town house? He would be far more comfortable with us than at a hotel."

"There's no need, my lady, I—"

The dowager poked him with her ebony-handled stick. "Come and stay with us, young man. Perhaps you can persuade my grandson to remain in his current position and leave the running of the household to me."

"I—"

Broughton stepped in front of his grandmother. "Did you say that you had some acquaintances you wished me to meet, Kurland?"

"Indeed." Robert smiled at the ladies. "A pleasure to meet you all."

"I'm sorry about that," Broughton said shortly. "My grandmother is not known for the gentleness of her tongue."

A characteristic that many of Broughton's contemporaries would recognize as having come directly down to the lieutenant.

"The previous generation were always rather more forthright with their opinions than our own. She didn't discompose me in the least."

Broughton sighed. "She certainly is an original. And while my father is away she considers herself in charge of the family, which is why she isn't anxious for my return. She doesn't approve

50

of my plans to study the sciences. She'd rather I stayed in the army and killed indiscriminately for a living."

"What do your parents think?"

"They are more than happy to have me home." He hesitated. "My grandmother is frailer than she appears and my brother is . . . fragile."

"Then I would consider it your duty to obey your parents and stay close to home," Robert said diplomatically. "Your grandmother is probably quite grateful, really."

Uncomfortable at being cast in the unlikely role of confidant, he allowed his attention to return to the matter at hand. "Let's go and play cards, and before supper, I'll introduce you to the Misses Harrington, Mrs. Giffin, and her mother. I'm sure they will be delighted to make your acquaintance."

Lucy was enjoying herself far more than she'd expected. She'd danced every dance, and not all of the gentlemen who'd asked her merely wanted information about Anna. Her aunt confided that Anna was a success and that she expected a flood of callers the next day and wanted Lucy and the Hathaways to be present to witness her triumph.

"And here comes Major Kurland, Lucy," her aunt murmured. "He's remarkably prompt."

"As are most military men," Lucy replied. "I wonder who the other officer is?"

"I think we're about to find out."

The major smiled at her aunt. "Countess, Miss Harrington, may I introduce you to Lieutenant Broughton? He served with me in the Tenth during the war."

Aunt Jane nodded. "Ah, yes, Broughton. I know your mother and grandmother. Are you also on leave, Lieutenant?"

"I'm selling my commission, my lady. I find my presence is required here to support my family." He turned to Lucy and bowed. "Miss Harrington, a pleasure."

Lucy studied the lieutenant's unremarkable face. Like the major, he was dark skinned from his time on the continent, but his eyes were brown and his hair had a reddish hue to it. She caught Anna's attention and brought her forward.

"Anna, here are Major Kurland and Lieutenant Broughton."

Broughton's gaze settled on Anna and stayed there as she placed her hand in his.

"Miss Anna, a pleasure."

"Oh yes, indeed."

Lucy glanced at Anna, who was staring up into Broughton's face, her lips slightly parted as he brought her hand to his lips and kissed her fingers.

Major Kurland's eyebrow went up and he cast Lucy a quizzical glance as the pair continued to simply stand and stare at each other. She could understand why Broughton was entranced by her sister, but what on earth was Anna seeing in his far from remarkable face? It must be the uniform. . . . She cleared her throat and Anna stepped back, blushing.

The orchestra struck up the supper dance and Broughton bowed. "Miss Anna, would you do me the honor of dancing with me?"

"Yes."

Before Lucy could remind her that she'd probably promised the dance to someone else, the couple headed for the dance floor and was soon swept away in the wave of dancers.

"Well," Lucy said, "how strange."

"Indeed," said Aunt Jane. "Broughton is the heir of an earl, you know, and from a very respectable family, as I'm sure Major Kurland can vouch."

"Indeed, my lady." Major Kurland offered his arm to Lucy. "Shall we go and find somewhere to sit so that we may converse more privately?"

"The supper room?" Lucy shook out her skirts. "We shall meet you there later, Aunt." Ignoring her aunt's look of quiet satisfaction, she allowed Major Kurland to take her through to the calmer part of the establishment and find them somewhere to sit.

"Would you like some refreshments, Miss Harrington?"

"No, thank you. Please sit down and tell me

how I can help you. Was Mr. Fairfax unacceptable? Has Mrs. Bloomfield given in her notice already?"

He took the chair opposite and regarded her for a long moment. "Mrs. Bloomfield is still in my employ, and Mr. Fairfax is currently evaluating the estate while I kick my heels here in London."

"Oh good." She let out her breath. "Then why did you want to speak to me?"

"To discuss another matter." He rested his cane against the side of his chair. "Do you remember declining a dinner invitation from the Prince Regent for me?"

"Yes, it was one of the first tasks I completed."

"Did you mean to send my reply directly to the prince?"

"I wasn't quite sure whom to address the missive to, so I wrote the name of the prince's private secretary and that of your regimental commander on the outside. Why, what happened?"

"The prince's private secretary received it. The prince himself happened to read your no doubt gushing story of my heroics, and decided he wanted to know all about me."

"I didn't *gush*. I simply said that you were unable to accept the invitation due to injuries sustained in battle." Lucy regarded him doubtfully. There was a grim set to his mouth, which didn't bode well for her. "It was an honest mistake. Did the prince ask to meet you? Is that why you are in London?"

"It's far worse than that. The prince has decided to ennoble me for my heroic conduct at Waterloo."

Lucy clasped her hands to her bosom. "Oh, Major Kurland, how exciting! That a small error of mine in addressing that letter brought you to the notice of the prince himself, and that he deemed you worthy of such a great honor!" She faltered. "Why aren't you pleased?"

"Because I've never wanted to draw attention to myself in this way. And I've certainly never wanted to join the ranks of the titled aristocracy!"

"So you are blaming me for your good fortune?"

"You're the one who wrote the damned letter."

Lucy glared right back at him. "You said that the prince asked his secretary to find out about you, which indicates that *others* thought you were worthy of the honor, too. I cannot believe I am being held responsible for *everything*."

"You started it."

She raised her eyebrows at him. "Really, Major, how juvenile."

He let out his breath and looked away from her. "You believe I am overreacting, but when I think of all the men I commanded during that *slaughter,* and all those who died and were far more heroic than I will ever be, I feel like an impostor."

55

"Then perhaps you might see the honor as one that represents all those men and can dedicate yourself to making sure those brave souls are never forgotten," Lucy said quietly.

He stared at her for a long moment and then nodded abruptly.

Lucy allowed a moment to elapse before she asked, "So you came to London at the command of the Prince Regent?"

"Yes, I am to meet with his private secretary, Sir John McMahon. Then I will be granted an audience with the prince himself where I will be honored with the title of baronet."

"Indeed."

"I've written to my aunt Rose to see if she wishes to accompany me to the ceremony."

"She will be thrilled beyond measure."

He managed a smile. "I know." He shifted in his seat. "And now let us talk of other things. How is London treating you?"

"I'm enjoying it greatly, Major."

"You don't mind all the people?"

"It is certainly a rather crowded city, but it has other qualities that make up for that."

"Is Miss Anna enjoying herself, too?"

"I believe she is."

"You are being rather short with me." He fiddled with the handle of his cane. "Have I offended you in some way?"

"Why ever would you think that?" She gave

him her best society smile. "How is everything in Kurland St. Mary? Do you think Mr. Fairfax will make a satisfactory estate manager?"

"I believe he will." He hesitated. "Miss Harrington, I apologize if I have offended you. My own distaste for the situation I find myself in is hardly an excuse to rail at you."

"When have you ever needed an excuse, Major? Your temperament is rarely sunny." She focused on the doorway that led into the ballroom and saw the flash of a blue uniform twirl by. "Is Lieutenant Broughton a good friend of yours?"

"I wouldn't say we know each other well, but we served together in the regiment for a few years. He was a stern but exemplary officer."

"Anna seemed rather taken with him."

"So I noticed. I don't think he'll do her any harm, and he is looking for a wife."

"He told you this?"

"Why else do you think I'm attending a ball? It's hardly a place I would choose to frequent for my own benefit. Broughton asked me to accompany him on his quest for a wife, and as I have plenty of time on my hands, I agreed."

"That was kind of you."

He shrugged. "I'm rarely kind, as you well know. Coming here gives me the opportunity to at least be *seen* by my peers and means that I don't have to waste valuable time making endless pointless morning calls just to prove I am alive."

She suspected it was also about him not wanting to expose himself in his present weakened condition to those who had known him before his accident, but she didn't intend to mention that. Unlike him, she did have some standards.

"So we shouldn't expect to see you at Clavelly House or in Dalton Street?"

"Of course I'll visit you there. I meant *other* people, not those whom I can tolerate. I'm rather glad Broughton took a liking to Anna."

"Why is that?"

"Because he was extolling the virtues of Miss Chingford yesterday, and admitting she was his first choice as a wife."

"Your Miss Chingford?"

"Mine no longer, but, yes, the same."

Lucy leaned closer. "She is here tonight."

"Good Lord, no." Major Kurland took a hasty look around the room. "I hope she doesn't see me."

"She's bound to notice you in that uniform. You are rather hard to miss." Her gaze drifted over his shoulder. "There *is* a lady trying to get your attention. Do you wish to acknowledge her, or shall we move away?"

He turned in his seat and then rose awkwardly to his feet as the elderly woman tottered toward him. "It's Broughton's grandmother, the dowager countess. I'll introduce you." He raised his voice.

"My lady, may I offer you a seat?"

The dowager came closer and scowled at him. "Thought you were my grandson from over there. I forgot my spectacles and everything is a little blurred."

"We do have similar uniforms." Robert held out his chair and the dowager sat down in a rustle of stiff black satin. "May I introduce you to an acquaintance of mine, Miss Lucy Harrington?"

Lucy smiled at the dowager, who didn't smile back.

"Harrington. Are you related to the Clavelly family, gel?"

"Yes, my lady. My father is the younger brother of the current earl."

"Good pedigree." The dowager stiffened as a woman approached their table. "And what do you want?"

Lucy turned to see a thin elderly woman with fading yellow hair glaring down at the dowager.

"Maude Broughton. I'm surprised you dare show your face about town!"

"You're the one who should remove yourself, Agnes. You are a thief and a liar!"

Lucy cringed as both the old ladies raised their voices and other people in the supper room started to turn toward their secluded corner.

"Me? A thief? You haven't changed your spots in years, Maude, and now I hear you're accusing me of stealing jewelry from you? Jewelry, I might add, that rightfully belonged to my husband's family and was never given freely to you in the first place!"

The dowager drew herself back like an enraged snake. "So you *did* steal it back!"

"I did no such thing! One would hope that your conscience would make you return the jewels to their rightful owners!"

"Ha! I always intended to be buried in them."

"You venomous, old—"

Lucy stepped between the two women. "Ladies, I hardly think this is the place for such a discussion. Perhaps you should continue it at a later time when you will not be on such public display."

The dowager glared at her and Lucy stared right back. Major Kurland had taught her a lot about standing her ground.

"Humph." The dowager turned away with a toss of her head.

Lucy turned to Agnes Bentley, whose cheeks were bright red. Her bosom was heaving and her eyes were narrowed slits of rage.

"Ma'am?"

"All right! I'll take my leave of her, but this thing is not finished. I will not have her maligning my reputation and that of my family with malicious gossip and innuendo. She's worse than the scandal sheets!"

She stalked off, leaving the dowager cackling with undisguised glee. "Agnes never could stand up for herself for long. Far too meek and mealymouthed."

Lucy resumed her seat. It was amusing that despite appearances, the aristocracy behaved just like the old ladies in Kurland St. Mary when they fought over who should do the church flowers for the harvest festival.

"Perhaps she decided that a retreat now would gain her a better position in the next battle. I believe that was the Duke of Wellington's strategy, too."

"That might be true, my dear." With the major's assistance, the dowager pushed down on her cane and rose unsteadily to her feet. "I'm feeling rather tired. Perhaps you might take me back to the ballroom to find my daughter-in-law."

"Certainly, my lady." Major Kurland tucked her hand in the crook of his arm. "I'll return in a moment, Miss Harrington."

Lucy sank back down and watched the dowager until she was safely through the door before letting out a sigh of relief. When Robert returned, he brought another man with him, one Lucy recognized.

"Miss Harrington, how delightful."

"Mr. Stanford. I didn't realize you knew Major Kurland."

He smiled. "We were allies at school against the majority of the boys who thought we weren't quite up to snuff and should've been sent to the local village school instead of Harrow. And how do you know the major, Miss Harrington?"

"We live in the same village. My father is the rector of the parish of Kurland St. Mary."

Mr. Stanford nodded at Major Kurland. "I must come and visit you at Kurland Hall, Robert, now that I know the inhabitants are so charming."

Lucy vigorously plied her fan. She suspected she was blushing. She liked Mr. Stanford. He had been charming during their dance and more than happy to make the acquaintance of Sophia and her mother, and had promised to call on them.

"What brings you to London, Robert? I thought you had an aversion to the place."

Robert sat down across from Lucy, and Mr. Stanford joined them. "I had business with my regiment. I'm selling my commission."

"Was that your decision?"

Robert glanced at his old friend and then down at his left leg. "Yes, I wasn't forced out. But I can't imagine ever being fit enough to engage the enemy again. I have an estate to run and a house to renovate, which will keep me very well occupied."

Andrew Stanford chuckled. "I can't quite imagine you striding around your acres, discussing the livestock and what sermons the rector should preach in your church." He paused. "Begging your pardon, Miss Harrington, I'm sure your father doesn't need any advice on that subject at all."

To Robert's surprise, Miss Harrington merely smiled and murmured something diplomatic rather than taking Andrew to task for his remark, as she would certainly have done if he'd made it. He looked from her to Andrew and noticed they were still smiling at each other. What was it about London that had this effect on people? Did everyone become a simpering fool when they came to Town? He'd never thought to see Miss Harrington behaving like all the other young ladies of his acquaintance.

He cleared his throat. "You are, of course, welcome to visit me, Andrew. I've been busy repairing the roof of the manor house so that my future guests won't have to worry about leaking ceilings and mildew."

"I'm glad to hear it. I assume you'll be returning home quite soon, then?"

"I have some other commissions to fulfill in Town, so I might be here for a week or so."

Miss Harrington leaned forward. "Major Kurland has been ennobled by the Prince Regent! He will be a *baronet*. He has to stay in London to attend the prince in person."

"Good gracious, Robert. Is this true?"

"Yes, but for God's sake, don't tell anyone yet." He glared at Miss Harrington, who had the grace to look guilty. "I'd rather keep it quiet."

"But it is such a well-deserved honor! I can't believe Prinny had the intelligence to offer it to you." Andrew reached over to shake his hand. "Well done, sir."

"Thank you."

"I assume it will be announced in the papers?"

"I suppose so."

Andrew winked and rose to his feet. "Then I'll keep it to myself until then."

"I'd appreciate that."

"A pleasure to meet you, Miss Harrington." He bowed. "I hope to continue our acquaintance."

Robert waited until Andrew was out of earshot and then turned to Miss Harrington, who was looking rather wretched.

"I'm sorry, Major. I won't blurt out your good news like that again, I promise."

"No harm done. Stanford's a lawyer. He's used to keeping secrets." He sighed. "The news will come out eventually. It always does."

Miss Harrington closed her fan. "He seems like a very respectable man."

"Who, Andrew Stanford? He is."

"I understand he is a widower with two small children."

"I believe that is correct." He frowned. "Why are you asking about him?"

"Why do you think?"

Realization dawned. "You think he might make you an amiable husband?"

"Don't you?"

"Well, as to that—"

"Don't turn around!" Miss Harrington hissed. "Oh my goodness, it's too late, she's seen you."

It was, of course, Miss Chingford. Robert rose and bowed.

"Miss Chingford."

His former betrothed clutched a hand to her throat and stared at him as if he'd grown two heads.

"You? Here?" She shuddered. "Am I to be hounded by your presence *forever?* After ruining my chances of marrying once, have you returned to London to ensure that if you can't have me, no one else will either?"

Her throbbing voice was attracting attention. Robert cast an anguished plea at Miss Harrington, who was watching the scene with great interest.

"With all due respect, Miss Chingford, I have no desire to prevent you from—"

"And yet you brought that creature to London with you to steal away another of my potential husbands!" She pointed back into the ballroom where Miss Anna was just concluding her dance with Broughton.

"I beg your pardon?"

"Miss Anna Harrington."

"I did no such thing, I—"

Miss Harrington stood up. "I can assure you that my sister was invited to London by our aunt

65

and uncle, *not* by Major Kurland. And she may dance with whomever she pleases."

"I should've known you would all be in this together. You are determined to ruin my existence." Miss Chingford looked distraught. "It was probably your plan all along, for you to marry my darling Robert and for your sister to marry his friend."

"I think you should go and lie down, Miss Chingford," Miss Harrington said firmly. "I fear your imagination is running away with you. As far as I can ascertain, Major Kurland relinquished all interest in you and your matrimonial prospects when you decided you would not suit."

"So why has he followed me to London to blight my attempts to find a new husband?"

Robert decided it was time to intervene. "I came to London to settle matters with my regiment. That is all. I have no intention of interfering with you or your matrimonial prospects. In truth, I wish you every success!"

Miss Chingford recoiled from Robert's rather biting tone and turned to Miss Harrington.

"He is an unfeeling brute. I am glad to be rid of him. Perhaps you may deal with him better, but I cannot wish you well. I wish all of you had stayed in Kurland St. Mary!" She tossed her head and flounced away to where her mother and a group of young ladies were gathered just inside the door.

"I wish I'd stayed there, too," Robert muttered. "Silly woman."

Miss Harrington sighed. "She lives her life as though she were on the stage and everything is about her needs and her wishes. It must be so fatiguing."

"And if she considers Broughton her beau, him making sheep's eyes at Miss Anna probably didn't help."

"That was certainly unfortunate," Miss Harrington agreed. "Perhaps now that she's said her piece, Miss Chingford will keep away from us."

"I doubt that," Robert said, his glance again straying to the door of the supper room where Miss Chingford was still talking and casting angry looks in his direction.

Miss Harrington shivered. "Whoever thought a visit to a London ball would prove so exciting?"

"Certainly not I, Miss Harrington. I knew there was a reason why I avoid the place. There are far too many people here whom I know." Robert stood up and bowed. "I see your aunt talking to Broughton and Miss Anna at the door. If you will excuse me, I'll take my leave before anything else can occur. Would you like me to escort you back to your party, or do you wish to stay here and save your seat?"

"You're leaving?"

"Yes."

"When it is just getting exciting?"

"I don't have your stomach for such drama, Miss Harrington, and prefer to retire to my bed with a good book and a glass of port. I will, however, call on you and Mrs. Hathaway and expect to receive a full report of the rest of the night's doings."

"Which I will be happy to supply."

He took her hand and kissed her fingers. "Good night, Miss Harrington."

"Good night, Major."

He made his escape with as much speed as he could manage, avoiding both his acquaintances and the hostess, who would insist on introducing him to young ladies of character. In truth, he was exhausted and would willingly cede the field to Miss Harrington, who was obviously enjoying herself. He wasn't surprised. She had always thrived in an environment full of excitement.

Out on King Street he had a footman find him a hackney cab and went back to Fenton's and the tender ministrations of Foley. In a few days he was meeting the Prince Regent's secretary and he needed to be at his best for that.

Chapter 4

I knew she'd come," Lucy murmured to Anna as Miss Chingford entered the drawing room of Clavelly House with her mother and at least two of her younger sisters. "She probably couldn't bear to keep away. At least Major Kurland isn't here."

Lucy surveyed Miss Chingford's charmingly cut blue coat edged with swansdown and the matching muff. Peacock feathers curling around the poke of the bonnet framed her face, which wore the sour expression of curdling milk.

Aunt Jane rose to her feet and went forward. "Mrs. Chingford, how lovely of you to call."

Miss Chingford's gaze swept over Lucy and alighted on Anna and Julia, who were in the middle of a laughing crowd of young people that included at least one heir to a viscount and the youngest son of an earl. The sight seemed to afford Miss Chingford no pleasure. Ignoring her sisters, she moved forward into the group, pushing one young lady to the side and claiming her place beside the viscount's heir.

Lucy fought a smile and instead congratulated herself on Anna's outstanding success. Several bouquets had been delivered to the house and a veritable shower of invitations that included both the Harrington sisters had also arrived. Lucy was well content with Anna's debut and quietly hopeful for herself.

Another newcomer entered the room and, as her aunt was still engaged with Mrs. Chingford, Lucy stepped forward.

"Lieutenant Broughton, my ladies." She curtsied to the dowager and a middle-aged woman who she assumed was the current countess and Broughton's mother. "You are most welcome."

The lieutenant bowed. "Miss Harrington, may I present my mother and grandmother, the current and dowager countesses of Broughton?"

The dowager snorted. "I've already met the gel. Now where's the sister you've been bleating on about?"

Broughton flushed. "Miss Anna Harrington is over by the window, Grandmother. I'll take you over and introduce you right now."

Lucy wondered if she should accompany the pair as the dowager leaned on her grandson's arm and tottered off across the room.

"Miss Harrington? How are you this fine afternoon?"

She turned to see Mr. Stanford smiling down at her. "Oh, Mr. Stanford, how nice to see you."

He bowed and held out a neat posy of violets. "I thought you might enjoy these."

She took the flowers and realized from the sudden heat in her cheeks that she must be blushing. "For me?"

"Indeed. I brought some for you and Mrs. Giffin." He winked. "I suspected the pair of you might be overlooked in the deluge of offerings for Miss Julia and Miss Anna, and I couldn't have that."

"That was very kind of you. I am particularly fond of violets, as is Sophia."

The sound of raised voices drew her attention to the party gathered around Anna. "Oh dear, I hope everything is all right."

Mr. Stanford looked over the top of her head. "Miss Chingford appears to be arguing with Broughton. I do believe the dowager countess is enjoying it, while the countess is wringing her hands and trying to intervene."

Sophia came up beside Lucy, her expression concerned. "What's going on over there?"

Lucy patted her hand. "I'm not sure, but I'm going to find out."

"Find out what?"

The deep tones of Major Kurland made her pause and look over her shoulder at the door. He was still in uniform, which was most unfair of him, and looked remarkably handsome.

"Major, you'd better stay where you are and converse with Mr. Stanford. Miss Chingford is obviously overwrought."

His rare smile made her blink. "Broughton's flown the coop, has he? This I have to see."

Lucy ignored him and headed across the

drawing room in the direction of the altercation. Miss Chingford was nose-to-nose with Broughton. He wasn't giving an inch; his face was flushed and his mouth a hard line as she continued to berate him. Of course, he'd grown up being belittled by the dowager and was unlikely to give in to such an amateur.

"You're as fickle and as uncaring of a woman's heart as Major Kurland."

Lucy stepped between the furious pair and held up her hand. "Miss Chingford—"

"Oh, not you again, Miss Harrington. Do you believe it is your life's duty to interfere in everyone else's business? I suppose I shouldn't be at all surprised. That's what old spinsters do, isn't it?"

Before she could get a word out, Anna was suddenly in front of her.

"How dare you say that about my sister, Miss Chingford. She has shown you nothing but kindness."

Anna's blue eyes were flashing. All the gentlemen in their corner of the room, including Broughton and Major Kurland, were now staring at her sister.

Miss Chingford took one look at the faces around her, gasped, and fumbled for her handkerchief. "Oh dear, I feel quite faint. . . ." She swayed becomingly and Broughton stepped forward to catch her in his arms.

Lucy sighed. "Please place her on the sofa,

Lieutenant. I have my smelling salts in my reticule." She glanced up at Anna, who looked conscience stricken, and Major Kurland, who looked amused. "Anna, why don't you take our guests to get some refreshments while I take care of Miss Chingford. Perhaps you might fetch her mother. She won't want a crowd around her when she recovers from her swoon."

"Yes, Lucy." Anna smiled at Broughton. "Would any of you care for some tea?"

Lucy uncorked her smelling salts and waved the bottle under Miss Chingford's nose, which had the desired effect of making her cough and sit bolt upright.

"Your mother will be here in a moment. Do you feel well enough to walk down to your carriage, or shall I find you some assistance?"

"You," Miss Chingford uttered with deep loathing.

"Who else? You can scarcely have imagined that Lieutenant Broughton carried smelling salts in his pocket. Luckily for you, I do." She looked up. "Ah, here is your mama to take care of you." She placed the smelling salt bottle in Miss Chingford's hand. "Please keep this with you for the journey home."

While Mrs. Chingford fussed around her daughter, Lucy stood up and surveyed the drawing room. Mr. Stanford was talking to Sophia and Mrs. Hathaway, Major Kurland was

73

with Anna and Broughton, and almost everyone else was attempting to leave, no doubt eager to carry the news of Miss Chingford's fainting and accusations to as many households as possible. In some ways, London resembled Kurland St. Mary all too closely.

"That Chingford girl is a fool."

Lucy turned to the window seat behind her and saw the Dowager Countess of Broughton perched there like a black crow.

"She is perhaps unwise to allow her emotions to flow so freely in such company."

"As is your sister, Miss Anna."

"Anna was simply defending me. I hardly think her behavior can be considered in the same light."

The dowager drew out a snuffbox, extracted a pinch of the brownish powder, and inhaled it from the back of her hand with a loud snort. Lucy's own nose wrinkled as she observed the dowager. Taking snuff was an old-fashioned habit that she for one was glad to see diminishing.

"Broughton will be well rid of the pair of them."

"I beg your pardon, my lady?"

"I don't want such emotional traits bred into my family." The dowager snapped the lid of the snuffbox shut. "I'll order Broughton to keep away from them both."

Lucy curtsied. "That is, of course, your

prerogative, my lady. Now, may I fetch you some tea?"

She walked away before she said something she shouldn't. What an interfering woman! She made Lucy look amateurish. She could only hope that Broughton was made of sterner stuff and would not allow his grandmother to influence his decisions at all.

Major Kurland came up to her and bowed. "Miss Harrington, I'll take my leave of you. I have an appointment with my solicitor."

"Then you definitely mustn't be late."

She held out her hand and he brought it to his lips. "A pleasure, Miss Harrington. I swear that whenever I encounter you I can be sure of some kind of excitement. It is quite remarkable."

"Your amusement at my expense is hardly edifying, Major. The dowager countess is determined to meddle in her grandson's affairs."

"I'm sure you'll soon put a stop to that." He saluted and had the audacity to wink before he went out the door, leaving Lucy staring after him.

For her appearance at Almack's that evening, Lucy decided to wear her favorite new dress, which comprised a gray-blue shot silk slip covered with British net and augmented by a deep flounce of blond lace at the bodice and the sash sewn under the high waist. Both Sophia and Anna said it complemented her coloring and her eyes and, although she was not one to be vain about her looks, she did look rather well in it.

Lieutenant Broughton had called during the preceding week, as had Mr. Stanford. There had been no sign of Major Kurland, although his friends intimated that he was busy with regimental business and the officials of the court.

The Clavelly party, which included the Harrington sisters, soon joined the Broughtons, who were expecting Major Kurland to meet them when he was done with his business. Both Lucy and Sophia had been granted permission to waltz by the patronesses of Almack's so they would not have to sit the dance out. Lucy wasn't quite sure of the steps and wondered whether she'd prefer not to be asked to attempt it after all.

Almost as soon as they entered the ballroom, Miss Chingford appeared at Lucy's elbow and smiled, showing far too many teeth.

Lucy merely looked at her and Miss Chingford tittered. "Oh, Miss Harrington, don't stare at me so. You are just the person I wanted to see."

"Are you quite sure?"

Lucy almost balked when Miss Chingford linked her arm through hers and dragged her away from her friends before turning to face her.

"I am a great believer in finding out the truth."

"What could I possibly know that interests you?"

"Is it true that Major Kurland is to be ennobled?"

"I am hardly likely to have such information, Miss Chingford. You'll have to ask him yourself."

"So there is something to ask about?"

"I have no idea."

Miss Chingford narrowed her eyes. "You're lying."

Lucy curtsied. "Good evening, Miss Chingford." She turned away, but Miss Chingford followed her right into the middle of the Broughton party.

"I insist on knowing the truth!"

Before Lucy could say anything, the dowager countess snorted. "And I insist that you go away. No one wishes to hear your loud voice, or witness your deplorable manners, young woman!"

"My manners are impeccable! It is your family who should be ashamed of themselves." Miss Chingford raised her chin at the dowager. "You are an outright bully, and your grandson is a coward who can't even stand up for himself!"

Lucy looked from the dowager to Miss Chingford but couldn't bring herself to step between them. It was rather like watching a battle from ancient Greek mythology. No one else intervened either, although Anna did take a tiny step forward.

"My lady—"

The dowager's cold gaze skimmed over Anna. "I'm going to speak to Lady Jersey and ask her to revoke *both* your vouchers for Almack's. I cannot have my grandson fought over like a bone in such a public place!"

Miss Chingford gasped. "You horrible old woman! How *dare* you! You would ruin my entire life, my entire *future* over your numbskull of a grandson? I could strangle you for this!" She made an impulsive movement toward the dowager, but Broughton stepped in front of her.

"It's all right, Miss Chingford. Let me escort you back to your mother."

Lucy thought Miss Chingford had done more to harm her own reputation than the dowager ever could. Threatening an old lady was hardly becoming behavior from anyone, let alone a peer's granddaughter.

"Good Lord." The dowager swayed and stumbled against Lucy, who instinctively caught her arm.

"Perhaps you should sit down, my lady." Lucy helped the dowager into a chair and studied her pale, sweating countenance. "Shall I fetch you something to drink?"

"Don't pretend to be nice to me, Miss Harrington. It won't save your sister or that awful Miss Chingford from expulsion from Almack's."

"I don't care what happens to Miss Chingford, but Anna has done nothing to offend you in the slightest."

"Apart from leach on to my grandson?"

"She can do much better than him, I assure you."

The dowager withdrew her snuffbox. "Then make sure she does."

Barely containing her temper, Lucy rose to her feet and saw Broughton coming back from delivering Miss Chingford to her mother.

"Lieutenant?"

Poor Broughton looked rather distraught. "Yes, Miss Harrington?"

"Would it be possible to fetch your grandmother a drink? She isn't feeling quite the thing."

"Of course, Miss Harrington. I'll find one of the staff and see to it immediately."

Lucy walked over to where Anna stood; her usual smile was missing and her troubled gaze fixed on the retreating Broughton.

She clung to Lucy's hand. "Oh, Lucy, whatever am I to do? Broughton's grandmother *hates* me."

"She is a loathsome old toad," Lucy whispered. "If Broughton really cares for you, he'll find a way to negate his grandmother's influence over him. It will be a good test of his true affection."

Anna managed to nod. "I suppose that is true, although we have hardly spoken of such matters yet."

"Then don't let it worry you and try to ignore all the gossiping fools around here. I doubt the dowager has the influence to have your voucher revoked after all."

Even as she spoke, the dowager heaved herself to her feet using her cane and set off toward the door of the club where two of the patronesses were still standing welcoming new guests.

"Oh dear," Lucy sighed. "She is rather like a runaway horse, isn't she? Impossible to stop. I still doubt Lady Jersey will listen to her. From what I hear, she doesn't like her authority being challenged by anyone, and I doubt the dowager will be diplomatic."

Robert came into the ballroom and paused to look about the assembled throng. He was due to meet the Prince Regent tomorrow and had hoped to go home and regroup after that. Unfortunately, he'd been drawn into consultations with the College of Arms about his title and new coat of arms. He'd also been included in several military dinners and meetings, which were impossible to refuse.

He'd spent rather too much of his spare time with the Broughtons. He'd never met a family who seemed to dislike each other so intensely, and would prefer to be on a battlefield than sitting across a dining table from the dowager and Oliver Broughton. It certainly felt far more dangerous.

The dowager seemed to delight in causing disharmony, and Robert had begun to wonder why Broughton wished to be home at all. Foley said that gossip insisted the atmosphere in the kitchens was no better with the household staff ranged firmly on the side of the family member they interacted with the most. The older retainers were for the dowager, while the younger were split between protecting the countess and the two brothers.

"Major Kurland!"

He looked down to see Miss Chingford waving at him.

She put her hand on his sleeve. "May I ask you something?"

"If you must."

"Do you have it within your heart to forgive me?"

"No, Miss Chingford, I do not."

"I was a fool to let you go."

"Hardly. We agreed we wouldn't suit. And as far as I am aware, nothing has changed." He bowed, detached her hand from his arm, and started walking slowly toward the Broughton party where he could also see the Miss Harringtons and Andrew Stanford.

Miss Chingford didn't follow him, but remained by the door, her hand pressed to her chest in a most affecting manner, which set all Robert's nerves on edge. When he glanced back, her gaze had shifted to the Dowager Countess of Broughton, who had paused to exchange what looked like angry words with her.

Robert kept going, his gaze settling on the unremarkable features of Miss Lucy Harrington.

She, at least, was an island of sanity and calm good sense that many of the young ladies here would do well to emulate. She was also smiling at something Stanford was saying to her, which made him pause.

"Miss Harrington?"

She looked up at him and curtsied. "Major, you've missed all the excitement again. The dowager countess is attempting to get Miss Chingford and Anna thrown out of Almack's."

"I doubt she will succeed."

"Why do you think that?"

"Because I just saw her coming this way after speaking to Lady Jersey and she looked absolutely furious."

"Oh, thank goodness," Miss Harrington said. "Anna is beside herself."

"And Miss Chingford?"

"Too busy looking for you to find out if you are to be ennobled."

"Ah, that's why she was trying to ingratiate herself with me again."

"She's already tried?" Miss Harrington shook her head. "Five minutes ago she was threatening to strangle the dowager, and now she's moved on to reattaching herself to you. One has to admire her stamina." She looked over his shoulder. "Where is the dowager now?"

"Talking to another old harridan and arguing with *her*. Does she ever stop?"

"That's Lady Bentley. Apparently, the dowager has accused her of stealing some jewelry from her."

"So I've heard over the dinner table all week." Robert considered the gaunt peeress, who was now pointing her finger in the dowager's face to emphasize each word. "I can't see Lady Bentley breaking into someone's house, can you?"

"No, but my aunt says they've hated each other for years, but no one quite remembers why. Recently, all-out war has broken out again."

"The dowager does seem to have a gift for bringing out the worst in people. They are coming toward us. Let's stage a retreat."

Miss Harrington turned with him and pretended to admire the potted palm trees and exotic flowers that decorated the ballroom. "It must be wonderful to see such things in their natural state."

"While your clothes stick to you, your skin is attacked and bitten by a million insects and you fear the native population are going to kill you?"

"You have no imagination, Major."

"That's because I've actually experienced such places, and know that in reality you'd be running away screaming."

"I would not." She raised her chin. "Although the chances of my ever being able to *prove* that to you, or any other man, are remote, as I'll never be given the opportunity to travel."

"Perhaps this mythical husband of yours had better be a world traveler. I believe Captain McNamara is looking for a new wife."

"And he is over fifty years old."

"I didn't realize you were inclined to be so particular."

"I suppose you assume I have no choice!"

"I—" He blinked at her. "I beg your pardon."

"Accepted. Will you please take me back to my aunt?"

Taking her elbow, he maneuvered her back into the circle around Anna and the Countess of Clavelly. Broughton looked up as his grandmother approached with Lady Bentley still in tow and groaned. He put down his almost full glass.

"Oh no, not again."

"Lieutenant, can you try and draw Lady Bentley off while I deal with your grandmother?" Miss Harrington asked. "She does look *rather* overwrought."

A tray with glasses of orgeat stood on the side table and she picked up the last two. Miss Harrington went up to the dowager, who was visibly shaking with anger, her narrow lips thinned, and her cheeks a hectic red.

"My lady, please take some orgeat and sit down. You look rather warm."

For a moment Robert tensed, ready to intervene as the dowager's black gaze fastened on Miss

Harrington. Then she abruptly held out her hand and took the glass.

"Thank you."

"I hope it chokes the old witch."

Robert glanced across at Oliver Broughton, who was glaring at his grandmother, his expression a mixture of embarrassment and contempt. With a muttered oath, Oliver turned on his heel and stalked away toward the card room.

"Good gracious!"

Robert switched his attention back to Miss Harrington, who was now staring down in consternation at the skirt of her blue gown.

He removed the empty glass from her hand. "You're supposed to drink it, Miss Harrington. Not throw it all over yourself, or were you aiming at the dowager countess?"

She held the wet fabric away from her. "Someone caught my elbow from behind. This was my favorite dress."

"I'm sure it can be fixed." Anxious to avoid another female expressing her emotions, Robert looked frantically around. "Shall I find your aunt or Mrs. Hathaway so that they can accompany you to the ladies' retiring room?"

"I can do that myself, thank you, Major. Oh good Lord." She glanced distractedly around the ballroom. "Now Miss Chingford is bearing down on us and Lieutenant Broughton has allowed Lady Bentley to escape him. They are both converging on the dowager and she really isn't well. All that rage comes at a price."

"That's not your concern, Miss Harrington. Let Broughton handle his grandmother and take yourself off to the retiring room. I'll stay here and tell you what happens. I even promise to intervene if it proves necessary."

"Thank you, Major." She gathered her skirts. "If you would be so kind as to tell my aunt where I've gone, I would be most obliged."

She turned away just as the dowager stood up again to confront Lady Bentley and Miss Chingford, who converged upon her.

"And what do you two want? Do you think I have time to listen to—"

With a strangled sound the dowager clutched at her throat and started to fight to breathe. Her face contorted and she fell forward, her cane clattering to the floor as she writhed and twitched like burning parchment and finally went still.

Around them the ball went on. Only those in the immediate vicinity seemed to realize that something was amiss. Robert went down on his knees and grasped the dowager's thin wrist. He bent even closer to observe her chest and finally stared into her wide black eyes.

"What happened? What's wrong?"

Miss Harrington knelt opposite him. Robert swallowed hard and raised his gaze to hers. He'd seen many die, but not in such bizarre surroundings as a ballroom. It made the sight even more obscene.

"She's dead."

"She *can't* be."

"Fetch Broughton and his mother and see if we can find a physician."

Chapter 5

Despite the shock of the dowager's death, Robert still had to present himself at Carlton House the next morning. His hackney cab pulled up at the guarded entrance to the palace. The prince's popularity with the general population was at an extremely low ebb, and since a mob had attacked him in January, he feared for his life. Robert produced the letter he'd received from Sir John McMahon and was waved through into a more secure courtyard at the rear of the property.

He wasn't allowed to wander, though, and was escorted through the lavish apartments of the prince's main residence until he was delivered to the private secretary's offices. As the footman knocked on the door and was granted admittance, Robert straightened his uniform and removed his hat. In terms of influence, the Prince Regent's secretary was at the pinnacle of power. He controlled all access to the virtual ruler of the country. One word from him could make a man's career or break him.

For a wild moment Robert considered asking Sir John if he could decline the honor and then dismissed it. The prince would consider it an insult and despite his own personal feelings as to the current monarch, Robert was a great respecter of authority.

"Major Kurland. Please sit down."

"Thank you, sir."

Robert took the offered seat, set his hat on his knee, and rested his cane against the side of the chair. Sir John sat down, too, his sharp gaze moving over Robert. He was a stout, older man with faded brown hair and a rather mottled purple complexion.

"You are still recovering from the injuries you sustained at Waterloo?"

"Yes, Sir John." Robert indicated his left leg. "My horse fell on top of me. I broke my leg in several places."

"So I was informed. You were lucky to survive."

"That's true, although I doubt I'll see active service again. My leg cannot support me properly anymore." It was still hard for him to say those words, but he'd decided he had to. It stopped him pretending that things would get better, and reminded him of the daily struggle simply to remain mobile.

"You intend to sell out?"

"It's already in hand, sir."

Sir John read something from the top piece of paper on the stack on his desk. "You have a property on the Suffolk-Essex border?"

"That's correct, sir. Kurland Hall in the village of Kurland St. Mary."

Sir John smiled. "The Prince Regent was very taken with the tale of your heroic actions."

"With all due respect, I hardly did anything that remarkable. In battle one does what is necessary to survive."

"You did a lot more than that." Sir John held up a sheaf of letters. "These are all recommendations from fellow officers."

"That's very . . . humbling, sir." Robert wanted to squirm in his seat like a schoolboy. "I still insist that what I did was nothing out of the ordinary."

"Which is exactly why the Prince Regent wishes to meet you and ennoble you." He consulted a leather-bound book. "Will you be available later today?"

"Of course, Sir John."

Sir John rose. "Then I will look forward to introducing you to his majesty."

Robert stood and saluted. "Thank you, sir."

At least he wouldn't have to wait around for too much longer. He'd already seen his tailor, his banker, and his man of business, and knew his fortune was safe and his financial credit good enough to fund the money needed for the large-scale agricultural improvements to the Kurland estate. He couldn't wait to get back there and inhale the fresh wind blowing in from the coast and the tartness of a spring morning.

When he reached Fenton's he paid off the hackney cab and made his way up the stairs to his room. Foley was bustling around in his bedchamber laying his clothes out on the bed.

"I wish you'd communicate your plans to me, Major. How am I supposed to get you all packed up before the Broughton carriage returns?"

"What?"

Foley gave him a reproachful stare. "The Countess of Broughton sent a message that you were moving into Broughton House today."

"I don't remember agreeing to that." He frowned. "And why would they want me there when there's just been a death in the family?"

"Well, the lady seemed quite convinced that she needed you and it was hardly my place to disagree with her." Foley paused as he folded Robert's long starched cravats into a neat pile. "Don't tell me you've changed your mind. I'm almost done!"

Robert sighed. "I suppose we might as well go. It will certainly help me to keep an eye on Broughton and ward off Miss Chingford."

"I beg your pardon, sir?"

"It's of no matter." Robert waved his hand at the bed. "Carry on."

Robert handed his hat to the butler at the Hathaways' residence and slowly climbed the stairs to the drawing room on the first floor. It wasn't the correct time of day to pay a call, but he assumed the Harringtons and the Hathaways would be too keen to hear his news to worry about such social niceties.

"Major Kurland, ma'am."

As he'd expected, they were all there, clustered around one of the scandal sheets that proliferated in the city streets. He was always amazed at how quickly the printers managed to discover and distribute the latest gossip about the upper classes. Miss Harrington turned to him and put down the sheet she'd been reading aloud from.

"Good morning, Major Kurland. How are the Broughtons bearing up on this sad day?"

He took the chair opposite her and surreptitiously stretched out his left leg to the warmth of the fire. His muscles were aching on such a damp morning and every step was a jarring agony.

"I believe they are still rather shocked. And just to make matters worse, Broughton was taken ill last night and the family physician was called to the house."

"Oh *dear*," Anna said. "Is he all right?"

"The doctor was still with him when I left, but

I believe he was on the mend." He hesitated. "The Countess of Broughton asked me if I'd stay at the house while Broughton was ill. I could hardly say no."

"Of course you couldn't. She will need your support." Miss Harrington took off her spectacles and held up the long sheet of paper. "Have you seen what the scandal sheets are saying?"

"No, I haven't. Why?"

"They are suggesting that Miss Chingford deliberately enraged the dowager countess to cause her death and that she laughed afterward and"—she consulted the sheet—"danced the night away without a care practically on the dowager's grave."

Robert snorted. "If anything killed that woman, it was her own spite and venom."

"Miss Chingford will be mortified to have her name associated with such a terrible tragedy."

"I doubt it will bother her in the slightest."

"Then you don't understand how precious a woman's reputation is in this very judgmental world."

"Are you defending Miss Chingford, Miss Harrington?"

"I suppose I am." She hesitated. "While you were dealing with the Broughtons last night, I spoke to the physician who confirmed the dowager's death."

"And?"

"He said that it seemed odd to him that the dowager had died like that."

"Of a heart attack?"

She frowned. "No one mentioned the dowager had a weak heart."

"Broughton told me she was not in the best of health, that's probably what he meant. Miss Harrington, are you trying to make a scandal out of nothing?"

"Of course not, Major!" She hesitated. "Although it does seem unfair that Miss Chingford might have to bear the stigma of causing another's death through no fault of her own. Lady Bentley might be considered equally to blame."

"Miss Chingford has a family to protect her, and this 'scandal' will be forgotten as soon as someone else in society does something untoward—and you can guarantee they will."

"I suppose you're right," Miss Harrington said. "Is the Broughton family receiving visitors? Mayhap you could take us back with you to offer our condolences."

"I suspect Broughton is still too unwell to receive anyone, but I will pass on your regards and your request." He rose to his feet and leaned hard on his cane to regain his rocky balance. "I'll call when I have more news on the patient."

Miss Harrington stood, too. "I'll come down the stairs with you, Major, if I may. I have to speak to the butler."

She followed him out, slowing her pace to allow him time to get down the stairs. In the hallway he paused to pick up his hat from the table and turned to find her still studying him.

"How is your leg bearing up?"

He scowled at her. "It's perfectly fine. The cold air just makes it a little stiff in the mornings."

She nodded. "Ask Foley to rub some warm oil into your skin every night. It will help relieve the pain."

"As if I'd let Foley anywhere near my leg," he snapped. "I'm perfectly fine, Miss Harrington, and no longer trapped in my bed where you can bully me."

She folded her hands and looked at him. "Have you ever noticed that you become far more difficult whenever you are in pain? I have, and that is the only reason why I am willing to forgive your offensive tone."

He rammed his hat on his head and saluted her. "Good *day,* Miss Harrington."

Turning to the door, he made his halting way across the marbled hall.

Her voice followed him. "If you don't want Foley massaging your leg, ask him for a hot cloth to place over your thigh."

"Damned interfering woman," Robert muttered as he barely managed the steps outside without falling. The fact that a hot compress on his leg sounded vastly appealing simply made matters worse. She had no right to dictate to him.

His temper remained sour on his journey back to Broughton House and was not improved when he was immediately asked to go up and meet the countess in her morning parlor. All he wanted was a hot bath and a shot of brandy to help withstand the pulsing agony in his thigh. He was due at Carlton House later, so he couldn't even put himself to bed.

The countess was alone in the small morning room. The velvet curtains remained shut, leaving the room in half darkness. As his hostess had also chosen to don a black gown, it was difficult to see her clearly. Robert bowed and remained standing in front of her chair.

"Lady Broughton, how may I help you?" He hesitated. "If you wish me to return to my hotel in this time of sorrow, I will leave immediately."

"Oh no, please don't go." The countess brought out her handkerchief and inwardly Robert tensed. Dealing with crying females was one of his least favorite occupations. "With Broughton sick, and Oliver disappeared, you are the only man I can turn to."

"Oliver has *disappeared?*"

"Well, I have no notion where he is, and his bed wasn't slept in last night."

"Does he even know that his grandmother died? I seem to remember him leaving the ball before anything occurred. Perhaps he is staying at an acquaintance's house and has no idea what is going on." He paused. "Do you wish me to inquire?"

"That's very kind of you, but Oliver isn't my main concern."

"Then, how may I help you?"

The countess dabbed at her pale cheeks. "The stupid new physician that Broughton *insisted* should replace our old one declares that Broughton might have been poisoned!"

"Poisoned?"

"Yes, I know it's ridiculous, isn't it? But he is determined to speak to you about it."

"Now?"

"The sooner the better, he said. Although what there is to remember, or forget, about what Broughton was doing last night when one was forced to watch a horrible old woman choke to death on her own venom is hardly worth noting."

A note of hysteria crept into the countess's voice and Robert took a step backward. "Shall I fetch your abigail, my lady? You seem rather distraught."

"No, no, I'm perfectly fine." She raised her head. "Would you speak to the wretched man? He doesn't want to tell Broughton what he suspects until he is feeling more the thing."

"I'll certainly speak to him, my lady. Is he still on the premises?"

"Yes, he's upstairs with Broughton."

"Then I'll go up to them and hopefully I'll be able to set your mind at rest."

The countess rose and gripped his hand with both of hers. "Thank you, Major."

"It's nothing, my lady. I'm just glad to be of service in this difficult time."

He disentangled himself from her frantic grip and headed for the door and up yet another flight of stairs. At least now when he was finished with this nonsense he could escape directly to his own bedchamber, which was on the same floor.

The door to Broughton's suite of rooms was slightly ajar. Robert knocked anyway and went inside to find a man pacing in front of the fire.

"Are you the consulting physician?" Robert asked. "You look younger than I expected."

"I'm Dr. Redmond." The man came to a halt and bowed. "I only recently qualified."

"Oh dear." Robert leaned heavily on his cane. "Now what's all this nonsense about Lieutenant Broughton being poisoned?"

Chapter 6

An hour later, after having enjoyed the warmth of a much-needed bath, and endured Foley's fussing, Robert was ready to leave for his meeting with the Prince Regent. He'd also taken a moment to scribble a note to Miss Harrington to ask her permission to visit her again later that day. After speaking to the physician, he was curious to see what she would make of the issue in hand. Her perspective was always interesting. He'd rely on her good sense before making any decision to proceed.

He also instructed Foley to heat some cloths to put on his thigh, which had helped immensely; not that he would be mentioning *that* to Miss Harrington. He could already imagine her satisfied expression if she knew that she'd been right again.

This time his entrance into Carlton House went more smoothly and he was escorted to Sir John's office without any hesitation, or demand to know his business. Sir John welcomed him and offered him some refreshments, but Robert refused. Despite his personal distaste for the Prince Regent, meeting one's reigning monarch, albeit the mad King George's eldest son, was rather overwhelming. Of course he'd seen the prince before from afar when he'd reviewed the regiment, but never on a more private basis.

The inner door of Sir John's office opened and a footman dressed in the royal livery came out and bowed to Robert.

"His Highness will see you now, Major Kurland."

Robert gripped his cane tightly in his left hand and followed the private secretary into the prince's inner sanctum. The windows were tightly closed, the curtains were drawn, and the sickly smell of perfume hung over the room like a dank fog.

"Major Kurland."

Robert saluted and then bowed low. "Your Majesty."

The Prince Regent came toward him, his remarkably podgy face wreathed in smiles. The prince was fifty-six years old and looked nothing like the portraits Robert had seen of him as a young man. Good Lord, he was even more corpulent than the cartoons made him out to be, and that was saying something.

To his surprise, the prince reached out and took Robert's hand between his own. "Major Kurland, our nation owes you a debt of gratitude for your outstanding courage and bravery during the Battle of Waterloo."

"I merely did my duty, sire."

The prince fixed his earnest gaze on Robert. "You did much more than that. I've read all the reports. You saved half a regiment from annihilation by that French battery."

"Thank you, sire."

"Offering you a baronetcy is a poor reward for your sacrifice, but I do hope you will accept it as a gift not only from your nation, but from your regiment's commanding officer?"

Robert found himself captivated by the Regent's fervent gaze and promptly forgot why he'd ever wished to disappoint the prince and refuse the title.

"I would be honored, sire."

The prince released Robert's hand and placed his own hand over his heart. His rather bulbous blue eyes were full of tears. "The honor is all mine." He looked over at Sir John. "You'll arrange a suitable time for the ceremony?"

"I've already put the event in your calendar, sire."

"Good." The Prince Regent nodded. "I look forward to it."

And with that, a slightly dazed Robert was led out of the room and into Sir John's spacious office, where he took the seat offered to him and tried to think of what to say. After a moment, the prince's secretary chuckled.

"You seem a little overcome, Major."

"I . . . didn't expect to, to . . ."

"Receive your baronetcy so quickly?" Sir John shrugged. "When the prince sets his mind to something, he is remarkably hard to dissuade. In this case you are the lucky beneficiary of his good will. The ceremony will take place within the next month. I'll send you the details nearer the actual date."

Robert accepted this information with a nod of thanks and felt grateful that he hadn't blurted out what he really meant about finding the prince so *charming*. He'd heard the prince could be quite captivating but hadn't believed it until he'd stared into the man's eyes and seen such emotion.

"Then I'll send you a note when we are ready to go over the details of the ceremony, Major."

Robert stood up and saluted. "Yes, Sir John. Thank you for your consideration."

He managed to make his way out to the courtyard behind the palace and into the waiting carriage, then asked the driver to take him to the Hathaways', where he hoped Miss Harrington would be awaiting him.

She was there in the morning room with Sophia Giffin and Andrew Stanford, who seemed quite at home with the two ladies. Robert gratefully accepted the seat Miss Harrington offered him by the fire and a cup of tea. Despite it being spring, the weather was still treacherous and far too cold for his liking.

After he'd satisfied his thirst, he thanked Miss Harrington, who relieved him of his teacup and sat forward expectantly.

"You saw the Prince Regent today, didn't you?"

"How do you know?"

"Our butler happened to see Mr. Foley out in the park this morning, and he passed on the news!" Miss Harrington smiled. "I do hope you are going to tell us what happened!"

Robert attempted to straighten his left leg as he considered his reply.

"I did see him and he was most . . . gracious."

"You sound surprised." Miss Harrington maneuvered a footstool under the heel of his left boot and sat back.

"As you know, I hardly hold the man in high esteem."

"You didn't refuse the honor, then?"

"I'd thought about it, but somehow, when the prince thanked me on behalf of the nation, I found it impossible to disagree with him."

"I have heard that the prince is very personable," Miss Harrington said diplomatically.

"He is."

"Are you returning to Kurland St. Mary now?"

"No, I have to be formally invested with the baronetcy, which will happen in the next month or so."

"And then you'll leave London."

"Yes, why?" He glanced at her properly for the first time. "Do you wish to be escorted home?"

"Oh no, I'm enjoying myself far too much to do that." She looked over at Sophia and Stanford, who were talking quietly to each other. "I don't think Sophia wishes to leave yet either. She still hasn't found a husband."

"Neither have you."

"Exactly." She smoothed down her skirts. "I do appreciate you coming to share your experience with the Prince Regent with us, Major. It is quite thrilling."

Shaking off his unexpected reaction to the

prince, Robert remembered his main purpose in coming to see Miss Harrington.

"Actually, I didn't come to tell you about my meeting with the prince. I wanted your opinion on another matter."

"You wanted my opinion?"

"Yes, Miss Harrington. You might be a little forthright at times, but there is no one I know with better sense."

"I think that's the nicest thing you've ever said to me."

"I'm not trying to be nice. I'm merely seeking your thoughts on a matter regarding the Broughtons."

He glanced over at Sophia, but she appeared to be oblivious to the conversation going on between him and Miss Harrington. "The countess asked me to meet with the Broughton physician."

"And what did he have to say for himself?"

"He suggested that Broughton was poisoned last night."

"What?"

"Exactly. I was all set to tell the man he was an underqualified idiot when he confounded me by proving to be nothing of the kind. In fact, he trained in Europe and Scotland under some of the best surgeons and healers in the profession."

"Some profession, Major."

"I know it's still considered to be the realm of butchers and blood letters, but this man, Dr.

Redmond, has made a very specific study of heart disease and poisons. That's why he believed Broughton was poisoned and didn't merely eat spoiled meat or any of the other more obvious solutions I suggested to him."

"Oh dear." Miss Harrington tapped two fingers against her cheek. "And what does the Broughton family have to say about that?"

"The countess is adamant that nothing needs to happen at all."

"And what about Lieutenant Broughton?"

"I have a suspicion that if his doctor insists on telling him that he was poisoned, he will not be willing to let the matter rest."

"But he will recover?"

"Apparently." Robert hesitated. "The physician also asked if he might view the dowager's body."

"View it or eviscerate it?" Miss Harrington shuddered.

"He wants to be able to tell Broughton exactly what she died of—for scientific reasons, I believe he said." Robert frowned. "He asked me if I noticed anything odd about the way the dowager died. All I could tell him was that she clutched at her throat rather than at her chest as she fell, which seemed rather irrelevant."

"And her pupils were so wide that her eyes looked black with rage."

"I'd forgotten that, but you are correct. The thing is, should I support the physician's desire to disturb the dead and advance science, or should I simply side with the countess and let the old harridan be buried and forgotten about altogether?"

Miss Harrington fixed him with her clear hazel gaze. "That's not your decision to make, Major, is it? I can understand that Lady Broughton wishes to let the matter rest, but you and I both know that rumors are already flying about the circumstances of the dowager's death. It would be wrong for an innocent bystander to be blamed for this when the truth might be something far more shocking."

"I thought you might say that, Miss Harrington."

She folded her capable hands on her lap. "Which is why you sought my opinion. You don't want the truth to be buried either, especially if it concerns Miss Chingford."

He blinked at her. "Miss Chingford has nothing to do with it. I merely don't appreciate seeing a fellow officer being poisoned."

"But at least he's alive."

"That is true."

"One has to ask why anyone would want to poison Lieutenant Broughton?"

"Perhaps someone merely thought to scare him."

"Broughton seemed generally well liked, but almost everyone hated the dowager." Miss Harrington considered him. "Perhaps the wrong person became ill. Do you suspect who the culprit is?"

"If it was a prank that went wrong, I can think of one person," Robert said.

"Who?"

"Oliver Broughton. He hasn't been seen since the ball at Almack's either."

Miss Harrington studied his no doubt grim expression.

"Why do you think it has something to do with Oliver?"

"Because he hated his grandmother, and Broughton revealed to me somewhat reluctantly that his brother is considered . . . unstable."

"I suspect he has a hot temper like many young men of his age, but I can't say I saw any malice in him."

"I did." Robert grimaced. "Also, at the ball, just before he departed he made a rather unpleasant comment about his grandmother."

"What exactly did he say?"

"That he wished the drink you were handing her would choke her."

"My goodness. No wonder you think he might be involved. Perhaps he meant both of his relatives to become ill, and the dowager ended up dead." Miss Harrington made an odd sound and went still.

"What's wrong?" Robert asked.

"*I* handed her that glass of orgeat."

"So you did."

"What if everyone thinks *I* poisoned her?"

Chapter 7

Lucy stared at Major Kurland, who stared back at her in return.

"Don't be ridiculous, Miss Harrington. Why would anyone think you wanted to murder Broughton, or his grandmother?"

His brusque tone was remarkably heartening and Lucy let out her breath.

"The dowager was threatening to have Anna's Almack's voucher taken away. Perhaps I thought to get back at her for that?"

If possible, the major looked even more disgusted. "And kill her grandson, the very man who was courting your sister? You are many things, Miss Harrington, but a fool is not one of them."

"Thank you."

"I meant it as a compliment."

"And I took it as one." She took a deep breath. "I'm being silly, aren't I?"

"Especially when we don't even know if this physician is correct about whether Broughton was 'poisoned' or how the dowager countess might have died. We could be dealing with two completely separate incidents."

"Which just happened to the same family on the same evening." Lucy snorted. "I don't think you believe that any more than I do."

His dark blue gaze collided with hers. "I'll feel better after I've spoken to Broughton, and find out what has happened to Oliver."

"Do you need my help?"

"Not at this moment." He rose to his feet. "I'm far more capable than I was last time we attempted to solve a riddle."

She stiffened. "I suppose you expect me to sit and ply my needle until you deign to come around to discuss something else with me?"

"Actually, if I can arrange it, I'd prefer that you persuade your sister and Mrs. Hathaway to visit the countess. I'd appreciate your insight into the family."

Her smile held a hint of surprise. "I'm quite sure I can do that."

"I'll send you a message when I arrange something."

Andrew Stanford stood up at the same time as the major and glanced over at Lucy.

"You have monopolized Miss Harrington, Robert, and now I have to go." He mock-frowned at Lucy. "I'll come down with you if I may. My carriage is at your disposal."

Lucy smiled at Mr. Stanford. "I'm sure Mrs. Giffin was an excellent replacement for me."

"Please don't ask me to answer that, Miss Harrington. How could I choose between two such wonderfully enchanting ladies?"

Major Kurland cleared his throat. "If you've quite finished, Stanford?"

"I believe I have." Mr. Stanford bowed low to Lucy and then to Sophia. "Good-bye, ladies. I will be back tomorrow to take you both to the park as promised."

The two men left together and Sophia gathered up the spent cups and saucers, and placed them on the tea tray.

Lucy stood staring at the door, her mind whirling with possibilities, none of which was very pleasant. If the physician was correct and Broughton had been poisoned, who was responsible? If it was Oliver's idea of a prank, it had gone disastrously wrong and ended up taking his grandmother's life. *His* life would be over at three-and-twenty. If it wasn't Oliver, did someone else hate the Broughton family so much that he or she was willing to kill more than one of them to achieve their goal?

And which Broughton had been their target?

By all accounts, the dowager was one of the most disliked women of the *ton*, but what about Broughton himself? Major Kurland had described him as an excellent and efficient officer, which meant he probably had many enemies from the lower ranks. But Anna liked him, and despite her sweet nature she was no fool. . . .

"Lucy?"

She turned to see Sophia hovering in the doorway.

"I'm sorry, I was wool-gathering. What did you ask me?"

"You might be interested to hear that Mr. Stanford spent most of our time together asking me about you."

"He did?"

"Yes, he was very interested in your family and Kurland St. Mary. I hope you don't mind that I shared such personal information with him."

"Why would I mind?"

"It's just that you are looking rather fierce."

Lucy walked over to her old friend. "I was just thinking about what Major Kurland came to tell us."

"About the Prince Regent?"

"Yes, and about the Broughtons." She registered the sound of a carriage stopping outside the town house. "I wonder if that is Anna and your mother?" She walked over to the window and peered through the curtains. "It is. Did Nicholas Jenkins manage to behave himself? By the look of Anna's expression, I suspect not. Oh dear, he's throwing the reins to his groom in a most ill-tempered fashion, and hurrying up the steps before Anna can have the door shut in his face."

"Then we must sit down and not be caught snooping at the window!" Sophia returned to her seat by the fire where she immediately picked up her abandoned sewing and looked industrious.

Lucy came to sit opposite her as the door opened and Anna came through, her face flushed and her blue eyes flashing.

"Nicholas is insisting on coming in." She yanked her bonnet off her head. "If you wish him to survive, may I suggest you talk to him? I am going upstairs to lie on your bed with a headache!"

Nicholas entered with Mrs. Hathaway. His expression darkened as Anna swept by him without a word.

"Anna—"

He bit his lip as she didn't respond and Lucy immediately felt sorry for him. After exchanging greetings, Sophia engaged her mother in conversation while Nicholas sat beside Lucy and simply stared into the fire without a word.

"May I offer you some advice, Nicholas?" Lucy said mildly. "Sulking won't endear you to any lady, let alone my sister."

He glanced up at her, a stricken look on his handsome face. "Oh, I do apologize, Miss Harrington, I didn't mean to be rude. It's just that—" He swallowed with some difficulty. "Whenever I open my mouth, I appear to put my foot in it."

Lucy patted his arm. "Which is exactly why your grandparents wished you to come up to London and learn how to go about in society."

"I didn't come because of that. I came because Anna, I mean Miss Anna Harrington, was here."

"I know."

"But she is determined not to acknowledge the connection between us."

"That you are old friends who grew up in the same village?"

"I thought we were more than that, I *assumed*—"

"Well, perhaps that was your first mistake. No young lady likes to be taken for granted."

"I simply tried to tell her that she didn't need to chase after titled old men at Almack's."

"You told her that? Oh dear." Lucy sat back. "How did she respond?"

"Not well." He tugged at his neckcloth. "She said I had no right to order her around, and then things just got worse until we were practically yelling at each other."

"Anna was yelling?" Lucy tried to imagine that. Mayhap her sister's feelings for Nicholas were more complex than she liked to admit. It was rare for Anna to raise her voice to anyone.

"And *now* she says she never wants to see me again."

The pain and confusion in Nicholas's gaze made Lucy feel far more sympathetic toward him than she perhaps ought.

"I'm sure she didn't mean it."

He sighed. "I'm fairly certain she did. You

know your sister better than anyone, Miss Harrington. Is there anything you can think of to help me make amends?"

"A written, heartfelt apology and a posy of flowers would be a good place to start." Lucy considered carefully what to say next. "I'd also attempt to treat her more like a new acquaintance than a long-standing friend."

"Thank you, Miss Harrington. I'll do that. She does look rather different here in London, actually." He gave a gusty sigh. "I suppose that if she wants me, she knows where I am. If she finds someone else here she prefers, like that stodgy old Broughton fellow, then at least I'll know that I tried to warn her off."

"Perhaps you should look around for a bride yourself, Nicholas, instead of propping up the wall and glaring at anyone who has the effrontery to ask Anna to dance."

He blushed. "Wouldn't that make her jealous?"

"If she truly cares for you, it might. And if she doesn't, and you find yourself attracted to another young lady, then you can both move on with your lives with no regrets."

"That's an excellent point, Miss Harrington. Thank you." He rose to his feet and bowed. "I won't stay and see if Anna wishes me to drive her back to Clavelly House. I have a strong suspicion she'd rather walk."

Lucy patted his hand. "I suspect you are right.

We'll make sure she arrives back at Clavelly House safely."

He took his leave of Sophia and her mother and positively bounded down the stairs and out into the square. Lucy watched his carriage depart and then turned to Mrs. Hathaway.

"Did they really have an argument in public?"

"Oh no, my dear, they had the decency to wait until they were in the carriage." Mrs. Hathaway chuckled. "If any young man had ordered me around like that, I would've lost my temper, too. But Anna set him back on his heels."

"She can be quite forceful when she puts her mind to it."

"I'd forgotten that." Mrs. Hathaway's smile faded. "Although, I must admit, I did feel quite sorry for young Nicholas. He is obviously head over heels in love with her and simply lacks the maturity to let her know it without coming across as a pompous, all-knowing idiot." She paused. "I believe that's what Anna called him."

"The thing is, I can't help thinking that in time he would make an excellent husband for her. He certainly brings out her temper, and that must mean her *feelings* are engaged."

"I agree." Sophia nodded. "Charlie used to drive me batty, but I loved him anyway. But what can we do? Anna has to make up her own mind about whom she wants to marry."

"Yes." Lucy smiled. "But perhaps with a *little* connivance from her sister."

Robert sat back in Andrew Stanford's luxurious carriage and eyed his old friend.

"For a man who claims to be perpetually busy, you seem to be spending a lot of time at the Hathaways'."

Andrew shrugged. "I can always find time for the things I enjoy."

"And what draws you there in particular?"

"The same thing that draws you, I imagine. Interesting company."

"Mrs. Giffin is certainly that. To be widowed at such a young age was very hard for her."

Andrew's face went blank. "I know."

Robert exhaled. "Of course you do, I apologize."

"It's all right. My Harriet died three years ago attempting to give me a son."

There was nothing Robert could think of to say that wouldn't sound either clichéd or insincere.

"I understand that Miss Harrington had the care of her younger siblings since their birth," Andrew said.

"That's correct. The twins have known no other mother. Thankfully, the little hellions have been sent off to school now and Miss Harrington finally has the opportunity to widen her horizons."

"She's remarkably competent for her age."

"She's twenty-six and this is a most improper

conversation to be having about an unmarried lady."

Andrew's eyebrows rose. "You're preaching propriety at me, Robert?"

"She is a good friend of the family."

"I understand that she organizes your life, too."

"She certainly helped with my recovery."

"Which raises her even higher in my esteem. If she can deal with you in a temper, my friend, she can probably deal with any man." Andrew looked out of the window. "We're at Broughton House. Are you quite sure you don't want to come and stay with me?"

"I promised the countess I'd support her through this ordeal. Thank you for the offer, but no."

Robert slowly descended from the carriage and leaned on his stick to look up at Andrew.

"Thank you for the ride."

"You're welcome." Andrew winked. "I'll see you tomorrow no doubt. But do remember I'm taking the ladies for a drive in the park at three. Perhaps we'll see you there instead?"

Robert didn't reply and turned to make his way into the house. The butler was passing through the hall and he stopped the man.

"Has Mr. Oliver come back yet?"

"No, Major, he has not."

"Is Lieutenant Broughton awake?"

"I believe he is. Do you wish me to inquire if he is receiving visitors?"

"Yes, please." Robert started up the stairs. "I'll be in my room."

Half an hour later, after talking to Foley and being scolded for staying out in the rain, he made his way along the corridor to Broughton's suite of rooms and knocked on the door.

"Good afternoon, Major."

Broughton's valet let him in and positioned a chair close to the four-poster bed where his employer lay propped up against the pillows. Broughton's face was pale and his eyes were ringed with dark purple shadows. He sipped at some water but seemed to find even that difficult to keep down.

"How are you?" Robert asked.

"Surviving." Broughton put down the cup with a hand that shook. "My stomach is still in turmoil and my head hurts abominably."

"Have you spoken to Dr. Redmond?"

"Yes; apparently he believes I was poisoned."

"And what do you make of that? Do you think the man capable of proving such an outrageous statement?"

"Earlier this year, after discovering that my grandmother had taken it upon herself to dose everyone with her own concoctions and brews, I personally employed Dr. Redmond as our new family physician. I met the good doctor at a lecture in Cambridge we both attended, and he impressed me with his modern scientific thinking."

"So you believe he might be right about the poison?"

Broughton sighed and his eyes closed momentarily. "I suspect he is correct."

"Did he mention anything about what happened to your grandmother?"

"There's no need to be so tactful, Kurland, it's not like you. Dr. Redmond asked leave to examine her body." Broughton met Robert's gaze. "I gave him my permission."

"And what does he hope to achieve by that?"

"He is beginning to wonder if she was poisoned, too. He maintains that if you know what you are looking for, such traces are easy to identify."

"And if he believes he has found evidence of poisoning? What will you do then?"

Broughton's hand clenched into a fist. "Find out who did this to us, and make them pay."

"Your mother believes it would be in the family's best interests to simply ignore what has happened, and bury your grandmother with all the necessary ceremony."

"She's not the one lying in bed weakened by the administration of poison, is she? I want to know the truth, Kurland."

"And I will help you discover that to the best of my ability. I know all too well the frustration of being tied to one's bed when one needs to be up and about dealing with things."

"I'm glad you said that, because there is one thing I'd like to ask you." Broughton licked his lips and Robert handed him the glass of water. After he'd taken another sip and grimaced, he fixed Robert with an anxious stare. "Where in God's name is Oliver?"

"I don't know."

"Blenkins, my butler, said he hasn't been seen since the night of the ball."

"Has Blenkins consulted with Oliver's man-servant?"

"I'm fairly certain that's where he got his information from."

Robert considered how to pose his next question and then decided that Broughton was blunt enough to hear his worst suspicion. "Do you think Oliver might have something to do with this?"

"As I said, he has a vicious and uncontrolled temper. He might have thought it amusing to make us both ill."

"Amusing?"

"He's not right, Kurland, there's something inside him that enjoys watching others suffer. Even as a child one couldn't leave a puppy or any small animal in his care. They always ended up dead."

Robert rose to his feet. "I'll find him for you, never fear."

"Be careful." Broughton swallowed hard. "He might not even remember what he's done. It wouldn't be the first time."

"I'll bear it in mind."

"Thank you." Broughton closed his eyes and sank back on his pillows. "If it's all right with you, I'll ask Dr. Redmond to report back to you about my grandmother's body if I'm not available when he calls."

"Of course."

Robert nodded to the valet, who went to the door to let him out. "When you have settled your master in, would you send Mr. Oliver's man-servant to my room? I'd like to speak to him."

"Yes, Major."

"Thank you."

Robert made his way back to his room, the sound of his cane hitting the wooden floor the only interruption to the quietness of the house.

When Robert went in, Foley was folding cravats and putting them away in one of the drawers. He'd barely opened his mouth before Foley abandoned his task and came hurrying over.

"Major, come and sit down by the fire."

For once he didn't argue. He'd exceeded his strength hours ago and wanted nothing more than the oblivion of sleep. He kept trying to remind himself that he'd made considerable progress in the last few months, but it still wasn't enough. He resented his lack of mobility with a stubborn rage that refused to die.

"I'm going to fetch your dinner on a tray." Foley held up his hand. "And no arguing with me either. You're worn out, sir, and I won't have it on my conscience if you drop dead in front of me. Your aunt Rose would have my head."

Robert leaned back in the wingchair and let out a slow breath. "I'm not arguing with you, Foley. I'm too exhausted. That's why I'm sitting here meekly absorbing your pearls of wisdom and anticipating my dinner in front of the fire."

Foley moved closer and frowned down into Robert's face. "Should I send for the doctor? It's not like you to admit you're not feeling well."

"I didn't say I wasn't *well*. I said I was tired and hungry."

"Of course, Major. You sit there quietly, and I'll fetch you up a nice dinner."

"And don't forget to send my apologies to the countess."

Foley sniffed. "As if I would forget the social niceties, sir."

After Foley departed, Robert yawned and stretched his legs out toward the warmth of the fire. A discreet tap on the door had him sitting up again to face a young dark-haired man who came to stand in front of him.

"I'm Silas Smith, Major Kurland. Mr. Oliver's man."

"Thank you for attending me here. I understand that Mr. Oliver has not been seen since the night of the ball at Almack's?"

"He certainly hasn't been back home, sir." Smith shuffled his feet and dropped his gaze to Robert's cane. "But that's not unusual. He's a young gentleman with a wide acquaintance."

"I can imagine." Robert studied the manservant. "Do you have any idea of his particular haunts?"

"Some of them, sir."

"And does he have any close friends he might have taken refuge with?"

"Not really, sir. He has a bit of a temper on him that tends to alarm folks."

"So I've heard." Robert paused. "Have you ever seen him in a rage?"

"Yes, sir." The manservant touched a livid scar on his cheek. "He threw a bowl of soup at me once, and knocked me out cold."

"Would you say he's been acting oddly at all recently?"

"Yes, sir. He's always been one to hold grudges and let himself brood over matters, but recently he seems to have gotten worse."

"In what way?"

"He imagines things, sir, like he's being watched, or that someone is after him."

"Someone in his family?"

"There's certainly no love lost between my master and the rest of them."

"I had noticed," Robert said drily. "Do you have any ideas where Mr. Oliver might be?"

"That's quite a long list, Major." Smith scratched his head. "You'd probably be best to start with the brothels, and then the gambling dens and—"

"I'll want to go out tonight and look for him. I'd appreciate it if you would accompany me."

"Yes, Major." Smith hesitated. "Mr. Oliver's not a bad man, sir. He just needs to grow up a bit."

Robert nodded. "Well, let's just hope we can find him and offer him the opportunity to do just that, shall we?"

Chapter 8

D o you notice something odd, Anna?" Lucy whispered to her sister.

"Are you talking about Miss Lewis's purple gown?"

"No, about Miss Chingford."

"She looks perfectly well turned out to me."

"I'm not talking about her dress. I'm talking about the fact that no one apart from her mother and sisters is speaking to her."

They were attending a musical event in a private home with a smaller guest list than usual. To Lucy's secret relief, it was a welcome respite from all the large balls and entertainments. She found it much easier to converse with other guests in a more intimate setting and felt less on show like a prize turkey at the county fair. Mr. Stanford had escorted her and the Hathaway ladies, and they'd met up with Anna and the Harringtons.

Miss Chingford sat with her mother at one of the small tables in the dining room. Although all the other tables were full, no one was taking up the empty spaces at Miss Chingford's table.

"How peculiar," Anna whispered. "She doesn't look very happy either."

"She never looks particularly cheerful, though, does she? Perhaps she's found out what the gossip-mongers are saying about her."

"I wonder. I should imagine that her mama wouldn't let her read the scandal sheets." Anna sounded quite sorry for Miss Chingford. "Do you think we should go and warn her?"

Lucy cast Anna a horrified glance. "And what do you think will happen if we do that? She already loathes us. She's hardly going to welcome us telling her she's suspected of murdering a little old lady."

"She hardly *murdered* her, Lucy. And Lady Bentley was as much at fault as Miss Chingford for upsetting the dowager countess."

"But slightly more discreet."

"How can you say that when they were both

converging on the dowager just before she died?"

"Lady Bentley is a widow who doesn't need to catch a husband, and can say whatever she likes and merely be thought of as an eccentric. Miss Chingford is not in that position. You know such a slur on her character could affect her chances of making a good marriage." Lucy waved a hand in Miss Chingford's general direction. "Why do you think everyone is giving her such a wide berth?"

"It's not fair." Anna's expression took on a mulish look that Lucy had learned to dread. "I'm going to speak to her."

Before Lucy could say another word, Anna started to make her way across the floor to where Miss Chingford sat in solitary splendor. With an irritated sigh, Lucy followed her.

"What do you want?" Miss Chingford didn't exactly look welcoming.

Anna smiled. "Are you all right?" She glanced around the room at the other guests who continued to ignore the vacancies at the table.

"Why shouldn't I be?"

Lucy stepped up beside Anna. "Because you are being ignored, and we both know how important social success is to you."

Miss Chingford scowled at Lucy. "Of course, having spent all of two weeks in London, you would know everything about that, wouldn't you?"

"It's much the same anywhere, Miss Chingford. No one likes being ostracized."

"Ostracized?" Miss Chingford raised her eyebrows and tittered. "Me? This silly crisis will resolve itself and the gossips will move on to something else."

"I doubt that will happen until this particular matter is properly resolved. I just hope it is in time for you to recover your standing in the eyes of your peers." Lucy hesitated. "Being accused of provoking an old woman until she died is hardly a laughing matter."

"I did no such thing! If anyone is to blame for her death it is your sister!"

Lucy raised her eyebrows. "And how did you work that out?"

"She's the one who stole Broughton from me, and forced me to act to resolve the situation. The dowager countess was agitated because her grandson was consorting with a *nobody*."

Lucy put a restraining hand on Anna's arm. "She isn't worth arguing with, Anna, and she's just trying to provoke you." Lucy met Miss Chingford's defiant gaze. "Despite everything, we will still try and make sure that you are exonerated of all blame for this appalling situation. But you might seek to examine your conscience, Miss Chingford, and perhaps accept some responsibility for your part in this matter. Good afternoon."

She linked her arm with Anna's and walked her back to their table.

"There's no point trying to engage her further. She'll just make matters worse."

Her sister sat down with a decided thump. "And now she'll be going around telling everyone it's *my* fault. Why did I ever feel sorry for her in the first place?"

"I'm not sure." Lucy patted her hand. "We tried to be charitable, and Christian, and forgiving of her appalling nature. That's what counts. Father would be proud of us."

Anna didn't look convinced. Luckily, at that moment, Julia and Sophia returned to their table and she was soon chatting happily to them. Lucy continued to stare at Miss Chingford, who had somehow managed to insert herself into a group of people. From the way her mouth was moving and the angry glances she sent in their direction, Lucy could only assume that Anna's reputation was being shredded. When Miss Chingford caught her eye, Lucy smiled graciously.

For once, she had no intention of trying to defend her sister. Didn't Miss Chingford understand that her ill will toward others made her appear most unattractive, particularly to men of marriageable age? None of them would want to bring a bride into their family who abused their elders. Miss Chingford was in a lot more trouble than she realized. Lucy only hoped it wouldn't drive her back to Major Kurland.

The major had sent her a note earlier inviting the Harringtons and the Hathaways to visit Broughton House. Anna was more than willing to go, and Sophia and her mother had agreed to come, too. Lucy was quite eager to visit the house herself and learn what Major Kurland had discovered. She was convinced that the dowager's death and Broughton's suspected poisoning were linked in some way. But how to proceed if they were? She was not at home in Kurland St. Mary, where she knew everyone and could wander into their houses at will. It was extremely frustrating. Here she would have to rely on Major Kurland to take the lead. He was ideally situated in the Broughtons' home. She almost wished she were there, too. . . .

"Miss Harrington? I understand we are to call on the Broughtons on the way home. Is that correct?"

She turned to find Mr. Stanford smiling at her. He wore a dark olive coat that brought out the green in his eyes and black top boots that gleamed. He always looked presentable and, unlike many men, he always treated her as an intelligent being, entitled to have an opinion about serious matters such as politics and warfare. She suspected he might make her a good husband, but she wasn't convinced he realized it yet.

"If it doesn't inconvenience you, sir."

"Not at all, Miss Harrington." He offered her his arm. "Shall we go and find your aunt and assure her that we will return Miss Anna to her in time for dinner?"

The ride to the Broughtons' house was fairly short, which was just as well with them all crammed together in one carriage to avoid the rain. Mr. Stanford gallantly took the center seat with Lucy and Anna on either side of him, while Sophia, and her more rotund mother, sat opposite. It was strange to feel the warmth of a male body all along her side. When Sophia winked at her, it simply made matters worse.

Mr. Stanford got out first and helped all the ladies down the steps and into the cavernous hall of Broughton House. The knocker on the front door was tied with black crape and the curtains had all been drawn. A footman took them through to the drawing room where the countess sat sewing in a chair by the fire. Major Kurland sat with her. He immediately stood and bowed.

Mrs. Hathaway went straight across to the countess and held her hand.

"We won't stay above a minute. May I express our condolences and inquire about the invalid?"

"Thank you." The countess patted Mrs. Hathaway's hand and gestured for her to join her on the couch. "Please sit down. Broughton is feeling much better. I believe he intends to join us for tea."

"I'm very glad to hear he is on the mend," Mrs. Hathaway said. "I'm sure Major Kurland has been of great comfort, but there is nothing like having your family around you at such a terrible time as this."

The countess looked across at the major. "He has indeed been very kind. I only wish my dear husband could be with me, too. I have sent a letter to him in India, but it will be months before he receives the news."

The butler returned with the tea tray and Lucy rose to help the countess. She took her own cup and brought another over to Major Kurland.

"Thank you, Miss Harrington."

"You are most welcome, Major." She took the seat beside him. "Have you heard back from your aunt Rose? Will she be able to join you at your investiture?"

"I haven't heard yet, Miss Harrington, but I'm fairly certain she will do her best to be there. An opportunity to meet the Prince Regent can hardly be ignored."

"How nice for her." Lucy looked back at the door. "Is Lieutenant Broughton really well enough to leave his bed?"

"He is determined to do so." Major Kurland hesitated and then lowered his voice. "He is also determined to find out who poisoned him."

"Ah, he doesn't mean to let it lie, then, like his mother wishes. I wonder why? Does he suspect anyone in particular?"

"At the moment, he's convinced it has something to do with Oliver. I spent last night looking for the young rapscallion at all his usual haunts, but he was nowhere to be found."

"That does make things more problematical."

"It is highly likely that Oliver *was* involved. According to Broughton, he has a history of malicious pranks against his family."

"Surely this goes beyond the malicious and into the murderous?"

"I quite agree, Miss Harrington. If he were my brother, I'd—" Major Kurland broke off. "Broughton's here."

Lucy watched as the poor man came into the drawing room and quickly sat down by the fire. His skin looked as clammy as a death mask, his eyes were black holes, and he was sweating profusely. Anna immediately rose and went to sit by his side, her expression concerned. After a while he appeared to rally and even attempted to smile at his solicitous companion.

Seeing that Broughton was engaged with her sister, Lucy leaned closer to the major and lowered her voice. "Has the physician examined the dowager's body yet?"

"I believe he was doing that today. He'll

probably come to the house this evening to let us know his findings."

"But Broughton believes they were both poisoned and blames his brother?"

"Yes, Miss Harrington."

"And do you agree?"

"It sounds likely. Why, do you have a different opinion?"

"Not really. I know from living in Kurland St. Mary that the most likely suspect in a suspicious death is a husband, a wife, or a close family member."

"So I believe. It is very different from the experience of warfare where one mostly kills complete strangers."

There was nothing Lucy could say to dispel the bleak look on her companion's face. Anna beckoned to her and with a word of excuse, she crossed over to her sister's side.

"Lucy, the lieutenant would like to take a short stroll into the garden. I wondered whether you and Sophia would accompany us?"

Lucy glanced at Broughton's gaunt face. "Are you certain that you feel well enough to venture outside, Lieutenant? It is rather cold."

"I've been inside for several days now, Miss Harrington, and would appreciate a breath of fresh air."

"If you are sure, sir, I'd be happy to accompany you and Anna." She glanced over at Major

Kurland, who raised a quizzical eyebrow, and increased the volume of her voice. "Major Kurland was just expressing a similar desire to escape the confines of the house."

Sophia and Mr. Stanford joined them and the party went out of the long windows that opened into the expansive gardens behind the house. Major Kurland took Lucy's arm.

"I never said I wished to escape."

"Major, you always look as if you wish to flee. You said London does not agree with you."

"That's true." He took a deep breath of the frigid air. "I asked Broughton if he remembered what he drank at Almack's. He thought he'd sipped at some weak orgeat."

"There was a tray of orgeat on the table. I remember one of the footmen bringing it over to us. That's what I gave the dowager."

"Didn't you drink some?"

"No, if you recall, someone jogged my elbow and the whole lot ended up all over my favorite gown." She shuddered. "Which I'm heartily glad of now."

"Did anyone else touch the orgeat?"

"I don't think so." Lucy frowned. "It is rather too sweet and syrupy for most people's tastes."

"Thank goodness."

"To be honest, I'm surprised to hear of Broughton drinking it, but at the time I believe he was rather too agitated with his grandmother's behavior to care what he was consuming."

"I can understand that. She really was an appalling woman."

Lucy glanced up at him. "One shouldn't speak ill of the dead."

"Why not? It's not as if she can hear me." The major avoided the trailing root of a tree, steering Lucy around it. "From what I can tell, everyone in the Broughton family will breathe a little easier without that particular dragon on their backs. I wonder where Broughton is heading? He didn't look well enough for a long trek."

His abrupt change of subject had Lucy returning her thoughts to where they were going rather than considering the issues the major had raised. His refusal to conform to the conventions of mourning the dead didn't really surprise her. In her opinion, anyone who had survived the battlefields of Europe was entitled to their own view on that matter. Such carnage would challenge any man's faith.

Broughton appeared to be heading for the building on the left. They waited as he found a key above the door and unlocked the heavy door. The sweet smell of herbs and dried hops flowed out into the frigid air, reminding Lucy of home. A sharp pang of longing for her garden at the rectory made her catch her breath.

"Are you all right, Miss Harrington?"

"Yes." She forced a smile. "I was just thinking of the rectory stillroom where Anna brews up the most effective potions for our various ills."

The major brushed aside a bunch of drying herbs that hung from a rack coming down from the ceiling. "If you gave me any of her concoctions I can certainly vouch for their efficiency."

Broughton's weak voice carried back to them. "Unfortunately, my grandmother's potions generally did more harm than good. Her eyesight was failing, and as she refused to let anyone help her read the ingredients for her mixtures she sometimes got them wrong."

"Which is why you replaced her with Dr. Redmond," Major Kurland said. He walked over to where Broughton leaned up against a large pine worktable and pulled out a chair. "Perhaps you should sit down. You look rather tired."

Sophia, Anna, and Mr. Stanford began investigating the dowager's stillroom and commenting on what they found as they walked through the space. Lucy followed the major over to the worktable where he stood looking down at a large leather-bound book. While Broughton sat and conversed with the major, she quietly opened the book. It was an herbal of great age with recipes and receipts written in several different hands. Some of the original script was faded, but it looked as if generations of women had added their thoughts and substitutions in the margins of the pages.

"Has this herbal been in your family for long, Lieutenant Broughton?" Lucy asked.

He nodded. "At least two hundred years. My grandmother set great store by it."

"And you?"

"I prefer to place my trust in the new science, Miss Harrington. Methods derived from the more rigorous and scientific approach of men."

"You don't think that this store of knowledge, knowledge that has been lovingly passed down for centuries by the women of your own family, has any value to it?"

"I'm sure some of it will be scientifically proven to be accurate, Miss Harrington, but until then, I'd rather not place my trust in the scribblings of women." He smiled at her as though trying to lessen the insult. "Please feel free to look through it while you are here. I believe my grandmother marked her favorites."

He turned to speak to Major Kurland as Anna came back to the table and Lucy began to leaf through the book. His assumption that the accumulated wisdom of generations of women was untrustworthy was slightly annoying, but not uncommon in this age of new science. Apparently, in order to be considered worthy, everything had to be proved anew. It seemed ridiculous to her. If willow bark cured a head-ache, and had done so for centuries, then why would one suddenly doubt it? It was typical of men to rewrite something just for the sake of it.

She turned another page, which was marked

with a red ribbon, and read the title, *Convallaria majalis* (Lily of the Valley), which was followed by a small drawing of the tiny, waxen white flowers and the long, straggling, slightly shiny leaves that reminded her of a bluebell.

"'Place the leaves of the lily of the valley in water and leave to soak overnight,'" Lucy murmured. "'Discard the leaves and boil the water, reducing the quantity by half, and bottle the remaining liquid.'"

In the margin of the page a different hand had added more information. "'In small quantities this "tea" can be used to alleviate the symptoms of an irregular heartbeat or a weakness of the heart. But use sparingly. It is deadly if drunk to excess.'"

Lucy looked up to find that Broughton had moved away to speak to Anna and that Major Kurland was standing right at her shoulder looking down at the text she had just quoted.

"Lieutenant Broughton said that his grandmother marked her favorite pages with red ribbon."

"A strange page to mark, then," Major Kurland commented.

"Not if she had a heart condition. Perhaps she used this concoction on herself." Lucy scanned the packed shelves. "We can check in a moment."

Major Kurland reached past her and turned to another marked page. "Here we have a remedy for lack of sleep, and another here about the uses of privet berries."

"*Privet* berries?"

The major stopped turning the pages and went back. "Yes, why?"

"They are *extremely* poisonous. Didn't you know that some of the young children in Kurland St. Mary have died after accidentally eating those bright red berries?"

"I was not aware of that. Privet hedges are extremely easy to find in the countryside and impossibly expensive to replace with more permanent structures." Major Kurland frowned. "Can't the schoolteacher warn the children not to eat the darn things?"

"There isn't a school, Major."

"I am aware of that. Rest assured I do have the matter in hand."

"I'm glad to hear it. If you need any help . . ." Lucy paused.

"You probably won't be there to help me, Miss Harrington. You are here to find yourself a husband, are you not?"

"Yes." She shut the book and straightened her spine. "Thank you for reminding me. I'm sure your new land agent will deal with the matter perfectly well."

Major Kurland glanced over at Broughton, who was looking ready to swoon, and raised his voice. "I think we should be getting back, don't you? I for one am getting tired and would appreciate a cup of hot tea."

Even as she applauded the major for offering Broughton the opportunity to retire back to the house, Lucy gave him a dubious glance. It was unlike him to admit to having any weakness. Was he coming to terms with his own limitations, or merely attempting to help his friend?

She waited until Sophia and Mr. Stanford left behind Anna and Broughton and shut the door, locking it with the key and standing on tiptoe to restore it to its hiding place on the ledge.

Major Kurland waited for her and then proffered his arm. "Shall we?"

"As long as I won't overbalance you." She glanced doubtfully at his weakened leg. "You did say you were tired."

"I wouldn't offer my arm if I thought I was going to bring you down with me, would I?"

"I suppose not, but in my experience, men can be incredibly stubborn about such things." Lucy accepted his arm and then walked slowly forward, her attention distracted. "Oh, I forgot to check for the bottle of lily of the valley water."

Major Kurland sighed. "Go ahead. I'll wait for you here."

She reused the key and went back inside the stillroom. Whatever the state of her health or her eyesight, the dowager had kept her supplies in immaculate order. It took Lucy very little time to discover a bottle labeled lily of the valley and one filled with dried red privet berries. Replacing the bottles on the shelves, she left the stillroom and returned to Major Kurland.

"Well?" he demanded.

"She had a bottle of privet berries and a bottle for the lily of the valley water." Lucy took a breath. "The lily of the valley water was all gone."

"Which proves nothing, except that she hadn't made a new batch."

"But she labeled and dated the empty bottle."

"And?"

"She only made that particular batch the day before she died, so where did the contents go?"

Chapter 9

A nd so I would conclude, Lieutenant, that your grandmother was poisoned. I can understand why the attending physician assumed she'd had heart failure. Her symptoms *were* rather similar. I suspect from the additional information Major Kurland and Miss Harrington supplied to me that she imbibed the poison."

"Imbibed? As in drank?" Broughton demanded.

"Yes, sir. That would seem most likely."

"Would it be possible to disguise the taste of

poison in a drink?" Robert asked. "I believe that Broughton's grandmother drank the orgeat Almack's provided."

Dr. Redmond stopped pacing. "Orgeat is a syrupy concoction made from orange flower water, almonds, and barley water. It has a very sweet, sickly taste and would be perfect to hide something in." He turned to Broughton, who sat back, his hands clutching the arms of the chair. "Did you drink the orgeat?"

"I did, but not very much of it. It was far too sweet for my taste."

"Which might explain why you lived and the dowager countess did not."

"The dowager drank a whole glass. Miss Harrington gave it to her," Robert confirmed.

Broughton looked up. "Miss Harrington?"

"Don't look like that, Broughton. I can vouch for her. She's no killer." Robert looked back at the doctor. "Do you have any idea what kind of poison might have been used?"

"It's difficult to say. I'd have to investigate more closely to determine exactly what it is."

"But you must have your suspicions."

Dr. Redmond pursed his lips. "Many poisons can be distilled from quite natural ingredients that are found all around us."

"So I noticed in the dowager's stillroom. I never realized privet was so dangerous."

The doctor turned his attention to his patient. "I

thought your grandmother was supposed to be kept out of the stillroom, Lieutenant?"

"Indeed, she was, but it proved rather difficult to stop her getting in there." Broughton stirred in his chair. "I'm surprised she didn't argue with you about it on your visits to Broughton House to attend to our health."

"The dowager countess refused to speak to me, or allow me to treat her, sir. She told everyone I was in league with the devil."

"She was a woman of strong opinions, Doctor, I'll give you that."

"As you are, sir, although your mind tends more to the scientific bent." He hesitated. "If you are not offended by the notion, Lieutenant, I will consult my copy of Orfila's book."

"Why should we be offended?" Robert studied both of the men's serious faces.

"Because the author, Mathieu Joseph Bonaventure Orfila, is a professor in a French university and originates from Spain."

"Our quarrel was with Napoleon, not the French people," Broughton said quietly. "Professor Orfila is a brilliant man regardless of his nationality and choice of residence."

"What exactly did he write?" Robert asked.

"*Traité des Poisons*. It's the first scientific treatise about how to identify the most commonly used poisons that leave traces inside a body."

Robert managed to repress a shudder. "And

142

how does one go about detecting such evidence?"

"If one wishes to be polite, I would say one 'delves deeper' into one's subject." Broughton shrugged. "Science isn't always pretty, Kurland, but sometimes the end justifies the means."

"And you both believe that Orfila's book will help provide you with an answer as to what killed the dowager countess?"

"It might do, sir. It depends on what killed her," Dr. Redmond said. "But as we've already noted, there are many ways to make poison."

"Would privet do it?"

"As I said, Major, I can't yet be sure of the cause. Professor Orfila's book offers various methods to establish the identity of a specific poison."

"What about lily of the valley?"

Broughton cleared his throat. "There's no point in questioning the man, Kurland. He'll report back to us when he has concluded a proper and scientific analysis of the available evidence and not before. I wouldn't want it any other way."

"And in the meantime, unless there is anything else you wish to tell me, I'll keep looking for young Oliver." Robert nodded and rose to his feet. "He has to turn up eventually."

"Unless he is guilty."

Robert glanced briefly at Dr. Redmond, who was looking troubled, but it seemed that Broughton didn't mind speaking in front of his physician.

"There could be any number of things preventing him from coming home, Broughton. It is a thoughtless age. I rarely bothered to speak to my parents unless I needed more money."

"That sounds just like Oliver."

Robert patted Broughton's shoulder. "Don't despair quite yet. We'll find him."

"Thank you." Broughton let out his breath. "I am beginning to fear the worst."

Robert was, too, but he didn't think that Broughton in his current weakened state needed to hear his thoughts on the matter yet. He'd agreed to meet Silas Smith at nine in one of the taverns on Fleet Street Oliver had liked to frequent. He glanced at the clock on the landing chiming the half hour. If he could avoid the countess, he'd go and speak to Miss Harrington before he left on his mission to recover Oliver.

Lucy was sitting in the drawing room with Mrs. Hathaway when the butler announced a visitor. She had decided not to go out with Sophia and the Clavelly party to yet another ball. A rather enthusiastic dance partner the evening before had bruised her foot, and she'd decided to stay home and rest it rather than potentially making it worse.

"Major Kurland, ma'am."

Mrs. Hathaway went to rise, but the major held up his hand. "Don't get up, ma'am. I do hope I'm not disturbing you? I wanted to have a word with Miss Harrington about a Kurland St. Mary matter."

"You're always welcome here, Major." Mrs. Hathaway gestured at the tea tray. "Would you like some tea, or perhaps something else to drink?"

"A brandy would be most acceptable, Mrs. Hathaway. Thank you."

While his hostess spoke to the still-hovering butler, the major came over to Lucy.

"Why aren't you out dancing?"

She indicated her slippered foot, which reposed on a footstool. "I injured my foot last night at a ball we attended after our visit to the Broughtons."

He cast a critical gaze on her elevated limb as he took the seat beside her on the couch. "It looks perfectly fine to me. Is your ankle swollen?"

She hastily smoothed down her skirt. "That is none of your business."

"I assume it isn't broken. Otherwise Mrs. Hathaway would've called a doctor to attend to you." He smiled. "You must recall that I am something of an expert on the malfunctioning of a limb, Miss Harrington."

"Not my limbs. And I am fairly sure that your toes have never been crushed on the dance floor by an overweight man."

He glanced down at his gleaming top boots. "Not while I'm in uniform, although I have had a few memorable encounters on the dance floor with some remarkably clumsy women."

"Do you miss that?" she asked impulsively.

His smile faded. "Dancing? Yes, rather more than I thought I would, actually. I miss a lot of things." He turned to the butler, who set a bottle of brandy and a glass at his elbow. "Thank you."

Mrs. Hathaway settled herself on the other side of the fireplace and had her nose in a book and a cup of tea at her elbow. She waved a lace-mittened hand at Lucy.

"Don't mind me. I'm far too engrossed in this story to make intelligent conversation. You'll have to make do with each other."

Lucy hoped Major Kurland didn't notice the wink Mrs. Hathaway gave her. She didn't understand why all her female relatives were constantly imagining there was anything between her and the major other than a great deal of irritation. Couldn't they tell the difference between a man in love and one who sought out an intelligent opinion? She'd never met a man who seemed able to do both. She was beginning to believe such a man didn't exist.

"Miss Harrington, Dr. Redmond believes the dowager *and* Broughton were poisoned at Almack's."

"Does he know how?"

"He suspects the poison was in the orgeat. He said it was strongly flavored enough to conceal anything added to it."

"Which makes a horrible sense." Lucy sipped at

her tea. "Did he reveal what kind of poison he thought it was?"

"He refused to be more specific than that. He insisted he needed to consult some new scientific book about detecting poisons before he could be absolutely sure what was going on."

"That must be Orfila's book." Lucy nodded. "I've read some of it."

"You have?"

"Naturally. My father ordered a copy as soon as it became available."

"And what did you think of it?"

"That it was fascinating, although I'm still not sure why proving *how* something works in a chemical manner makes a difference to the effect it has on the body. The person is still dead after all."

"But the ability to identify which poison was used could rule out more natural causes of death and convict a killer."

"We're all going to die of something, Major. I still don't see how it changes anything."

Major Kurland shifted in his seat. "To get back to my original point, Miss Harrington. If the dowager and Broughton were both poisoned by the orgeat, who put the poison in there?"

"I assume Lieutenant Broughton still thinks it was Oliver?"

Robert refilled his brandy glass. "Well, Oliver did have access to his grandmother's stillroom.

He could've taken the privet berries, or the lily of the valley water, or whatever else the dowager was making, and used it to poison his own family."

"I suppose he could've done."

"Why do you sound so doubtful?"

Lucy put down her cup and considered. "Any of the Broughton family *or* their servants could've gone into that stillroom and taken something."

"The door was locked."

"But the key was hidden in a very obvious place."

"That's true, but Oliver had a grudge against the whole family and was known to have a vicious streak. Poisoning sounds just the sort of dramatic thing he would do," Major Kurland countered.

"Yet, it is still considered a woman's weapon. Think of Catherine de Medici or Lucrezia Borgia, or—"

"Yes, yes, but in this instance we're dealing with an overemotional boy, not an exaggerated view of a historical figure."

"Mrs. Peters in the village poisoned her husband."

Major Kurland began to tap his fingers on the head of his cane. "What does that have to do with anything?"

"She was a tiny woman and her husband beat her. She didn't even deny poisoning him. She said that it was the only way she could stop him from hurting her and their children."

"So you've managed to convince yourself that the murderer is a woman?"

"If the dowager was the intended victim, everyone at odds with her apart from Oliver was female." She counted them off on her fingers. "There's Miss Chingford, Anna, although she is certainly not guilty, the current Countess of Broughton, and Lady Bentley, who all had good reason to dislike the dowager."

"Dislike her, yes, but *kill* her? And what about Broughton? Are you quite sure that *he* wasn't the one who was supposed to drop dead? Oliver hates him *and* his grandmother."

"So if it *is* Oliver, you could be right. I'm not convinced."

He scowled down at her, but she refused to be cowed.

"It's not a competition, Miss Harrington. I'm merely speculating as to the motives and identity of a murderer."

"So am I." She held his irritated blue gaze. "You must also recollect that a stillroom is very much a female's domain. If Oliver was indeed in his grandmother's stillroom looking for ways to dispose of his brother, someone might have noticed. Have you spoken to the servants yet?"

"No, I'd rather find Oliver first before I start spreading suspicion and doubt among the Broughton staff."

"Very wise, Major." Lucy nodded. She could

sense that he was becoming irritated with her circuitous reasoning. "There is, of course, one other option that we should perhaps consider."

"What's that?"

"The dowager had specifically marked those poisons in her herbal, hadn't she?"

"Yes."

"Then one might assume that she was either planning to make them or often made them."

"Agreed."

"Then might one also speculate that she was conversant in their usage?"

"We already agreed that she might have used at least one of them as a home remedy to regulate her weak heart."

"That's true, but is it also possible that she accidentally poisoned herself?"

Major Kurland shook his head. "Sometimes your meandering path of reasoning astounds me, Miss Harrington. How on earth did you come up with that melodramatic claptrap? This isn't a gothic novel."

Lucy raised her chin. "The dowager's eyesight was bad, her temper and disposition were abominable, and she enjoyed tormenting people. Perhaps she was the one who decided she'd had enough of Broughton, the countess, or Oliver?"

"Which would mean Broughton is lucky to be alive."

"I gave *her* the glass of orgeat, Major, when she

was confused and she was extremely reluctant to take it from me. Perhaps she meant to pick up her own, and the ones with the poison in them were meant for Broughton and Oliver."

"That would require a degree of planning and forethought that I doubt the dowager could have accomplished in such a public setting."

"Well, someone did. Why not she? She did seem to be seriously unwell and became confused. Perhaps she even added the poison to her own glass and meant to hand it to Oliver, and drank the wrong one?"

"This is all fascinating, Miss Harrington, but also extremely far-fetched, and with all due respect simply the typical product of an overactive female imagination."

Lucy sat back and folded her arms. "Says the man who feared he was imagining a shadow against the church wall and begged me to investigate."

The look he gave her was scorching. "That's not the same thing at all, and you know it."

"But I at least gave you the benefit of the doubt, and didn't assume you had an overactive imagination, did I?"

"Of course not. You knew that as a military man I wouldn't . . ." He stopped speaking and sighed. "All right, then. I'll take your lurid imaginings and bear them in mind as I search for Oliver."

"Thank you, Major Kurland. All I ask is that

you keep an open mind. Has a memorial service been arranged for the dowager yet?"

"I don't think so, why?"

"Has the body even been released to the family?"

"The last I heard, Dr. Redmond was examining it. I suppose it depends on whether he makes his suspicions public and asks the coroner to investigate."

"What do you think Lieutenant Broughton will do if his brother is indeed the culprit?"

"Possibly nothing. I suspect he'd be reluctant to drag his family's name into such a sordid matter."

"Then you really need to find Oliver soon."

"I'm doing my best, Miss Harrington. London is rather a large city." He put his brandy glass down. "In fact, I'm off after the young fool this evening." He consulted his pocket watch and slowly rose to his feet, one hand gripping his cane. "It's always a pleasure to speak to you, Miss Harrington. I appreciate your insight."

"And I always appreciate your company, Major."

"Liar." His sudden smile was unexpectedly charming. "We fight like cat and dog." He bowed. "Good evening. I'll let you know if I discover anything new."

"I'd appreciate that."

She watched him make his halting way over to

Mrs. Hathaway and make his adieus and then returned her attention to her hands that were folded in her lap.

"Lucy?"

"Yes, Mrs. Hathaway?"

"Come and sit by me, dear."

Lucy concealed a sigh and went to sit by her chaperone. "I know it isn't proper to have such a long conversation with one gentleman, especially at this time of night, but Major Kurland is an old family friend and I feel obliged to offer him my advice when he seeks me out."

"As I was sitting here chaperoning you the whole time Major Kurland was present I'm hardly going to be lecturing you about that, now am I?" Mrs. Hathaway patted Lucy's hand. "What I was going to say was that some men, actually most men, don't like to think that women are intelligent. It frightens them."

"So I've noticed," Lucy said gloomily.

"Which is why a lady on the lookout for a husband must *conceal* her intelligence until she has safely hooked her man and married him."

"That seems remarkably deceitful."

"Oh no, dear. It's simply good advice. Every man needs to be flattered a little and told that he is right even when he isn't."

"A little?" Lucy snorted. "Major Kurland wouldn't believe me if I did flatter him. He'd simply think I was after something."

"You might be surprised, my dear. He does keep coming to see you."

"Only because he values my opinion. You must not be imagining anything else, ma'am."

"Wouldn't you like to be the lady of Kurland Hall?"

"I've never thought about it."

"Then I suggest you do. I'm not the only one who believes Major Kurland's intentions toward you are becoming very marked."

"Oh good Lord. Who else?" Lucy asked.

"Your aunt and uncle for certain, and Miss Chingford hasn't a pleasant word to say about you and Anna stealing her admirers. I wouldn't be surprised if the earl doesn't ask Major Kurland about his intentions fairly soon. Now that he is to become a baronet, your uncle considers him a worthy match for the granddaughter of an earl."

Lucy simply stared at Mrs. Hathaway. "Major Kurland won't be amused if my uncle starts asking him about his intentions. It will make things very awkward between us."

"I wouldn't worry about it, dear. The menfolk will decide these matters in their own way."

"Which is ridiculous in itself. I'm not a pig being bought or sold at market!"

Mrs. Hathaway chuckled and patted Lucy's knee. "Now don't fly into alt, Lucy. *Lady* Kurland does have rather a nice sound to it, don't you think?"

• • •

Robert paid off the hackney and stepped into the grimy street. The lamps had been lit, but their flickering glow barely penetrated the dark corners of the row of tall buildings on both sides of the road. The smell of beer, sweat, and the stables drifted past Robert's nose and he turned toward the sign swinging over the archway entrance to the mews behind the Red Dragon Inn.

Smith fell into step beside him. "Do you want me to go and ask the landlord whether the young master is here, sir?"

"I can do that myself."

Smith cast a dubious glance at Robert's uniform. "You might not want to be seen in such a place, Major. The locals don't take kindly to the military around here. Let me go and ask around."

"There's not much I can do about my attire now, is there?" Robert sighed. "You go and talk to the landlord. I'll take a quick glance inside."

"You'll wait for me to investigate further, though, sir?"

"If you think it wise."

Smith disappeared into the mews, and Robert turned toward the scarred oak door that led into the inn. He had to bend his head to avoid the low-hanging beams in the narrow passageway that separated the tavern proper from the coaching side of the business. The door into the public bar reverberated with a low rumble of sound that

155

occasionally became raucous. Robert decided not to enter and glanced toward the right. In the daytime the large room would be filled with busy travelers awaiting their conveyances or acquiring a room for the night. At the moment it was empty apart from a rush basket on the end of one of the trestle tables that appeared to contain a forgotten chicken.

At the far end of the passageway, there was a staircase that obviously led up to the rooms for rent above the inn. Seeing no one around, Robert went up the stairs and found himself on a landing surrounded by six numbered doors. A single lantern swung back and forth illuminating the cramped space.

"Oh, I do beg your pardon, sir."

Robert almost lost his balance as a maidservant emerged from the door behind him with a bundle of bedclothes almost as big as she was clutched in her arms. He managed to grab hold of one of the vertical beams that framed the staircase and steadied himself.

"Are you after a room, sir?"

"Actually, I was after an acquaintance of mine, a Mr. Oliver Broughton. Is he still here?"

The maid took a hurried step backward. "I couldn't say, sir. I'm not allowed to share the names of our guests."

"I have an urgent message from his brother about a death in the family."

The young woman hesitated. "Well, he was in number four, sir, but I don't know—"

"Thank you." Robert stepped out of her way and gestured at the stairs. "I'll follow you down in a moment." He retrieved a coin from his pocket and handed it to her. "No need to worry the landlord."

After one scared glance back at him, the maid carefully descended the stairs, leaving Robert in the silence. He moved as swiftly as he could to the fourth door and knocked. There was no answer. He knocked again and then brought his hand up to the latch and gently pressed down.

The door swung inward, and Robert almost recoiled at the stench of human waste and sickness. He gripped the door frame hard enough to hurt his fingers and forced back the memories of battle and the chaos of a hastily improvised medical station in a ruined French chateau.

A man lay facedown on the bed, one arm trailing on the floor. A bucket stood close to his head and his nightshirt was filthy. Holding his breath, Robert advanced into the small, sloping space and looked down at the unmoving figure.

"Major!"

His attention snapped back to the door where Smith stood panting as if he'd run up the stairs.

"Yes?"

He swallowed hard. "He ain't dead, is he?"

"No thanks to you. How long have you known he was here?"

Smith joined him by the bed. "What makes you think I knew anything?"

Robert met his gaze. "Because this is the first time you've tried to dissuade me from involving myself in the search. I've dealt with a lot of young men during my military career. I can usually tell when I'm being lied to."

Smith sat gingerly on the side of the filthy bed and took hold of Oliver Broughton's wrist. An expression of alarm flooded his face.

"Major? I can't tell if he's breathing anymore."

Robert rolled Oliver over onto his back and stared into his waxen countenance. He'd seen far too many men near death not to recognize it even in civilian surroundings. "Go and find the landlord, and call us a hackney cab. We need to get him home at once."

Chapter 10

I'm not sure if your brother will live, Lieutenant, but I've at least made him comfortable."

Dr. Redmond drew the covers over his patient's naked chest and smoothed Oliver's hair away from his face before moving away from the bed, his expression strained. He started to pack away his instruments with hands that shook.

"Are you all right, Dr. Redmond?" Robert asked.

"I'm fine, Major. It is always a shock to see a young man in such a pitiful state, especially when one is well acquainted with the family."

After a nod from Broughton, one of the maidservants took up her station by the side of the bed, ready to watch over Oliver. Robert followed the doctor and Broughton out into the hallway and down to Broughton's suite of rooms.

"Thank you for finding him, Kurland." Broughton nodded as he subsided into one of the chairs by the fire. He didn't look much better than his brother.

"It was simply a process of elimination," Robert said. "I just wish that thoughtless manservant of his had told us where Oliver was immediately."

"The stupid young fool," Broughton said. "I've cast him off without a reference. He'll find it very difficult to find another job in London."

Robert studied Broughton. "That seems a little harsh. His loyalty was to his master."

"I'm his master, I pay the bills. Smith answered only to me."

Robert wisely didn't argue with that, although to the best of his knowledge it was the dowager and Broughton's father who managed the finances of the family. Or it had been. He supposed Broughton was in charge now by default.

"Has Oliver been poisoned, too, Dr. Redmond?"

"I beg your pardon?"

The doctor swung around from his contemplation of the fire. He still seemed rather distracted. "It's highly possible. According to his manservant, he was taken ill shortly after he arrived at the inn, and hasn't left his bed since the night of the ball."

"Did Smith tell him what had happened to Broughton and his grandmother?"

"I didn't ask, Major. I didn't consider it my business."

"Did you ask him, Broughton?"

"No."

Robert looked at them both. "Would you object if I sought Smith's opinion before he left?"

"Not at all." Broughton nodded his permission. "I assume you think it might be important, although I'm not sure why. As I mentioned, Oliver tends to remember only the things that show him in a favorable light."

"Which is why it might be important to see if he received that information and how he reacted to it. Excuse me, won't you?"

Robert made his way along to his own room and found Foley there sewing a button onto one of his shirts.

"Major Kurland? What's wrong?"

"There's nothing wrong, Foley. I just need your help."

"Naturally, Major. What can I do for you?" Foley put the sewing aside.

"Can you find Silas Smith?"

"I believe he's been dismissed."

"I know that, but can you see if he's still in the house? I need to speak to him." Robert walked over to the fireplace and contemplated the burning coals.

"I'll go and find out immediately. Do you want me to bring him here?"

"If you would, please."

"And do you require anything else while I'm forced to go up and down these stairs again, sir?"

Robert looked over his shoulder. "Do you want me to go instead?"

"Not at all, sir, not with your leg in the state it's in."

"Good. Then I'll await you here." Robert sat in the nearest chair and stretched out his booted feet to the blaze. Foley didn't appreciate all the levels of the Broughton town house and had made that very clear. In truth, Robert didn't appreciate them either. Stairs and steps made his life a misery.

Within a few minutes, Smith came into his room and stood before Robert. He was dressed for traveling and carried what appeared to be all his meager possessions in a knotted sack that he placed at his feet.

"Major Kurland."

Robert studied the manservant's face. "If your employer dies it might be your fault. Why in

God's name didn't you tell someone where he was?"

Smith's expression tightened. "He made me promise not to tell anyone."

"Why?"

"I don't know, sir. I just know that he begged me not to tell his family where he was. He was terrified."

That didn't sound like the actions of an innocent man. "Did he know the dowager countess had died, and that his brother was sick?"

"I didn't tell him, if that's what you mean, sir. He barely woke up after that first night."

"So it's possible that he doesn't know?"

"I suppose so, sir."

Robert considered the firm set of Smith's mouth. He'd got to know the young man reasonably well on their nightly quests to find Oliver and found him steady, dependable, and loyal to a fault. "Do you have anywhere to go, Smith?"

"Not really, sir, not without a reference." His mouth twisted. "I'll have to go back home and help out on the farm."

"Perhaps you might consider doing something for me first. I'll pay you for your trouble."

"Like what, sir?"

"Take a message to my house in Kurland St. Mary and bring me back any reply."

"I'd be right happy to do that."

Robert went across to the writing desk set against the wall. "Just give me a moment to write the letter and you can be on your way."

He scribbled a note to his potential new land agent, apologizing for his continuing absence and asking if Mr. Fairfax could remain in place for a while longer. He sealed the note with wax, pressed his signet ring into it, and turned back to Smith.

"Take this to Mr. Fairfax, my land agent at Kurland Manor. Foley will give you further directions. I suggest you stay at a coaching inn tonight and leave in the morning."

"Thank you." Smith took the letter and slowly counted the coins Robert handed him. "I think this might be too much, sir."

"Then keep an account of your spending and we can settle up when you return."

"How do you want me to contact you?" Smith cleared his throat. "I can hardly come back here."

"That's a good point. I'll give you the address of a family I'm acquainted with here in London, the Hathaways. You can meet me there."

"Thank you, Major Kurland."

Robert nodded as Foley reappeared clutching his heart as if the stairs had finally defeated him. "My butler will walk you out."

So what had Oliver Broughton meant when he'd begged his manservant not to reveal his location to his family? Whom was he more scared of, his brother or his grandmother?

Eventually, Foley returned, his breathing even more ragged. "I gave Smith the Hathaway address, sir, and sent him to the correct inn to connect with the Saffron Walden coach tomorrow morning."

"Thank you, Foley."

"He seemed a nice enough lad."

"He's certainly loyal, but in this instance, that loyalty might cost his former employer his life." Robert accepted the brandy Foley poured for him and slowly sipped it. "If he completes this task satisfactorily, I might consider taking him on myself."

"As your valet, sir?"

"Possibly, but I'd want to see whether he likes Kurland St. Mary first and that he won't pine for the city. I have no intention of spending much time here in the future."

"But surely once you take your place in the House of Lords, you'll have to be in London quite regularly, sir." Foley hesitated. "You do wish to take your seat?"

"Baronets aren't entitled to a seat in the Lords, Foley. But I might consider a run for Parliament instead." Robert frowned. "Devil take it, if I do that I'll have to find somewhere more permanent to live, won't I?"

"Do you wish me to inquire as to suitable

properties, sir?" Foley literally brightened. "I am rather lacking in occupation at the moment. The Broughton butler is resistant to my offer to help him restructure this house in a more efficient manner."

"You can certainly begin some inquiries for me, Foley." Robert sighed. "I'll have to pay closer attention to the matters being addressed in the lower house and decide whether I wish to become involved, and on which side."

"I'd be delighted to help out, Major." Foley refilled the brandy glass. "Do you wish to own a town house or an apartment, or will you merely be leasing something until you settle down more permanently?"

"I have no idea."

"Then I'll simply investigate all potential avenues." Foley rubbed his hands together. "Now, if you'll excuse me, sir. I must start making some lists."

"Good night, Foley. I can put myself to bed."

"And leave that uniform on the floor so that I have to spend hours brushing it? I don't think so, Major. I'll pop in later to make sure everything is put away properly."

"Thank you."

After Foley's departure, Robert rose and made his way out to the corridor. Pausing to check that there was nobody around, he walked along to Oliver's bedchamber and let himself inside. The maid who'd been sitting by Oliver's bed was nowhere in sight.

Robert paused to study Oliver's ghastly pallor. He didn't look like a murderer, more like a young boy at peace with the world. But Robert already knew that innocents could kill and die just like any other man. He'd been one himself. Moving closer to the bed, he listened to the slight rasp of Oliver's breathing and observed the faint flicker of his eyelashes.

"Oliver?" he whispered. "Can you hear me?"

He almost flinched when his hand was grabbed, almost pulling him down on top of the boy.

"Don't let her do it."

"Do what?" Robert leaned closer.

"Grandmother. Don't let her meddle."

Robert considered the boy's frantic gaze. "What did you do, Oliver?"

"*Nothing,* I just know there's going to be trouble, and I hate it. I *hate* it." His eyes closed again and he swallowed hard.

Robert straightened and placed Oliver's hand back on top of the coverlet. His skin was covered in scabs and his nails were ragged as if he'd been clawing at the walls. His frantic words were hardly a confession of guilt, but did signify that Oliver was aware of the tensions in the Broughton household. What had he feared his grandmother might do, and what might he have done to prevent his worst fears from happening?

"Kurland?"

Robert turned his head to see Broughton dressed in his banyan leaning heavily against the door frame. He looked far too ill to be out of bed.

"Good evening. I was just wondering where the maid had gone. I wanted to ask her how Oliver was doing."

"I sent her out to get some warm water to bathe his face. She should be back in a moment." Broughton moved closer. "Did he say anything? I thought I heard his voice."

"Nothing that made any sense to me," Robert replied diplomatically. "I should imagine we'll have to wait a few days to see what he has to say for himself. Has he spoken to you yet?"

"No." Broughton smoothed a hand through his hair. "To be honest, Kurland, I'm not sure I want to hear what he has to say. I'm terrified he'll admit to poisoning us, and then where will we be? Will I have to publicly denounce my own brother?"

"It's a difficult situation." Robert turned to the door. "I'll leave you in peace."

"Did you speak to Smith?"

"Yes, he confirmed that Oliver became ill that first night and was hardly conscious at all after that. He denies telling him that his grandmother is dead."

"Do you believe him?"

"It depends on what your brother says when he wakes up."

"If he wakes up." Broughton swallowed hard. "Perhaps it would be better if he didn't recover. At least then we'd be spared the indignity of a family scandal. As it is, even if he does get well and, God forbid, is not guilty, it might be better to ship him off to India to be with my father for a few years."

"That might also be the making of him."

"I damn well hope so." Broughton looked over Robert's shoulder. "Here's the maid coming back with the warm water."

Robert clasped Broughton's shoulder. "You should go to bed. You are in no condition to be wandering the halls at night."

"I know." Broughton's quick smile was strained. "I'm really quite exhausted."

Robert left his friend talking to the maid and made his way back to his own room. He had an appointment the next morning at the College of Arms to discuss his new family crest and motto, and was having difficulty in coming up with anything he wanted to include in such an unexpected honor. A pile of dead French and English soldiers topped by a bloody bayonet as a warning to his heirs not to go to war would probably not be acceptable.

And as for a family motto . . . He pushed open his door and contemplated his neatly turned down bed. He'd think about that in the morning.

• • •

Lucy counted the new guests who had arrived at her aunt's home, and walked over to introduce herself and offer them some tea. Not that anyone would accept a beverage. A call was supposed to last no more than fifteen minutes, and was a simple matter of being seen in the right place, speaking to the right people, and for the men, to be seen courting the Season's beauties, of which Anna was definitely one.

It was quite unlike Kurland St. Mary, where a visit to a neighbor involved a lengthy discussion of everyone's health, all of their relatives' whereabouts both living and dead, and an update on the local gossip. Such outings were liberally enhanced with endless cups of tea or something stronger, and wedges of fruitcake, scones, and clotted cream.

Lucy cast a longing look back at the teapot, which sat forlornly on the tray.

"Can I trouble you for a cup of tea, my dear? I'm rather thirsty."

She turned to see one of the new arrivals smiling up at her.

"Of course, Lady—?"

"Lady Bentley. I believe we met at Almack's, Miss Harrington."

"That's correct. I was with Lieutenant Broughton's party."

"And I was arguing with that awful old woman.

I do apologize for that. Maude Broughton brought out the worst in me."

Lucy handed Lady Bentley a cup of tea and poured one for herself. She spotted a pair of vacant chairs on the quieter side of the room and gestured toward them.

"Would you care to sit down, my lady?"

"Thank you." Lady Bentley settled herself in the chair with a rustling of petticoats. Despite her age she was a sprightly looking woman with a firm mouth and a way of tilting her head and looking at the world that reminded Lucy of an inquisitive hen. "I suppose you think I should be in mourning for the old harridan. At one point we were bosom beaus, but I'm not quite that much of a hypocrite."

"I assume you are referring to the sad death of the Dowager Countess of Broughton?"

Lady Bentley smiled. "I wouldn't use the word *sad* myself. In truth, when I saw her go down frothing at the mouth, I was quite thrilled."

Lucy glanced around to see if anyone else was attending to their rather unconventional conversation. "I thought your and the dowager's acquaintance was of long standing?"

"We used to be friends." Lady Bentley sipped her tea. "But as you might have noticed, we were at odds at the end."

Lucy considered her reply. "It is difficult when someone dies before you have the chance to sort out any grievances or misconceptions, isn't it?"

Lady Bentley finished her tea in one long gulp and put the cup down on the table. "Oh no, my dear. Sometimes it means that you win in the end. My eldest son and I planned to pursue her through the courts, but this has a far more biblical sense of justice to it, don't you think? An eye for an eye and all that?" She glanced past Lucy. "My son is waving at me. It must mean that it's time to go. It was a pleasure to meet you again, Miss Harrington."

Lucy rose and curtsied. "And you, Lady Bentley. Will you attend the dowager's memorial service?"

Lady Bentley chuckled. "I might just do that. One has to make sure that she is truly dead and buried." She smoothed down the skirt of her olive green gown. "I might even wear a nice red dress to commemorate the occasion. It will not be the same without the rubies she stole from me, but it will make me feel so much better."

"You believe the dowager stole your rubies?"

"Amongst other things." Lady Bentley drew on her gloves. "I'm sure the Countess of Broughton knows all about it. Be sure to ask her to tell you her version of the story and while you're about it, ask her to search the dowager's jewelry box for my rubies."

"Mama? Are you coming?" A tall man with a

rather forbidding stare came up behind Lady Bentley and nodded at Lucy.

"This is my eldest son. Miss Harrington, have you been introduced? He is of a similar age to Lieutenant Broughton."

"I haven't had that honor, Mama, but it is a pleasure to meet you, Miss Harrington." Mr. Bentley gave her a glacial nod. "Now, if you will excuse us, we have another call to make."

"Miss Harrington is acquainted with the Broughtons. Nigel, I was just asking her to find out if the dowager still has my jewels."

If possible, Mr. Bentley's expression grew even colder. "This is hardly the place to be discussing such a matter, Mama."

"Why not? The despicable woman is dead, and even if we can't take her to court, I'd still appreciate having my jewelry returned."

Mr. Bentley gripped his mother's elbow very firmly and urged her toward the door. "Good afternoon, Miss Harrington."

Lady Bentley winked at Lucy over her shoulder. "It seems I must be off. A pleasure, Miss Harrington."

Lucy sat down again as soon as Lady Bentley disappeared. She'd looked nothing like the angry woman Lucy had first seen at Almack's. Her rival's unexpected death seemed to have relieved her of her fury. With the dowager gone, there would be no more threats about stolen or misplaced jewelry to deal with. No more costly lawsuits or slurs on the Bentley family name. . . .

And there was certainly a lack of remorse, or sadness for the dowager's demise. Lady Bentley seemed positively joyful. But was that enough for Lucy to wonder whether the lady had taken to murder? Her son looked ready to murder anyone who stepped in his path. She'd noticed him hanging around her cousin. But Julia had never mentioned the man or displayed any partiality for him.

"Miss Harrington."

She looked up to find Mr. Stanford smiling at her.

"Mr. Stanford. Do you know a Mr. Nigel Bentley?"

"Yes, as a matter of fact, I do. He's a lawyer, supposedly a very good one, why do you ask?" His lazy gaze wandered over her face. "Do you wish to be introduced?"

"His mother introduced me to him."

He took the seat opposite her. "And what did you think of him?"

"He seemed rather impatient to be gone."

"Bentley's not known for his charm and since his father died, he is the head of the family. I suspect he rather relishes having the opportunity to control his mother's spending."

"Do you think it is possible that the lawsuit against the Broughton family was initiated by him rather than his mother?"

"Oh, you know about that, do you? I'm quite certain he was the instigator. His father and mother's extravagant lifestyle left him in poor financial straits and without even a title because his father was a mere knight. He'd probably be willing to do anything to restore his fortunes." He leaned forward. "Has Bentley been showing interest in your sister, Miss Harrington? I wouldn't recommend him as a suitable spouse at all. His temperament is difficult and his financial future requires that he marries an heiress."

"Oh no, I don't think he is interested in Anna at all."

"I wouldn't recommend him as a husband to any woman of sense." Mr. Stanford rose. "Now, I must pay my compliments to your aunt and be on my way. It's always a pleasure to see you, Miss Harrington."

She watched him walk across the room to her aunt and take his leave. What if Lady Bentley was working with her son to get rid of the dowager? Legal action was expensive and could drain a family's resources. Wouldn't it have been quicker to get rid of the woman and attempt to reclaim the jewels from the Broughton family afterward? She could imagine the countess and her son being willing to negotiate such a deal to avoid the scandal of a court case.

Nearly everyone had left now except a gaggle

of admirers clustered around Anna, Julia, and Sophia. Lucy glanced over at the circle. She really should go and join them. Her aunt would expect it. Just as she stood up, Major Kurland came into the drawing room and looked around; his gaze fell on her and he saluted.

"Miss Harrington."

"Major Kurland." She looked over at the group around Anna. "Do you wish to speak to my sister, or my cousin?"

"I'd rather speak to you, actually."

His voice was used to carrying over battlefields and rang out far too loudly in the confines of a London drawing room. Lucy's aunt looked up and came toward Robert, her hand extended.

"Major Kurland, how lovely to see you. I was hoping you'd come today."

He bowed over her hand. "My lady. How may I be of assistance?"

Lucy tried to melt away, but Aunt Jane flicked a commanding glance at her. "I was wondering if you'd like to come to dinner tomorrow night."

"That is very kind of you, my lady." Major Kurland hesitated. "I assume you don't expect me to bring the Broughtons?"

"Not at all, Major. I thought you might like an evening away from a house in mourning. It must be difficult for you."

"I promised the countess I would remain until Broughton is fit to take care of matters. I don't expect to be there much longer, but it's the least I can do."

"And reflects very well on you." Aunt Jane tucked her hand into the major's elbow and walked him determinedly toward where Lucy was standing poised for flight. "Ah, Lucy, do pour the major a cup of tea. He looks rather chilled."

Aunt Jane sat on the couch and Major Kurland had no choice but to join her. Lucy could tell from his expression that he'd rather be anywhere than cornered by a society hostess. But she assumed her aunt knew that, too, and was relying on his good manners to keep him by her side.

Lucy poured the tea and handed him a cup without meeting his eyes.

"Will you excuse me? I'll just go and ask the butler for some more hot water."

Aunt Jane patted the seat beside her. "Don't go quite yet, Lucy. I believe our guest wished to speak to you about something."

"Oh, I'm sure it was nothing of importance," Lucy said, and looked hopefully at the major. "Wouldn't you agree, sir?"

His blue eyes snapped sparks. "I would hardly have bothered to call if I hadn't deemed it necessary. I suppose it depends on your definition of what is important."

Lucy tried for a lighthearted laugh. "Which means that as I'm a woman it was probably something very trivial indeed."

"I never underestimate the contribution an intelligent woman can make to solving a problem, Miss Harrington, but if this is an inconvenient time . . ."

Aunt Jane rose to her feet. "Of course it isn't. You and Lucy are such old friends that no one will remark upon you sharing a quiet conversation. I'll leave you to converse for as long as you wish."

Lucy watched her aunt walk away and rejoin the crowd around Sophia and Anna. She felt far too conspicuous and found herself looking anywhere but at the man sitting opposite her.

"Are you feeling quite well, Miss Harrington?"

"I'm perfectly fine, thank you, Major."

"Are you sure?"

Summoning her courage, she turned to face him. "Yes, now what did you wish to speak to me about?"

"I thought you might like to know that I'd found Oliver Broughton."

"Alive?"

"Barely. He might even have been poisoned himself."

"Oh dear. Has he explained why he didn't return home?"

"According to his manservant, after Almack's, he went straight to an inn off the Strand and fell ill there later that night."

"Did he claim not to know his grandmother is dead?"

"He's not claiming anything. He's barely clinging to life and not in a position to be confessing his sins or his lack of them to anyone."

Lucy contemplated her gloved hands. "And what does Lieutenant Broughton think of that?"

"He's still convinced Oliver is the culprit."

"Even though Oliver is sick himself?" She shook her head. "I suppose one will just have to wait until Oliver regains his senses to question him more thoroughly. What will Broughton do if he is guilty?"

"Like most of the aristocracy, he'll ship the problem off to India and hope it resolves itself out there or never comes back."

"Without making him face justice here?"

Major Kurland shrugged. "There's no need to sound so judgmental. I didn't say I agreed with him, just that in my experience it's what usually happens."

"That's appalling."

"That's why I never wanted to be part of the aristocracy."

Lucy bit down on her lip to stop herself from getting into an argument with him about that again. Anyone might think that his honor from the Prince Regent had ruined his life.

"I spoke to Lady Bentley today."

"And who might she be?"

"The dowager's ex-best friend. The woman she

was fighting with at Almack's last time we were there."

"Ah, yes, I remember her."

"She is delighted that the dowager is dead."

"Of course she is."

Lucy set her jaw. "She was intending to take the dowager to court to retrieve her jewelry."

"But I thought the dowager claimed Lady Bentley had stolen it from her?"

"I don't know the full story, but I *do* know that Lady Bentley stood to lose her social standing if the dowager's version of events was believed."

"Which is still hardly a reason to resort to murder."

"You really don't understand women at all, do you? Sometimes our reputation is all we have left." She gathered her thoughts. "Lady Bentley's son needs to restore the family fortune. Mr. Stanford believes that *he* was the one behind the threat to go to court to retrieve the Bentley jewelry."

Major Kurland straightened. "What does any of this have to do with Stanford?"

"I asked his opinion of Mr. Bentley."

"You shouldn't be asking him about anything to do with this matter."

"Why not?"

"Because it is private."

"But he is a friend of yours."

179

"Miss Harrington, if I'd wanted his opinion, I would've asked him myself. Now can we get back to the matter in hand?"

"You were the one who started talking about Mr. Stanford."

"Because you—" He sighed. "I've completely forgotten what I came here to say now."

"Then perhaps if I am proving to be such an unsatisfactory companion you should go and speak to Sophia and Anna."

He raised his eyebrows. "Why? They are surrounded by admirers. They hardly need to speak to me."

"Because coming here and seeking me out and no one else isn't socially acceptable."

"You are in a strange mood this afternoon, Miss Harrington. Who would care or notice whether I talk to you or anyone else?"

"You are about to become a *baronet,* Major. That makes you a catch on the marriage mart. Haven't you noticed all the matchmaking mamas smiling at you recently?"

"No, I haven't because such a thing would be ridiculous."

"Why?"

"Because"—he glared down at her—"I'm not willing to be married for my title, my lands, or my social position." He readjusted his grip on his cane. "I'm not exactly much of a catch, am I, Miss Harrington? An awkward cripple who has something of a temper and is afraid of getting back on a horse. Most of these young girls would run away in terror the first time I growled at them."

"Some might, but not all of them."

"Because some of them value a title more than the man who owns it. I've already learned that lesson from Miss Chingford, Miss Harrington. I refuse to be conned again." He checked the clock on the mantelpiece. "I must be going. I've spent the last few hours at the College of Arms trying to decide how my coat of arms should look and come up with a family motto."

"How interesting. I've never thought about how such things come about before. One just assumes all family titles are old and their meaning resonant with history."

He half-smiled. "Apparently, including any direct reference to the fortune I inherited from my grandfather's mills is not appropriate. If you think of anything meaningful I might wish to bestow on future generations of my family, Miss Harrington, please don't hesitate to share your thoughts with me."

"I will, Major, and in the meantime, if you do not dislike it, I will further my acquaintance with the Countess of Broughton and Lady Bentley and see if I can discover exactly why she and the dowager were at war."

"If you must." He carried on speaking before

she could get a word in. "I'd rather wait to see if Oliver confesses all."

"I wonder whether Lieutenant Broughton will allow you to be present at such an interview?"

He hesitated. "What do you mean?"

"If he intends to send Oliver away regardless, he probably won't want you knowing the truth, will he?"

"Broughton isn't like that. He's quite a disciplinarian and set in his ways."

"But, as you said, not necessarily with his own family." Lucy sighed. "I wish Oliver would wake up and confide in you and then you can decide what to do."

Major Kurland paused as he rose to his feet. "He did say one thing to me, but it didn't make much sense."

"I thought you said he hadn't spoken to anyone?"

"I can hardly call it a conversation. He was merely babbling due to his fever. He insisted that his grandmother should not be allowed to meddle."

"I wonder what he meant." She looked up at him. "Maybe my theory is correct and the dowager is the one who poisoned herself."

"You do have a terrible tendency to leap to the most far-fetched conclusions, Miss Harrington. Oliver might simply have been suggesting he'd taken care of that problem once and for all."

"Oh, I didn't think of that."

His complacent smile was particularly infuriating. "Let's wait to hear what he has to say, shall we?" He bowed. "Good afternoon, Miss Harrington. Thank you very much for the tea."

Chapter 11

Lucy smiled at the Countess of Broughton and poured her another cup of tea. It hadn't taken her long to gain the countess's permission to visit her at home. Insisting that it was an honor to be of assistance, she'd tucked a blanket over the countess's knees and a fine paisley shawl around her shoulders. Being the daughter of a rector had taught her how to care for the bereaved and the lonely, and she sensed the countess was both.

"You are very kind, my dear."

Lucy patted her black mittened hand. "I'm just doing what my father would wish, my lady. He always insisted that Anna and I place the needs of others above ourselves." Particularly *his* needs, but the countess didn't need to know that.

"An estimable man," the countess murmured. "Most young women today seem far too intent on pursing their own pleasure rather than caring for their families."

Lucy had persuaded the countess to give up her place in the large draughty drawing room and take refuge in her sitting room at the back of the house, which not only caught the morning sun, but also was a lot easier and smaller to heat.

"I met a Lady Bentley at my aunt's house yesterday. She asked to be remembered to you."

The countess shuddered. "I have no wish to be remembered by *her*. She and the late dowager ruined many a social occasion for me recently with their ridiculous feud."

"Lady Bentley referred to some rubies that she believed belonged to her. Is it true that she meant to take the dowager to court over such a small matter?"

"It's a rather complicated story."

Lucy assumed her most interested expression and the countess continued. "They came out in the same year and were considered inseparable. Then Maude, my future mother-in-law, set her cap at a certain man, and managed to wring a proposal of marriage from him despite everyone knowing that he really preferred her best friend, Agnes."

"Oh dear."

"Lady Bentley was not the sort of woman to accept such a situation. She managed to persuade the man in question to marry her instead. As you might imagine, the dowager didn't take that very well, and her family considered legal action against the Bentleys. Luckily, it came to naught because Maude met the Earl of Broughton and married him instead. She always insisted that her choice was far superior because she'd married an earl, whereas Agnes had settled for a mere knight."

"But what does that have to do with rubies?"

"Well, Bentley gave Maude some of his family jewelry during their betrothal, and she refused to give it back after the arrangement ended. Lady Bentley insisted it should be returned to her, and the matter has remained one of heated discussion for the last forty years."

"So why did Lady Bentley finally decide to resurrect the matter and turn to the law?"

"Because Maude insisted that Agnes had recently *stolen* the jewels from her. Lady Bentley, of course, denied it, and the dowager took her grievances and decided to air them in front of the *ton*."

"I cannot imagine Lady Bentley charging in here and stealing jewelry, can you?"

"No, because the dowager barred her from the house years ago." The countess shivered and gathered the shawl more closely around her shoulders. "It's far more likely that my mother-in-law misplaced the jewels and decided to blame her old enemy."

"And gave you yet another thing to worry about, my lady," Lucy said gently, and set the countess's empty cup down beside her. "When do you expect your husband to return?"

"Not for many weeks, my dear. If he decides to come." The countess sighed. "Although as his mother's financial affairs were rather complex, it might force him to return."

"Indeed." Lucy sipped her own tea and toasted her toes on the hearth of the fire. "I presume you won't wait for him to bury the dowager, then?"

"If it were up to me, Miss Harrington, I'd have my mother-in-law buried tomorrow, but Broughton is insisting we wait until Oliver recovers."

Lucy looked sympathetic. "It must be very hard for you to deal with this when your own health is so delicate."

"It is very difficult, indeed, and yet no one thinks of me. Major Kurland has been very kind, but it's not the same as having one's family around one, is it?" There was a whining note to the countess's voice that rose with every word. "Unfortunately, my only daughter is away in Wales awaiting the birth of her second child."

"So you have no one here to help and support you." Lucy took a deep breath. "I wonder if I might make a suggestion? I would be more than willing to help you with any tasks that require a more *delicate* approach. I have a lot of experience in these matters from helping my father's parishioners."

That was at least the truth. She could be very helpful to the countess, who appeared to find everything an effort.

"But what of your Season?"

Lucy smiled. "I really came to support my sister. I'm rather too old to expect to find a husband for myself."

The countess regarded her carefully. "You have many wonderful qualities, Miss Harrington, as does your sister. I cannot imagine you won't be sought after."

"Then let me help you when I can. My father would be most disappointed if I didn't at least offer my services." Lucy kept going. "For example, I'm sure the idea of setting the dowager's possessions to rights and cataloguing them for the benefit of the estate would tax your strength enormously. In fact, if I *did* help to sort out her affairs, we might find those missing jewels again, and settle the matter once and for all."

"That would be nice." The countess stared into the fire, her expression thoughtful.

"Then I could aid you with that at least." Lucy tried to look dependable. "It wouldn't impede on my social invitations at all."

The countess patted her hand. "You are very kind. I will speak to Broughton and see if he is amenable to the idea. He seems to hold your family in high esteem, so I doubt he will prevent you from helping me." She hesitated. "If you are sure, that is? And if your aunt and Mrs. Hathaway can spare you?"

Lucy squeezed the countess's thin fingers and smiled. "It would be an honor, my lady."

In an effort to avoid the well-meaning attentions of the staff and Dr. Redmond's unending lectures, Robert had taken to visiting Oliver's bedchamber late at night when it was comparatively quiet. He'd even sat with Oliver while the nurse carried out various tasks that required her to leave the room.

After an hour of listening to Foley explaining the delights and downside of the current London property market, he'd finally managed to escape to the relative peace of Oliver's suite. Having been bedridden himself, he had a particular understanding of the frustrations of the situation and was more than willing to help out. As he approached Oliver's door he heard voices and slowed his steps. If he wasn't mistaken, Broughton was in there and speaking quite desperately to his brother.

"Oliver, tell me the truth. Devil take it, *tell* me! What did you see?"

Robert couldn't hear the weak answer well enough to make sense of it and took another cautious step closer to the half-open door.

"It didn't make any sense." Oliver sounded stronger now. "Why would she—" He coughed, and there was the sound of water being poured into a cup.

"She's dead, Oliver."

"Grandmother is?" Robert tensed as Oliver started to laugh. "That's wonderful."

Robert's cane struck the door and he quickly caught it before deliberately rattling the door handle and walking in.

"Broughton?" He turned his attention to the bed, where Oliver lay propped up against his pillows, his face flushed and his eyes glittering. "Good to see you are recovering, Oliver." He paused. "Am I interrupting?"

Broughton gestured to a chair. "No, please come in. Your appearance is highly propitious. I was about to question Oliver about what happened after Almack's."

His brother's face clouded. "As I said, I had a few drinks and then felt ill. Silas got me a room at the inn. I stayed there until I woke up and realized I was in my own bed again. Where is Silas, by the way?"

"He's been dismissed."

"For helping me? That's *typical* of you, Broughton, you are far too harsh."

Broughton sat up straight and stared at his brother. "Aren't you going to ask what happened to your grandmother?"

"Why should I? She's dead, isn't she? That's the best news I've had all week. I'm not going to pretend I cared about her. Everyone knew we were at odds. Did she finally drop dead in one of her rages? I'm just sorry I missed it." He glanced at Robert. "Why are you both looking at me like that?"

"She died just after you left the ballroom at Almack's," Robert said.

"Well, she had been stirring up trouble, hadn't she? Fighting with Broughton about his choice of wife, with me about my allowance, and with Lady Bentley threatening to take her to court . . ." He trailed off. "What's wrong?"

Robert glanced at Broughton, who seemed content to leave the questioning to him. "As far as we can tell, she didn't die of rage but of something far more sinister."

"Don't tell me someone shot her in the middle of Almack's? What a lark! I almost wish I'd stayed to watch."

Robert winced at the callous tone. "She wasn't shot. The doctor believes both your grandmother and your brother were poisoned."

Oliver's mouth closed and he lay back on his pillows. *"Poisoned?"*

"Yes."

"But"—Oliver stared at Robert and then at his brother—"that's absurd."

"Did you ever help your grandmother in her stillroom?"

"Of course not! Are you trying to suggest I had something to do with this?" Oliver turned to Broughton. "Aren't you going to defend me?"

Broughton's mouth twisted. "I wish I could. You hated her, Oliver. You were seen by one of the maids leaving the stillroom last week."

"Dammit, Broughton, we were all in there sometimes, even you! She gave me something for my cough, some concoction of rose hips and honey, that's all." He fell back against his pillows, his face flushed and his mouth a hard line. "I wanted her dead, but I would never have chosen that route."

Broughton brought something out of his pocket. "Then why did Smith have this amongst his possessions?"

Robert studied the label on the empty glass bottle, which was covered in the dowager's distinctive crabbed handwriting.

" 'Privet. Use sparingly.' " Robert squinted hard and managed to make out the words.

"Maybe Silas killed her! I don't know! This is ridiculous!"

"I doubt Smith was able to get into the ballroom at Almack's," Robert said drily. "This is rather incriminating."

He wondered what other evidence Broughton was refusing to share with him. It seemed that Miss Harrington might be correct about his friend trying to exclude him from finding out the truth.

"I didn't kill her, Broughton." Oliver scrubbed a hand across his face. "I left the ball in a rage, went straight to the inn, and fell ill. That's all I remember."

"How much had you had to drink before we even arrived at Almack's, Oliver? Can you even be sure of what you did?" Broughton hesitated. "It wouldn't be the first time you have no memory of a night of carousing, would it?"

"Damnation, I think I'd remember if I'd tried to murder my brother and my grandmother!"

Broughton sighed and put the bottle back in his pocket. "I suggest you think about this matter while you recover? When you are prepared to be completely honest with me, I will be glad to hear anything you wish to share and will do my best as your brother to ensure that no harm comes to you." He paused. "Or you might care to wait until our father returns and explain yourself to him."

Oliver's face blanched. "Oh God, not him. He's never been on my side. He believes everything you and Grandmother tell him."

Broughton stood and patted Oliver's clenched fist. "Then think very carefully about what you want to do." He glanced over at Robert. "I think it would be best if we left him to sleep now, don't you?"

"Of course." Robert nodded at Oliver and followed Broughton out into the hallway and down to his suite of rooms. "You look better today."

"Thank you." Broughton sank into a chair and Robert sat opposite him. "I'm sorry that I didn't tell you about what I found in Smith's bags. I wanted to see Oliver's face when I showed him the bottle."

"I understand." Robert kept his gaze on the fire. "Are you still convinced that Oliver is responsible for this matter?"

"After finding that bottle of poison, I'm fairly certain, aren't you?" Broughton groaned and buried his face in his hands. "I can't believe it's come to this."

"Don't give up hope. He hasn't confessed to anything yet. Perhaps he is innocent as he claims."

Broughton slowly looked up at him. "Do you think so?"

"There are others who disliked the dowager just as much as Oliver did."

"Such as?"

"Lady Bentley for one. Wasn't she threatening to take your family to court?"

"I hadn't thought of that. But surely that would mean my grandmother would've been the one doing the poisoning."

"That *was* another possibility that had occurred to me."

"Good Lord! That my grandmother poisoned herself?" Broughton went still. "She certainly had the knowledge."

"Maybe she simply meant to scare Lady Bentley and misjudged the dose?"

"That's a remarkably charitable interpretation of my grandmother's actions. If she'd meant to kill with her poison, she would've been successful."

"And I suppose she was. She just happened to give the poison to the wrong person. Herself." Robert stood up. "This is all pure speculation, of course. I just wanted to give your thoughts another direction to consider rather than worrying about Oliver."

"That's very good of you, Kurland. You've been very kind to me and my family over the past week." He swallowed hard. "I suppose if Oliver won't confess, and Dr. Redmond can't identify exactly what killed my grandmother, we will never know what happened, will we?"

"Unfortunately not. Have you considered that such a scenario might be for the best?"

"I suppose it might, but I hate injustice, you know that. I'd much rather see the culprit suffer."

"Even if it is your brother?"

"Even then, although I suspect my father might have something to say about that. He would probably prefer to keep it quiet and take Oliver back to India with him."

"Naturally."

Broughton's smile was tight. "I don't expect you to understand that, Kurland, but to my father our family name means everything."

"Then perhaps it would be better if we could prove the dowager poisoned herself after all." Robert headed for the door. "Good night, Broughton."

Deep in thought, Robert made his way down the stairs into the front hall and then down the servants' stairs to the kitchen. As he entered the kitchen, a sudden scraping back of chairs and of conversations shut off greeted him. He cursed under his breath when he realized the staff was eating their dinner and that he had disturbed them.

He remained by the door as the butler bowed to him, and Foley, who was seated at the butler's right hand, pretended not to notice his existence.

"Major Kurland, how may we help you?"

Robert waved a hand at them all to sit down again. "I apologize for bothering you at this time of night. I wanted to speak to the dowager's maid. Is she still employed here?"

One of the women stood up again. "I was the dowager's maid, sir."

Robert nodded at her. "After you've finished your dinner, could you come and speak to me in my room? Thank you."

He turned and retreated as quickly as he could as the conversation returned and his interruption was either quickly forgotten or was being avidly discussed. He'd meant to speak to the dowager's maid earlier in the week and had forgotten to do so. Switching his cane into his right hand, he slowly mounted the stairs and headed for his bedchamber. At the pace he went, the maid would probably beat him upstairs. It was interesting that Broughton had reacted to the idea that the dowager might have poisoned herself without ridicule. Perhaps Miss Harrington's idea wasn't quite as far-fetched as he'd first thought.

Robert grimaced as he finally reached the top of the staircase and waited for his left leg to recover. Miss Harrington would appreciate that.

"You wanted to see me, Major Kurland?" The maid curtsied. "I'm Hester Macleod."

"Thank you for coming. I apologize for interrupting your dinner."

"Think nothing of it, sir." She gave him a competent smile. She was far younger than he'd anticipated and hardly a suitable companion for an elderly lady. "How can I help you?"

"I wanted to ask you about your duties. Did you serve as the dowager's abigail or were you with her for most of the day?"

"When my mother died I took over her job as the dowager's abigail, sir. As the dowager grew older, my duties expanded to include accompanying her around the house and offering my help when needed."

"I'll wager she didn't accept help too easily."

"That's true, sir, but she is to be commended for refusing to allow her age to stop her from enjoying life to the fullest."

"Did you aid her in the stillroom as well?"

"Yes, sir. Her eyes were failing. I often had to read out the ingredients from the herbal and make sure she was certain of the dosage required before she started handing out potions to the household." Hester cast a furtive look behind her and continued in a low voice. "There was one incident recently when she insisted the whole household needed to take her worming medicine. Everyone who did so became ill. After that Lieutenant Broughton insisted she had to have someone with her in the stillroom at all times."

"Which was usually you."

"Yes, sir."

"I assume she didn't take well to Lieutenant Broughton's decree."

A faint flush appeared on the maid's cheeks. "Not really, sir. She said there was nothing wrong with her potions and that the younger generation were a bunch of lily-livered weaklings."

"Do you remember what kind of potions the dowager was brewing in the last week of her life?"

"I'm not really sure, sir."

"Come now, if you were responsible for reading the instructions out to the dowager, you must remember what you were making. Lieutenant

Broughton was counting on you to keep the household safe."

"Sometimes she refused to let me see what she was brewing up and made me leave the room." Hester swallowed hard. "I was afraid not to do what she told me in case I lost my position."

"I understand. But can you remember anything you helped her make recently?"

"We made face cream for the countess, and some pills to help Master Oliver sleep, and some rat poison and—"

"Did you also make cough syrup for Master Oliver?"

"I believe he came in for some, sir, but we brewed that particular remedy all through the winter months and not just for him. Everyone gets a bit of a cold now and again, don't they?"

"Indeed, they do. Did Master Oliver ever help out in the stillroom?"

"Sometimes he came in to speak with the dowager countess and he'd ask me questions about the potions while he waited for his grandmother to attend to him. He never stayed long. They did tend to annoy each other."

"So I've heard." Robert thought about how to ask his next questions. "Do you know what was in the sleeping pills the dowager made for Oliver?"

"The usual things, sir, valerian, lavender, and feverfew for his headaches."

"And what about the rat poison?"

"It depended on what we had on hand, sir. The dowager always said there were hundreds of ways to get rid of vermin. She loved to tell me stories of famous folk who used poison to get rid of somebody important."

"Did she ever tell you which her favorite poisons were?"

"She liked the strength of the privet berries, sir, and the fact that lily of the valley was considered such a sweet virginal plant when it was actually quite deadly." She paused. "With all due respect, sir, is there any particular reason why you're asking me all these questions? You don't think I did anything wrong, do you?"

"Not at all. Did you think the dowager was becoming frailer?"

"I wouldn't say that. She seemed full of vim and vigor to me."

"I understand that she had a bad heart and that she took her own concoctions to help herself."

"She did, sir." Hester paused. "You don't think she brewed up something too strong when I wasn't looking and did something bad to her heart? I can't be held responsible if she ordered me out of the stillroom, can I? That wouldn't be fair."

Robert considered the trembling woman. If he told Broughton that the dowager's maid had left her to brew potions by herself, Hester's career would be over, and like Silas Smith she would be cast off as untrustworthy and without a reference.

"I certainly don't think that's the case, Miss Macleod, and it certainly wouldn't be fair. I'm sure you did everything in your power to keep the dowager countess safe."

"Thank you, sir." She bobbed a curtsy. "Can I go now, Major Kurland? I have to help Connie put her ladyship to bed."

"Of course, and thank you for your help."

Robert remained sitting by the fire and ran the conversation back through his head. It seemed that everyone had access to the stillroom and that Oliver was rarely there, but had shown an interest in what was being produced. But the dowager herself had already accidentally poisoned the whole household once. Was it too far-fetched to believe that Miss Harrington was right and that she might have made a more vital mistake and poisoned herself?

Chapter 12

C ome along, Anna, the countess is expecting us."

Lucy picked up her skirts and went up the steps of the Broughton town house. After some thought, she'd decided it was far better to bring

Anna with her to help out than to go alone. Anna was an excellent and tireless worker, and might prove useful if Lucy needed to lure Lieutenant Broughton away.

After establishing that the countess was still in bed, but was more than willing for Lucy to begin cataloguing the dowager's possessions, the sisters found themselves in the lofty apartment of the deceased dowager. It seemed that she had never relinquished the countess's formal apartment, forcing her son and daughter-in-law to occupy a far more modest suite on the other side of the house.

"Good Lord," Anna breathed. "This will take forever! Why on earth did you offer to help?"

Lucy had to agree. The suite of rooms was filled with large, old-fashioned, walnut and teak furniture from a different, more formal century. Boxes were stacked against the walls, and trunks were overfilled with gowns and petticoats made of brightly colored silks and satins that had long gone out of fashion. She opened the curtains, dislodging a week or so's worth of accumulated dust and brownish snuff and sneezed. To be truthful, the thought of finally being active and *useful* far outweighed her desire to discover anything she hoped to find.

"Well, we'd better make a start then, hadn't we? Do you have pen and paper?"

Anna cleared a space on the desk under the

window and laid her paper out. "Where do you want to begin?"

Lucy considered the huge rooms. "I wonder if we should speak to the dowager's maid and ascertain where her mistress kept her valuables? I suspect Lady Broughton would like us to start with those, don't you?"

Three hours later, when they'd employed the help of both the dowager's abigail and one of the maids, Lieutenant Broughton put his head around the door.

"Good morning, Miss Harrington, Miss Anna Harrington." He bowed. Lucy was pleased to see that he appeared to be regaining his health. "I was hoping to persuade you to share a nuncheon with my mother and myself." He smiled. "We cannot have you overworking on our behalf, although we are both incredibly thankful for your generous help."

"Thank you, Lieutenant. I was feeling rather peckish and I'm sure Anna is, too." Lucy dusted down the front of her brown Indian muslin gown and stood back as Anna went forward to greet Broughton.

"Are you really feeling better, Lieutenant?" Anna asked.

"Yes, Miss Anna, I am." He took her hand and brought it to his lips.

"And how is your brother? Major Kurland said he had been quite ill as well."

Broughton tucked Anna's hand into the crook of his elbow and patted it. "Oliver is recovering quite well. It is so kind of you to be so concerned about us all."

Lucy followed along behind the engrossed pair and down to the dining room where the countess already awaited them. There was no sign of Major Kurland. Had he returned to his hotel? She could hardly ask. That would be displaying far too much of an interest in the man.

After the meal, Broughton suggested a stroll in the garden. It was a remarkably clear day without the usual biting chill of a harsh spring, so both ladies acquiesced. Lucy was happy to listen to Anna and Broughton talk while she considered fresh places to search for the missing Bentley rubies.

The dowager did have a document listing some of her jewelry, but the list wasn't complete and the Bentley jewelry was not on it. When she returned to the dowager's rooms, Lucy decided to concentrate on discovering all the places she might have hidden any valuables that were not already accounted for.

She realized Broughton was leading them toward the second building in the garden and hurried to catch up. It was a shame he'd neglected to take them to the stillroom. She'd rather hoped to take another peek at the dowager's herbal.

"Ladies." Broughton stood back to allow the

sisters to pass into the building. "This used to be the dairy. I had it converted into a laboratory."

"You are truly a man of science, Lieutenant Broughton," Lucy commented as she studied the long wooden benches and tiled floors of the austere space. It was as unlike the dowager's stillroom as the sun and the moon. Everything had its place and was labeled and sorted into regimental straight lines. Major Kurland would approve.

"I *aspire* to be a man of knowledge and learning, Miss Harrington. I wouldn't consider myself a true expert, but I do my best to keep abreast of the latest scientific and botanical theories."

"You are to be commended, Lieutenant. Our father is of a similar bent."

Lucy moved farther into the room, noticing the sharp tang of lye soap and a hint of something that smelled like rotten eggs. She wrinkled her nose and turned to see the lieutenant smiling down at Anna. Swallowing down her next question, she caught a flutter of motion in one of the cages that lined the back wall, and went over to investigate. She found herself staring into the small black eyes of a sparrow. Other cages contained mice, rabbits, and her least favorite pest of all, rats. She wasn't sure if it was their pink tails or their red eyes that offended her most.

"Are you admiring my test subjects, Miss Harrington?"

Broughton had obviously finished gazing into Anna's eyes and had come up behind her.

"Test subjects?"

"These creatures help resolve the mysteries of the human condition."

"Which I assume means that you test your theories on them?"

"Exactly."

Anna shivered. "That doesn't seem very fair. Why should these creatures have to suffer to prove a scientific theory?"

"Unfortunately, Miss Anna, in order to progress as a species, we have to use whatever is at our disposal." Broughton spoke gently, but there was an underlying note of purpose in his words. "These dumb animals don't feel as we do, or experience pain in the same way. They are merely a tool to be utilized for the benefit of mankind."

Anna turned away. "I still don't think it's very fair, Lieutenant." She glanced over at Lucy. "Is it time for us to return to the house? I believe we should be getting on."

Without another word she turned on her heel and went toward the door, her lower lip caught in her teeth. Beside Lucy, Broughton sighed.

"I've offended her, haven't I?"

"My sister has always had a very soft heart, sir."

"But surely she has to see that in order to prove a theory one has to make sacrifices?"

"I don't suppose she thinks about it quite like that," Lucy said diplomatically. "Shall we go after her? It *is* getting rather late."

"Of course, Miss Harrington." He locked the door behind him and offered her his arm. "I was hoping that you and your sister would accompany me to an alfresco event on Friday."

"Are you sure you are well enough to resume your social activities, Lieutenant?"

He chuckled. "Indeed, I feel that if I don't get out of this house soon, I'll become quite unbearable. I'm not used to being caged up inside."

Lucy forbore to comment that the creatures in his laboratory might harbor similar feelings, and followed him into the house. She hated being cooped up herself. Apparently a young unmarried lady was not allowed to walk anywhere in London without being accompanied by at least a maid, if not a footman, which irritated Lucy immensely.

When Broughton set off to speak to his mother, she continued on upstairs to find Anna already busy unpacking one of the dowager's chests.

"Are you all right, Anna?" Lucy noted the vigor with which her sister was dumping the contents of the chest out onto the carpet. "Lieutenant Broughton was concerned that he had offended you."

Anna looked up at Lucy, a silken opera cloak clutched to her chest. "How could he treat those animals so?"

"He is a man of science."

"He is cruel."

Lucy sank down on her knees beside her sister. "Our father hunts foxes and shoots game birds, as do all gentlemen, why is this any different?"

"I don't know. It just feels so much more *detached,* as if he doesn't gain enjoyment from it, only knowledge."

"I still fail to see the difference. Is it better to enjoy the killing? The poor creature is still dead at the end of it."

Anna hunched a shoulder. "You lack sensibility, Lucy. I have often remarked upon it."

"Because I'm a pragmatist and you are a romantic. And I didn't think Lieutenant Broughton was completely detached about his experiments. He sounded quite fervent about them, actually."

"Which just makes it worse."

Lucy sighed and considered the contents of the chest. "Shall I write the list while you repack the chest?"

The alfresco event was held in a large mansion that sloped down toward a series of shallow man-made ponds that eventually fed into the River Thames. Lucy sat with Mrs. Hathaway while Anna chatted to Julia, and Sophia took the opportunity to walk her little dog around the gardens with Mr. Stanford.

During the luncheon, she spotted Lady Bentley

and discreetly made her way over to where the lady was sitting. She was spotted at once and waved into the vacant seat.

"Miss Harrington, what a pleasant surprise."

"Lady Bentley. Isn't it a beautiful day for such an event?"

"Indeed, it is. Are you here with your aunt?"

"No, she had a slight chill and decided not to come out today. My sister and I came with the Hathaways and Lieutenant Broughton."

"Broughton, eh? I heard a rumor that both he and his younger brother had been brought to their beds since the dowager's death."

"They have both been unwell."

Lady Bentley snorted. "Or struggling to hide their complete lack of remorse over that harridan's death. They should be thanking me and Miss Chingford for driving her into such a rage."

"You believe you caused her death?"

"In a manner of speaking, yes—at least I hope I had a hand in it. My son has a hot temper and threatened to strangle the old biddy for me. I told him a more subtle approach was needed."

Lucy swallowed hard. "And did he heed your words?"

"He is a very clever man, I'm sure he did." Lady Bentley poked Lucy's arm with her fan. "Did you speak to the countess about my rubies?"

"Actually, I've been helping catalogue the dowager's possessions, but there is no sign of your rubies. The dowager told the current countess that the jewelry had been stolen from her."

"Or she sold or pawned it to pay her debts." Lady Bentley's mouth thinned. "Although I doubt she would do that unless she was desperate, and she never struck me as a woman who was short of money."

"Are you talking about your lost jewels again, Mama?"

Lucy jumped as Nigel Bentley loomed over her. "Of course I am, dear. I want them back."

Her son took a seat opposite Lucy and studied his mother. "I hardly think this is a suitable place to discuss such a matter. The Dowager Countess of Broughton is dead."

"And she isn't going to win, Nigel. You agreed with me, you said you would do anything to—"

Mr. Bentley cut across her. "Is Lieutenant Broughton here today, Miss Harrington?"

"Yes, he is."

"Then perhaps it is time to take this matter up with him myself."

"Oh!" Lady Bentley's voice rose to a shriek. "I wouldn't recommend that, darling. He isn't the easiest of men to deal with now, is he? And he's a hardened killer straight from the battlefields of France!"

Mr. Bentley stood up. "And I doubt he'll draw his cavalry sword and run me through at a public event, Mama. I've always found him a reasonable man."

"But—"

He bowed and walked away. Lady Bentley grabbed Lucy's hand in a punishing grip.

"You have to go after him, or warn Broughton that he is coming! Nigel has a terrible temper; there's no knowing what might happen."

Lucy eased her hand free of the frantic grip. "I'll do my best, my lady."

"I should never have involved him in this matter. He is too quick to defend me at all costs."

"It's all right. I'll go and find Lieutenant Broughton."

"Thank you." For the first time Lady Bentley looked truly frightened. "I couldn't bear to lose my only son. I'll come with you."

Her concern sounded rather extreme to Lucy, but then she'd never been a mother and had no idea what Nigel Bentley might do. She couldn't imagine Lieutenant Broughton becoming involved in a brawl either. She spied Anna's yellow plumed bonnet down toward the edge of the lake and headed down the slope. If Anna was there, Broughton was probably close behind.

Robert was not having the best of days. He'd barely arrived at the party when Miss Chingford attached herself to his arm and refused to stop chatting to him as if they were the best of friends.

Short of shaking himself free and flinging her to the ground, he couldn't think of a single way to politely dispose of her company. She was also leading him down toward the boating area of the lake, and the uneven surface was proving difficult for his injured leg to navigate.

"Miss Chingford, will you, please—"

When she realized he was intending to lead her over to Broughton, she suddenly pulled out of his grasp and stomped off in a huff, upsetting his balance.

"Major Kurland, are you all right?"

He rocked back and forth and discovered Anna Harrington in front of him, one hand reaching out as if ready to stop him tumbling headfirst into her arms. He dug his cane into the soft ground and finally managed to stay upright.

"Miss Anna."

As he forced himself to continue down the slope, Broughton turned toward him and nodded at the boats. "Are you coming, Kurland? I could do with another pair of hands."

Dubiously, Robert regarded the boats. "I'm not sure if—"

"Lieutenant Broughton!"

The demanding tone had both Robert and Broughton turning away from the lake and back toward the house.

"What the devil does he want?" Broughton muttered.

"Lieutenant, I wish to speak to you." The man arrived at the bottom of the slope and strode toward Broughton.

"How may I help you, Mr. Bentley?"

Robert looked closely at the approaching gentleman. This was Lady Bentley's son? He didn't remember having met the man before.

"I believe we have a matter to discuss about your grandmother's estate."

Broughton stiffened. "At a *boating party?*"

Bentley flushed with annoyance. "As it has proved impossible to meet with you otherwise, then yes."

"I've been indisposed."

"So I heard, but don't you think this issue between our families has gone on long enough? I require a resolution."

"This *issue* as you call it has no foundation in fact and is merely a silly women's quarrel."

Bentley stepped in close, his eyes narrowed, his hands fisted at his sides. "The jewelry is missing from our family coffers. It belongs to us, and I request its return. If you don't wish to settle this matter amicably, I will continue with the court case."

"You'll lose."

"I doubt it, and I am a lawyer well-versed in such cases. We have evidence to support our claim."

"What *evidence?*"

Mr. Bentley bowed. "That, you will find out in

court, Lieutenant. I wish you good day. My mother wishes to try boating on the lake and I hate to disappoint her in anything."

"Bastard," Broughton muttered, but Robert was the only person who heard him. "And I know who is behind this. He's always been his mother's plaything. She is intent on hounding me into an early grave."

"What evidence could he have?" Robert asked quietly.

Broughton turned to Robert as if he'd only just remembered he was there. "I have no idea. The whole thing is preposterous."

"I agree." Out of the corner of his eye Robert saw Lucy Harrington and Lady Bentley approaching at some speed. Mr. Bentley reached them and took possession of his mother's hand. He appeared to be comforting her. Miss Harrington continued toward him and Broughton. She wore a blue gown and a tall bonnet that made it difficult for him to see her face properly.

He moved slightly away from Broughton to await her.

"Did Mr. Bentley speak to Lieutenant Broughton?"
"He did."

She pressed a hand to her chest, her breathing agitated. "I knew I wouldn't reach them in time. Thank goodness you were there. Did they fight?"

"In a manner of speaking, yes. After Broughton was forced to discuss the problem, Mr. Bentley threatened to continue with the lawsuit to recover his family's property. He said he had evidence to support his claim."

"Lady Bentley didn't mention anything about that." Miss Harrington frowned.

"Have you been meddling, Miss Harrington?"

"I told you I would speak to Lady Bentley about the missing jewelry. I didn't find any rubies at all in the dowager's rooms, or any mention of them in her accounts."

"I assume you also spoke to Mr. Bentley."

"He seemed quite well informed about the matter already, sir. I believe he and Lady Bentley are very close. She seemed quite frightened about what he might do to protect her honor."

Robert offered her his arm and they strolled toward the boats moored at the end of the short pier. Broughton was just handing Anna into one of them and Mr. Bentley was doing the same for his mother.

"So now you believe the Bentleys are in cahoots?"

"Possibly." She glanced up at him. "Lady Bentley suggested she might have deliberately enraged the dowager in the hopes that she might die of apoplexy."

"That scarcely counts as murder. I suspect we've all hoped that might happen to an appalling relative or acquaintance in the past. I also doubt it would stand up in court."

"I suppose you are right." Miss Harrington sighed. "Do you have anything else of interest to tell me?"

Robert guided her away from the boats. "I'm wondering whether you were right all along and the dowager countess accidentally poisoned herself."

Miss Harrington stopped walking and simply stared up at him. "But what about Oliver?"

"He's still the most likely candidate, but, apparently, the dowager already managed to poison half the Broughton household earlier this year, so your idea does have some merit."

"Thank you." She stared out over the lake. "Oh dear, I hope Lieutenant Broughton steers clear of Mr. Bentley. They are rather close together."

Robert shaded his eyes and observed the activity on the water. There were several boats out on the lake and none of them was being rowed particularly skillfully. Broughton was moving steadily, but the Bentley boat appeared to be on a collision course.

"Lady Bentley did say that her son had a quick temper."

They moved closer to the edge of the lake, just as the Bentley boat appeared to slow down and head off at another angle toward the artificial waterfall. Several other vessels were launched, and it became hard to see either Broughton or the Bentleys from their position.

"Shall we take a stroll around the lake, Miss Harrington?"

"Are you really worried that something might happen?"

He offered her his arm. "Better to be safe than sorry. I'd hate for Miss Anna or Lady Bentley to take a ducking because their male companions were behaving like schoolboys."

She placed her gloved hand on his sleeve and they moved off, their progress slowed by the loss of the path and the slightly muddy nature of the grass.

"I can't see them," Miss Harrington said eventually.

Robert paused as he caught a glimpse of the yellow ribbons of Miss Anna's bonnet. "Over there. Coming toward this bank."

A sudden scream rent the air and Miss Harrington started forward, almost toppling Robert into the water.

"What's happened? Where is Anna?"

"Broughton's boat has capsized. Where's Bentley?"

"Forget him!" Miss Harrington was untying her bonnet and pulling at the button of her pelisse. "I need to find Anna."

Robert caught her arm. "No, stay here, let me." He struggled out of his heavy coat and dived into the water, gasping as the coldness invaded his lungs. When he surfaced, he struck out for the center of the lake, narrowly avoiding the oars of the other boats that had gathered to watch the catastrophe. The wreckage of more than one craft floated on the surface.

He glimpsed Broughton diving for something and went down as well. The water wasn't clear, but he caught sight of a flash of yellow and dove toward it. His outstretched hands caught onto fabric and he hauled the extraordinary weight toward the surface with all his might.

"Major Kurland! I'm all right, I can swim!" Anna clutched at his arm. "But I have Lady Bentley. Help me!"

"I'll take her." He realized that she held on to another body and let her go to wrap an arm around the unconscious form of Lady Bentley.

Broughton reemerged from under the water and Robert shouted at him. "Take Miss Anna! Where's Bentley?"

"I got him on another boat along with the other two who collided with us."

"Then I'll bring Lady Bentley in." Robert set his jaw and began to swim backward with his unconscious burden toward the edge of the lake, which suddenly seemed a long way away. His injured leg started to throb with every stroke, but he had to kick out strongly as the weight of Lady Bentley's petticoats and heavy skirt dragged them both down.

As he approached the bank, several of the men

waded in to help and lifted Lady Bentley out of his arms and onto the pier. Barely managing to move, he forced himself to crawl out of the water on his hands and knees and collapsed onto his back, breathing hard.

"Major Kurland, are you all right?"

He opened his eyes to see Miss Harrington hovering over him, a soft blanket in her hands.

She knelt beside him and helped him sit up. He coughed up at least a bucketful of lake water while she draped the blanket over his shoulders. When he struggled to rise, she offered him her shoulder to lean on and gave him back his cane. She had his coat over her arm.

"Are you sure that you don't want to rest, Major?"

"No time."

He hobbled toward the pier where an excited crowd surrounded Lady Bentley, and shouted, "Turn her onto her side, don't leave her on her back!"

He managed to navigate the short journey to Lady Bentley's side and came down beside her. She wasn't breathing and he couldn't feel her heartbeat. He began thumping her on the back until his arm was wrenched behind him.

"What the devil are you doing to my mother?" Bentley demanded, his face pale, his brown hair still dripping with water. "Are you trying to strangle her?"

"Don't be a fool, man." Robert stared at him. "I'm patting her back. It's a trick I learned in the Low Countries to get rid of water from a person's lungs. It works, I assure you."

Bentley lurched at Robert. "Leave her alone, *damn* you!"

Robert's left leg gave way and he fell backward, leaving Bentley to gather his mother in his arms and rock her like a child. He stroked her ashen face. "Mama, wake up, wake up!"

Miss Anna Harrington appeared with Broughton and the other two soaked guests, and they all set off back up the hill toward the mansion where a fleet of servants were running out to greet them. The majority of the guests, uncomfortable with Bentley's excessive show of grief, followed them.

It appeared that someone had at least had the sense to call for a physician and some men to carry Lady Bentley's body into the house. Bentley was slow to release his mother. His wild gaze caught Robert's.

"Oh God, my damnable *temper.* I didn't mean this to happen. I just wanted to give Broughton a well-deserved ducking. I never thought the other boat would get involved and we'd all go down together."

The physician patted him on the shoulder. "It's all right, Mr. Bentley, calm yourself. Your mother is in God's hands now."

Bentley stood up, openly weeping as the

servants carefully placed his mother's body on the large blanket and lifted her up.

Wearily, Robert looked around for his cane and his coat.

"Here you are, Major."

"Thank you, Miss Harrington."

Damnation, he didn't think he could stand, and he couldn't lie here within two feet of the grieving Bentley for much longer or he'd start feeling sorry for himself. He waited for a moment, but Miss Harrington's sensible half-kid boots didn't move an inch. He put one hand flat on the ground and tried to raise himself up on his right knee. The pain was excruciating.

"Major?"

He focused on his outstretched hand until he had his breathing under control.

"Go away, Miss Harrington."

"But—"

"Please."

Silence followed his request and he briefly closed his eyes. When he opened them again, Miss Harrington had gone and his coat lay neatly folded beside his cane on the ground beside him.

"May I assist you, Major Kurland?"

A male voice this time. Robert looked up. "Yes, please. I appear to have damaged my leg."

Chapter 13

Major Kurland!" Foley's cry made Robert wince. "What happened to you?"

"Not now, Foley."

Robert allowed the two servants who had helped him up the stairs to lower him onto the bed, and closed his eyes. For a moment there was blessed silence and then he heard Foley's worried breathing coming closer.

"Do you want a hot bath, Major?"

"No, thank you. Just leave me be. I'll do well enough."

"Major, you are soaking wet and covered in mud. Your boots are ruined, and I have no idea if I'll ever be able to get the stains out of your new uniform."

Robert kept his eyes closed and focused his meager resources on mastering the tearing pain that shook through his left leg and entire torso.

Foley sighed loudly. "I'll send for some hot water anyway, sir. Just stay where you are and I'll be right back."

"Trust me, I have no intention of going anywhere, Foley."

He shied away from the insidious thought that he'd never go anywhere again and had finally condemned himself to life as a complete invalid in a chair. He lay still, holding himself tightly within himself, listening to the snap of the coal in the fireplace and the gentle ticking of the clock on the mantelpiece.

Had Bentley's immature attempt to annoy Broughton caused the death of his own mother? How would one live with that on one's conscience? Robert had killed in battle and understood the necessity of that, but to accidentally cause the death of a loved one through one's own lack of ability to keep one's temper? That would be a hard burden to live with.

"Major Kurland? It's Dr. Redmond. I happened to be in the house tending Oliver when your manservant came to find me. May I examine you?"

Robert opened his eyes and focused his gaze on the guilty face of his butler, who was peering over the doctor's shoulder.

"He shouldn't have bothered you. I'm just a little overtired."

Dr. Redmond was already feeling carefully down Robert's left leg. "You were injured here before, I take it?"

"Yes, I broke my leg at Waterloo."

His breath hissed out as the doctor and Foley relieved him of his boots and soaked breeches. Sweat broke out on his brow as the doctor manipulated the tight muscles of his left thigh.

"I don't think you've broken anything new. I suspect you simply overstrained yourself. The best treatment I can recommend is bed rest and warm compresses on the muscles. I can also leave you some laudanum to help reduce the pain."

"No laudanum," Robert said through his clenched teeth.

"Are you sure, sir? You are obviously in considerable pain."

"I'll survive. I've done it before."

Dr. Redmond drew the covers over Robert's lower body. "I'll leave the laudanum just in case you change your mind, and I'll check in on you tomorrow."

"Thank you."

Relief washed over him as the doctor turned away to consult with Foley. For one horrible moment, he'd imagined being told his leg would have to come off. At least his current level of pain reassured him that his leg was still attached, and merely complaining.

He shut his eyes again and tried not to think about Lady Bentley's white face and the way her hair had unraveled like seaweed in the water and clung to his fingers. But the image refused to leave his mind. Something Bentley had said . . . He was aware of Foley moving around the room and then approaching the bed to wash as much of the mud off Robert as he could reach. He accepted a large glass of brandy in lieu of the laudanum and then lay back down. The pain was receding a little. He let himself fall into it and finally found oblivion.

"It's all right, Anna." Lucy handed her sister the warm whisky and lemon punch Aunt Jane had ordered to be brewed for them. "Drink this."

Anna cupped her hands around the glass and breathed in the fumes of ginger and lemon that rose from the punch. She'd changed into her nightgown and had two blankets wrapped around her shoulders. Her long fair hair had been washed and was spread out over her shoulders.

"It was *horrible.*" Anna shivered. "And it isn't all right, Lucy. Lady Bentley is *dead.*"

"I know." Lucy patted Anna's knee. "Mr. Bentley was beside himself with grief. But perhaps he should've thought about the consequences of his actions before he decided to teach Broughton a lesson." She gave her sister a hard stare. "I find it rather difficult to forgive him myself. You might have ended up dead as well as his mother!"

"At least I could swim. From what I remember, Lady Bentley sank like a stone. When it was obvious that Bentley was all right, both Broughton and I went after her. Bentley was too hysterical to help us much. Broughton managed to haul her up to the surface and I helped keep her afloat. Thank goodness Major Kurland came to my rescue. I was struggling to keep hold of her while Broughton helped Miss Phillips."

Anna swallowed hard. "It was all so confusing. I'd already been trying to persuade Lieutenant Broughton to return to shore. But I suppose that even *suggesting* to a man that he might be a little too weak to be rowing a boat makes him believe he has to behave like a Greek hero."

"It's a shame he didn't turn back."

Anna took another sip of the boiling hot drink. "When Bentley altered course and seemed to be heading straight for us, Lieutenant Broughton didn't have the energy left to get out of the way fast enough. And when the Phillips boat came between us . . ." She shuddered. "It was a disaster."

"So Mr. Bentley definitely went after your boat?"

"Yes, I just said so."

"I wonder why?"

"He's hot tempered and overly fond of his mama."

Lucy sat back on the bed. "I wonder if she encouraged him."

"She looked as terrified as I'm sure I did as the boats crunched together. We both screamed."

"She was very worried when he decided to confront Broughton at the party. She begged me to stop him."

"And she was obviously right to be concerned. Poor Mr. Bentley will have to live with the knowledge that he caused his own mother's death."

"Indeed." Lucy rose from the bed and smoothed out the covers. "You should go to sleep, my dear. I'll come back and see you in the morning."

Anna obediently got into bed and lay down. "I don't think I'll be able to sleep very well after this." She hesitated. "Will you stay here with me tonight?"

Lucy put down her pelisse and reticule. "If you can lend me a nightgown and don't mind sharing your bed, then of course I will."

She lay beside her sister and watched the hands of the clock move around the dial as Anna finally managed to fall asleep. Perhaps she was a cynic, but it seemed very convenient that Lady Bentley had died right in the middle of the investigation as to what had happened to her lost rubies. Had Bentley's decision to ram Broughton's boat been more calculated than anyone might imagine? Had he wanted his mother to die?

It was another three days before Lucy was able to visit the Broughton family and finish up her inventory of the dowager countess's possessions. Anna had caught a chill from her encounter with the lake and couldn't accompany her. When she arrived, the countess told her that both Lieutenant Broughton and Major Kurland had been ordered to stay in bed by Dr. Redmond.

"Oh dear. You have a houseful of invalids." Lucy sipped at her tea. The countess was stretched out on the chaise longue opposite her with a shawl covering her shoulders and a blanket over her black skirts. "I do hope all of them recover soon."

"Broughton and Major Kurland are both recovering nicely, my dear, and hope to be downstairs today at some point."

"And how is Oliver?"

"He still seems very weak." The countess frowned. "Dr. Redmond is watching him very closely but has been unable to come up with a reason for his slow recovery when Broughton is doing so well."

"It must be very trying for you." Lucy set down her cup. She noticed the countess hadn't mentioned the death of Lady Bentley at all. Perhaps she hoped that it meant an end to the matter of the disputed jewelry. If that was the case, Lucy almost couldn't blame her.

"I wonder if I might visit the dowager's stillroom and see if she has anything that might help my sister Anna's cough? I'm worried that it might settle on her lungs."

"You are more than welcome to look, my dear, although you might wish to check with Hester, her maid, or even with Broughton when he comes down, to make sure that the potion is safe."

"Are the dowager's recipes generally unsafe, then?"

"Oh no, it's just that occasionally as she got older she made mistakes."

"Then I'll be sure to check with Lieutenant Broughton." Lucy rose and placed her cup beside the teapot. "Is the key in the usual place above the door?"

"I believe so." The countess smiled warmly at her. "You have been such a great help and solace to me, Miss Harrington."

"It's been a pleasure, my lady." She curtsied. "I'll finish writing up the inventory of the dowager's possessions and then I'll visit the stillroom."

Eventually, Lucy made her way out into the garden and down to the stillroom. Standing on tiptoe, she used her hand to locate the key and brought it to the lock. The smell of dried herbs and the tang of spices reminded her of her skirts brushing past the hedgerows in Kurland St. Mary. Perhaps it was time to admit it. She missed her home very badly. London had its share of amusements, but she suspected that at heart, she would prefer to live in the countryside and visit the capital occasionally. She couldn't imagine having to live there all year and engage in the exhausting social round. Truth be told, she also missed being her own mistress. Having to depend on the good-natured Mrs. Hathaway or her aunt as a chaperone was remarkably constricting.

The only man she'd met who seemed to appreciate her intelligence and enjoy her conversation was Mr. Stanford. He had made no effort to engage her interest more deeply, content to escort her and Sophia wherever they wanted to go and share his smiles equally between them. Perhaps spinsterhood and running the Kurland St. Mary rectory really were her lot in life. . . .

Shaking off this unpleasant conclusion, she studied the shelves of potions. Where was the cough mixture that the dowager had given to Oliver? She found a bottle labeled rose hip and honey, and set it on the worktable. Uncorking it, she cautiously smelled the contents and then sealed it up again. It seemed fine to her, but she would take the countess's advice and consult with the lieutenant before she gave any to her sister.

She spied the dowager's herbal and drew it toward her. Would anyone mind if she borrowed it? She suspected it might be missed if Hester, the dowager's maid, was still using it to make potions for the household. She remembered Broughton saying that the dowager's favorite recipes were marked with ribbon. Lucy flicked through the pages, noticing when comments had been added to the page and comparing them to the handwriting on the label of the bottle. It seemed that the dowager had a lot to say about her forbear's recipes and none of it was complimentary. There was also another hand that had recently added comments. Perhaps it was Hester's. . . .

"Good afternoon, Miss Harrington." Lucy twirled around to find Lieutenant Broughton smiling at her from the doorway. "My mother said I might find you here. Is it true that your sister is unwell?" He heaved a sigh. "If that is the case, I can only apologize for being the cause. I can assure you, Miss Harrington, I never planned for us both to end up in the lake."

"I'm sure you didn't, Lieutenant. Anna has a slight chill, but I see no signs of any fever, so I think she'll recover fairly soon."

"I'm very glad to hear it. Are you intending to take her some cough mixture?"

"Yes, if that is all right. The countess suggested you check to see if the recipe was correct."

He came to stand beside her and picked up the bottle to read the label. "There's no need in this case. I've already made sure that this potion is safe. Hester and I made up a new batch together." He pulled the herbal toward him and leafed through the pages. "Here's the original recipe and my grandmother's additions." He smiled and traced a finger along another line of text. "And here is one of the improvements I made. I added less sugar and more honey. Of course, my grandmother hated me suggesting anything, and despite my superior knowledge she usually ignored my suggestions."

"Then I will accept this bottle with pleasure and will ensure that Anna take some this very evening."

Lucy watched as he closed the herbal, and followed him reluctantly to the door. She wouldn't get a chance to look around the stillroom with him there, but she did know where the key was for a return visit.

He held the door for her and locked it before turning around.

"You seem rather interested in my grand-mother's stillroom, Miss Harrington."

"I'm a countrywoman at heart, sir, and have spent many happy hours comparing household remedies with others in my village. In fact, I noticed that your grandmother made her own version of rat poison. I have great trouble finding anything that keeps the rats away from the pantry at the rectory. Do you know what she recommended?"

"Oh, you don't want to use old-fashioned remedies for rats, Miss Harrington. There are far better and quicker solutions than that." He started off across the grass toward his laboratory. "If you have time, I can show you what I mean."

She followed him as he continued to talk.

"Of course, most natural poisons take a long time to work and, if you are like most of the women of my acquaintance, Miss Harrington, the thought of any creature suffering upsets you."

"It certainly isn't pleasant, sir, but—"

"It's much better to use, say, a concentrated, more industrial form of the product—a powder, for example, instead of a liquid. By boiling off the excess liquid, one improves the strength of the poison and, especially when dealing with vermin, makes it easier to use. And, if one *prefers* to use a liquid, a prepared powder can be dissolved into anything and at the strength you require, making it far more likely that you will have a successful outcome."

He gestured at the cages that lined the back wall of the room. "I've tested this theory quite extensively with the rat population of Broughton House. Using variable doses and strengths of poisons derived from both natural plant recipes and the more sophisticated mineral powdered form, I've taken notes about how long the rodent takes to die and how painful it appears to be for the creature. I'm considering writing an article and submitting it to one of the scientific journals."

"How fascinating," Lucy said weakly as she studied the caged rat in front of her. For the first time in her life, she actually felt sorry for a rodent. "I assume the dowager countess disagreed with your findings?"

"Naturally, but she was an old lady and somewhat behind the times. Her opinion and her validation of my work were not necessary.

The scientific method will always trump the old wives' tale." He offered Lucy his arm. "Are you coming in for tea? I believe my mother is expecting you."

After Broughton left to go to his club, Lucy sat and talked to the countess for a while longer until her hostess fell into a discreet doze. Rising from her seat, Lucy tiptoed out of the room and made her way up the stairs. She encountered a maid on the landing and asked if she might speak to Mr. Foley.

In less than a minute, she was accompanying Foley to Major Kurland's bedchamber while he told her how his master was doing and warned her about his uncertain temper. It was just like old times. . . . Promising to guard the door against intruders, Foley discreetly ushered her inside. Major Kurland was sitting up in bed in his night-shirt, the daily newspapers spread out around him.

"Miss Harrington!"

Lucy curtsied. "Major Kurland, how are you feeling?"

"I'm fine. You shouldn't be in here." He frowned as he whipped off his spectacles. "Did Foley make you come?"

"No, I wanted to talk to you myself, so I found him. He's outside making sure no one will see me in your bedchamber."

"Thank God for that. Where are all the Broughtons?"

"The lieutenant has gone out, the countess is dozing in her chair, and I assume Oliver is still in bed." She drew up a chair next to his bedside. "Don't you find it odd that Lady Bentley died at this point in time?"

"I do, but I'm not sure what to make of it." He pushed the newspapers to one side.

"I suspect Bentley killed his mother."

"Why on earth do you think that?"

"She was worried about him confronting Lieutenant Broughton. She *begged* me to intervene."

"Because she knew he had a bad temper and that if he pursued Broughton he might do something he'd regret. And she was correct."

"Perhaps she might have feared that if he spoke to Broughton, he'd realize that she hadn't been telling the truth. Maybe the story of the rubies was false, and she was alarmed that he intended to take it too far?"

"So she chose to drown herself in a fit of remorse? This makes no sense, Miss Harrington."

"But what if she told him when they were on the lake? Perhaps when the boats collided he decided not to save her so that he could extricate himself from a potentially damaging situation that would affect his career if he pursued her lies?"

"But, by all accounts, he loved her dearly."

"Maybe he loved her too much."

Major Kurland rubbed a hand over his jaw in an impatient gesture. "This whole scenario is based on nothing but your vivid imagination, Miss Harrington."

"Then why did Lady Bentley die? I searched through all the dowager's possessions. There was no sign of those rubies."

"I don't know why she died; perhaps both of the old ladies killed themselves and there is nothing more to say about the matter."

"Now that *is* a ridiculous suggestion, sir. Perhaps the question we should be asking ourselves is who would *want* both ladies dead?"

"Apart from all of the Broughton family and half of society who have grown tired of dealing with the squabbling pair?"

"Well, at least we can't blame Oliver for this one." Lucy sat back and folded her hands in her lap.

A banging on the door made her jump to her feet with a gasp, but it was only Foley. She was just about to ask him what was the matter when he fixed his gaze on the major.

"Major Kurland! There's a commotion coming from Master Oliver's room!"

Lucy could hear something now, and gathered her skirts. "I'll go."

Major Kurland threw back the bedcovers and

she hastily averted her gaze. "I'm coming, too."

She didn't wait for him, but ran out into the hallway and down to the open door where one of the maids stood screaming.

"What's wrong, Mairi?"

"Master Oliver! I just brought up his dinner. He's—"

Lucy brushed past her and then came to an abrupt stop. Oliver's bed was empty, and the nurse who tended him lay sprawled on the floor, either dead or unconscious. A gust of wind blew in her face and, stepping over the fallen figure, Lucy advanced toward the wide-open window where the curtains were open and flapping wildly.

"Miss Harrington, stay there."

Lucy looked over her shoulder to see Major Kurland, resplendent in his blue banyan, coming in through the doorway.

"But—"

"Don't argue with me." He held up his hand. "Let me approach the window first."

She managed to stay still as he went slowly ahead of her, his cane tapping on the wooden floorboards. He paused and then leaned slowly forward until he could see out of the window.

"Good Lord," he murmured. "He's out on the ledge."

"*Oliver* is?"

"Yes." Major Kurland turned to her. "And we're three stories up with the flagstone square below us. Find Foley and tell him to gather some of the male servants and get them to bring a large blanket out to the front of the house below this window."

"In . . . in case Oliver *jumps?*"

"I doubt he's sitting out there to appreciate the sunset, Miss Harrington."

"And what are you going to do while I'm organizing Foley?"

"I'm going to try and talk to him."

"*You* are?"

The doubt on her face almost made him smile. "Yes."

"You can't possibly be considering going out there yourself?"

He glanced down at his cane. "Of course not. I bloody well *can't,* can I? After you've found Foley, come back and see if you can revive the nurse. I've already sent for Broughton."

Lucy forced her trembling limbs to obey and ran to do his bidding.

Robert contemplated the open window and the hunched figure to the right of it. During the war he'd gained a lot of experience in how to talk to frightened young men. Boys who were afraid to go into battle for the first time, or soldiers who couldn't bear the thought of being in the middle of such senseless slaughter again. Usually a dose of calm good sense won the day. He could only hope his skills hadn't deserted him. . . .

He set a pillow on the window ledge and sat sideways on it, favoring his injured leg. The chill of the wind gusted through his hair, but it was a mere nothing to the winters he'd faced in Spain. He leaned out as far as he could and contemplated the hunched figure.

"Oliver?"

There was no response.

"It's Major Kurland. Do you wish to return to your bed now? It is getting rather cold out here."

He tensed as Oliver slowly turned his head toward him. His eyes glittered black and his complexion was flushed. He wore a white nightshirt and his arms were wrapped around his knees, which were drawn up tightly against his chest. Robert judged the ledge to be less than two feet wide.

"Are you in pain? Can I get someone to help you? I'm sure Dr. Redmond could give you something to make you feel better."

"No more potions. Can't trust him!" Oliver muttered. "Can't trust anyone. Think he's trying to kill me."

"You're obviously not well, Oliver; perhaps you should come back to bed. I can call my own physician if you prefer."

Oliver shuddered so violently that Robert instinctively reached for him before stilling the motion. He doubted that even with his arm extended to the fullest he could get hold of

Oliver's shirt, let alone something tangible like his elbow.

"I'm sure we can sort this out. Why don't you come back in and we can discuss it in a more reasonable manner?"

"No, I'm not going back in there! Broughton thinks I killed the old lady, but I didn't. I wanted to and I'm glad that she's dead, but I didn't kill her."

"If you say so, I'm sure you are right."

Oliver licked his parched lips. "You believe me?"

Robert held his gaze. "I'm willing to try."

"No, you're his friend, you believe all his lies." His gaze dropped lower. "No! They're both coming back!"

Robert looked down, too, and saw the top of a hackney cab from which Broughton and Dr. Redmond were emerging. Broughton looked up, his face white, and Oliver screamed and tried to press himself back against the unforgiving wall, his fingers scrabbling against the brickwork.

Robert leaned out even farther. "Oliver, look at me, don't—" Just as his fingers brushed frantically against Oliver's shirt, the boy jumped.

"God, *no!*" Robert closed his eyes as the sickening crunch of a body hitting the cobbled street below reached him. For a moment he thought he might vomit but managed to control himself and finally look down.

Oliver's body lay at an unnatural angle on the ground and even from his viewpoint, Robert could see the bright red of his blood draining away through the cobblestones and into the gutter. Several figures were running toward Oliver, including Dr. Redmond, who crouched down beside the body and immediately shook his head. He remained kneeling, his frantic hands feeling over Oliver's torso as if desperately seeking a heartbeat that was no longer there.

"What happened?"

Robert turned to face Miss Harrington, who had just come back into the room.

"I couldn't stop him."

She raised her fingers to her mouth. "Oliver's *dead?*"

"Don't look." He nodded as he eased away from the window and found his cane. "How is the nurse?"

Miss Harrington swallowed hard. "She has a bump on her head. She thinks Oliver must have hit her when her back was turned."

"Does she remember what happened just before that?" Robert's gaze fell on the bedside table where an empty glass and spoon stood beside a black bottle.

"She was giving Oliver his medicine and waiting for the maid to bring up his dinner."

Robert picked up the bottle and after checking that the cork was firmly in place, put the bottle in his pocket.

"What are you—?"

He put a finger to his lips. "I'll explain later. Miss Harrington, you need to remove yourself from this room. In truth, I don't want Broughton or Dr. Redmond knowing you were here at all."

Chapter 14

Oh, the poor lady, to lose her mother-in-law and her youngest son within such a few days." Mrs. Hathaway wiped her eyes with her lace handkerchief as Sophia patted her hand.

Lucy could only nod as she tried not to think of what had happened to Oliver. At Broughton House, she'd slipped back into the morning room and had sat quietly, gathering her shattered nerves until Lieutenant Broughton had burst into the room, awakening his mother, and told them both the bad news.

The countess had indeed been inconsolable. So much so that Lucy had helped her up the stairs, watching very carefully as a pale Dr. Redmond dosed her with laudanum and put her to bed. There had been no sign of Major Kurland, who she assumed had answered Broughton as to his part in the tragedy and gone back to his room. Why had he taken the medicine bottle from beside Oliver's bed? What further horrors was he imagining?

A knock on the door heralded the arrival of the butler, who bowed to Mrs. Hathaway.

"Ma'am, there is a man in the kitchens who says he was sent here by a Major Kurland to await further orders. Do you know of this person, or should I eject him from the house?"

Lucy looked up. "It might be a messenger from Kurland St. Mary who doesn't know that the major moved into the Broughtons' house. Did he give you his name?"

"Silas Smith, Miss Harrington."

Lucy touched Mrs. Hathaway's shoulder. "If you permit, ma'am, I'll speak to this man and ascertain what he wants. If he does have a message for the major, it might be better to keep him with us this evening rather than send him over to the Broughtons."

"That's an excellent thought, Lucy. We don't want to put them to any more trouble." Mrs. Hathaway blew her nose twice. "I think I'll take myself off to bed. It's been a horrible day."

"Then I'll go and speak to him, shall I? And if the matter is truly urgent, I'll send a message around to Major Kurland and ask him if he is well enough to meet Mr. Smith here."

After bidding Mrs. Hathaway a fond good night and promising to come back and speak to Sophia before she, too, went to bed, Lucy went down to the kitchens and was taken into the butler's pantry.

"Mr. Smith?"

The young man who stood up wasn't one she remembered from the village.

He doffed his hat. "It's Miss Harrington, isn't it?"

"Yes, I understand that you are looking for Major Kurland. He's not at Fenton's at the moment. He moved into a friend's house."

"I know where he is, Miss Harrington. That's why he told me to come here." He straightened his spine. "I can't show my face at Broughton House. I was dismissed by Lieutenant Broughton without a reference for aiding Mr. Oliver."

"Oh good gracious, I remember now. You were Oliver's manservant, weren't you?"

"Yes, Miss Harrington. Just after I was dismissed, Major Kurland asked me to take a message to his land agent and return with the reply. He thought it best if I came here."

She studied him for a long moment. "I'll send a message to Major Kurland telling him you have arrived. I'm sure he'll come immediately. Have you had your dinner yet?"

Robert alighted carefully from the hackney cab and threw the driver a coin before mounting the steps to the door of the rented house the Hathaways had retained for the Season. Within a few moments, he was taken in to the drawing room where Miss Harrington and her friend Mrs. Giffin awaited him.

After inquiring about Miss Anna and Mrs. Hathaway and murmuring some general replies to Mrs. Giffin's anxious questions about the state of the Broughton family, he became aware that Miss Harrington was not her usual self. Despite several attempts to engage her interest, she simply stared into the fire and nodded absently at all his remarks.

Eventually, to avoid spending the whole evening talking around the painful topic of Oliver, Robert was forced to ask the question outright. "I understand there is a messenger awaiting me here?"

"Oh yes, that's right!" Miss Harrington jumped. "If you'll excuse me, Sophia, I'll take Major Kurland down to the kitchens."

Sophia smiled at them both. "I was just thinking about going to bed, actually."

There was a knock on the door and the butler appeared again. "I apologize for interrupting you again, but a Mr. Stanford has arrived. He seems to think he was invited for dinner."

Sophia jumped to her feet. "Good gracious! I completely forgot that Mother and I asked Mr. Stanford to come for dinner tonight! I must see him and explain."

Robert bowed. "And while you do that, I'll go down and speak to my man. A pleasure, Mrs. Giffin, as always."

He headed for the door and Miss Harrington followed him. They passed Andrew Stanford coming up the stairs with the butler. He raised his eyebrows at Robert in a quizzical fashion, but thankfully didn't ask any awkward questions. Robert wondered if Miss Harrington would prefer to be back in the drawing room with Andrew. She gave no sign of it; her expression was distracted as she silently paced alongside him.

Had she seen more than he'd thought that afternoon? Was her mind busy playing those gruesome seconds of Oliver's jump from the ledge over and over again as his was? He knew that if he managed to sleep he would face a night full of horrors as he saw Oliver's terrified face the second before he'd leaped into the air. . . .

"I didn't tell Silas Smith about what happened to Oliver this afternoon."

Miss Harrington had stopped outside one of the doors in the dimly lit servants' quarters.

"That was remarkably sensible of you."

"It was more that I am a coward. I thought you would do a better job of it."

"I've had to tell many people that their loved ones are dead. It doesn't get any easier."

In the semidarkness, her hand fleetingly came to rest on his chest. "Then I apologize for expecting you to deal with such a loathsome task. I'll tell him myself."

"There's no need. You've been remarkably brave all day, Miss Harrington." He turned the door handle and went into the upper servants' sitting room. Smith sat at the table, finishing what looked like the remains of a large meal. He stood up when he saw Robert and wiped his mouth with his napkin.

"Major Kurland. Good evening, sir."

Robert gestured for him to sit back down and after setting a chair for Miss Harrington, he sat opposite Smith.

"I have a letter for you from Mr. Fairfax, Major, but he also said to tell you that he is quite content to stay on until you return."

"Thank you." Robert took the letter and placed it on the table in front of him. "How did you find the manor house and the countryside around it?"

"I liked it well enough, sir. The soil looks better than that of my family farm up north and the climate's a bit warmer."

"You still intend to return to farming?"

Smith shrugged. "It's not as if I have a choice, is it? Without a reference no one is going to take me on as a manservant, let alone an aspiring valet now, are they?"

"Actually, I am looking for a new valet myself."

"*You* are, sir?"

"I'd like you to consider taking the position. You might have to spend some of your time in London, but generally I prefer to reside at Kurland Manor."

"But why, sir? Why me? You of all people know what I did."

Robert held Smith's gaze. "Because I believe your loyalty to your young master did you credit, and in light of recent events, I regret ever having insisted that you bring him home."

"What's happened to Master Oliver?"

"He's dead, Silas."

"But I thought he was getting better. I sneaked in to see him before I left and he looked right peaceful as he lay there sleeping. Did his fever get worse?"

"I'm not sure," Robert said. "The circumstances of his death were quite unusual. He threw himself off the ledge outside his bedroom window."

Smith shot to his feet and started to pace the small room. "I told you he was scared to go back there. Mayhap he was right." He swung around to look at Robert. "Why would he do that? Jump to his death?"

"Because he was afraid. The trouble is, he was so distraught when I tried to talk to him that I couldn't understand exactly what he was afraid *of.*" Robert looked up. "Did he ever tell you?"

Smith sat back down with a thump and rubbed hastily at his eyes. "He hated and feared them all. He was convinced that he was such a disappointment that they wanted to get rid of him."

"Do you think he was correct?"

"To be honest, sir, I merely thought him over-young and rather self-obsessed, but maybe he wasn't." Smith raised his head. "Did Lieutenant

Broughton tell you why Master Oliver was almost expelled from Eton?"

"Not specifically, although Broughton did tell me that Oliver had a reputation for drinking, gambling, and stealing from a very young age."

"That's not all of it, sir." Smith let out his breath. "Oliver fell in love."

"Such things often happen to young men of fortune who assume that their introduction to copulation by an unsuitable woman means they are in love. I dealt with it all the time in the regiment."

"No, sir." Smith lowered his voice. "Oliver wasn't in love with a woman of any class. He told me it was another student, a much older boy."

"Ah." Robert looked warily over at Miss Harrington, but she didn't appear terribly shocked. "I should imagine that didn't go down very well with the Broughton family."

"They treated him appallingly, sir—like vermin." Smith shook his head. "I know that what he did was a sin, but they had no compassion or understanding for him at all. After that, he just gave up trying to please them. He used to tell me that as they already thought he'd gone to the devil, he might as well enjoy the ride and antagonize them as he went down."

"Do you think Oliver might have decided to rid himself of his family before they got rid of him?"

"I doubt it, sir."

"Then why did he steal the bottle of poison from the dowager's stillroom?"

"What bottle?"

"The one that Lieutenant Broughton discovered hidden amongst your belongings."

Smith opened his mouth and then closed it again. *"What?"*

"Do you not recall your master putting the bottle there?"

"Sir, there was no bottle. I swear it."

"And you didn't decide to rid Oliver Broughton of his unpleasant relatives yourself?"

Smith's hand clenched into a fist on the table. "Even if it means your offer of employment is withdrawn, Major, I will never lie and claim to be a poisoner, or one who aided one!"

"Is it possible that Oliver might have put the bottle in amongst your possessions without telling you? He did fall ill very quickly. He might not have had time to explain what he'd done."

"I suppose that could've happened, but I still don't believe he would have poisoned his grandmother, or his brother. They are both far more knowledgeable about such matters than my master is, I mean was."

"You have been most helpful, Smith." Robert looked over at Miss Harrington. "Do you think Mrs. Hathaway would object to Smith staying here tonight? I am anxious for him to return to Kurland St. Mary to await my homecoming."

"Mrs. Hathaway's staff has already prepared a room for him, sir." She rose from her seat in a whisper of silk. "I'll take you through to him, Silas."

Robert waited in the gathering gloom until Miss Harrington returned and took the seat Smith had previously occupied.

"Are you hungry, Major?"

He glanced at the remains of the pigeon pie and shuddered. "No, I thank you."

"Something to drink, then? I asked the butler to bring me some tea, but I'm sure he can find you something stronger if you wish it."

"Tea will be fine." He pushed the pie away from him. "This is fast becoming a horribly complex mess."

"I have to agree with you, sir. I was beginning to believe that the dowager countess accidentally poisoned herself and Lieutenant Broughton until Lady Bentley drowned and now poor Oliver . . ." She hesitated. "Died so *unnecessarily.*"

"I suppose now that everyone we suspected is dead, we should really give up all hope of ever understanding what has gone on."

"Maybe Oliver chose to kill himself because he was guilty."

"I almost wish I could agree with you, but the last thing he said to me was that he didn't kill anyone and that he was afraid." He shook his head. "I'm reluctant to mention it, but he did look quite mad. His eyes were like black holes into hell."

"Vermin."

Robert looked up. "What did you say, Miss Harrington?"

"Silas said that the Broughton family treated Oliver like vermin, and that's how you kill vermin—you use poison. Why did you take that bottle of medicine from Oliver's bedside?"

"Because the nurse said she'd just given him the medicine before he attacked her."

"Who prescribed it?"

"One must assume it was Dr. Redmond."

"A man who knows all about the Broughton family's personal lives and has the knowledge to kill. But why would he want to get rid of them?"

"Perhaps he views them as a scientific experiment?"

"But he wasn't at Almack's?"

"How do we know? He attended Harrow and Eton and is the fourth son of an earl, so he would certainly have been allowed in. Just because we didn't know he was present doesn't mean he wasn't there. And if he came to speak to Broughton, or any other member of the family, no one would've remarked on it."

"So if he was there, he had the opportunity to add the poison to the orgeat. I suppose we can check the subscription book for that evening and see if Dr. Redmond was present." Miss Harrington sighed. "I'll say it before you do. This is all pure supposition. Perhaps the dowager did poison everyone and everything that has happened since is simply because of that. It is none of our business anyway."

Robert raised an eyebrow. "When has that ever stopped you from meddling?"

She smiled at him. "After being trapped in a tomb last year I decided it would be prudent to keep my meddling ways to myself. But it seems as if I either attract trouble or have an overriding desire to be proved right. What's your excuse, Major?"

"I'm not sure anymore. I thought I was helping an old army colleague."

"And what about Lieutenant Broughton's part in all this?"

Robert met her clear gaze. "What about him?"

"He is very close to Dr. Redmond and was the person who introduced him into the household."

"After the dowager nearly killed everyone with her potions."

"Yes, but what does Broughton think about all these deaths?"

"I haven't spoken to him about Oliver yet. I got the impression from Dr. Redmond that he suspected some kind of pressure on the brain or a fever had taken over Oliver's mind and made him irrational, hysterical, and delusional enough to leap out of the window over nothing."

"And from all accounts that could be true,"

Miss Harrington said slowly. "Is it possible that Dr. Redmond is doing Broughton's bidding?"

"But Broughton was poisoned himself. He might have died."

"That's true, so perhaps the good doctor has decided to intervene on his benefactor's behalf and clear the decks around him. But why would he bother? What reason would he have to even consider such a series of actions?"

"I don't know." Robert sighed. "He is rather fond of the current countess, but she is still married to Broughton's father. Unless *they* are in cahoots and intend to lure the viscount back to England and dispose of him as well."

"I suppose that is possible. She *is* the only member of the family who wasn't poisoned. Unfortunately, she doesn't seem the sort of woman who would fall passionately in love with anyone."

"Agreed."

"And I can't really see Dr. Redmond killing *for* her, because he'd still have to dispose of Broughton and his father." Miss Harrington made a face. "I don't think we are ever going to understand what is going on."

"*I* think it's time I moved back to Fenton's. I don't want to be anywhere near Dr. Redmond at the moment."

"I agree, but there are a couple of things you might consider doing before you leave. . . ."

After bidding Major Kurland good night, Lucy made her way back up the stairs to the drawing room deep in thought. To her surprise, Mr. Stanford was ensconced in a chair by the fire still talking to Sophia.

He stood up when she came in and bowed. "Good evening, Miss Harrington. Mrs. Giffin has been telling me about young Oliver Broughton's unexpected death. I must confess to be shocked to hear of it."

Lucy sat beside Sophia on the couch. "It is always terrible when someone dies at such a young age, isn't it?" She considered him for a long moment. "Mr. Stanford, did you mention that you were interested in science?"

"I did, Miss Harrington. I belong to a club named Fletchers on Portland Street where we discuss new developments in the emerging scientific fields." He smiled. "I must admit that my interest is not purely impartial. As a lawyer, I am always looking for new ways to ensure a conviction in a murder investigation. For far too long, many murderers have gotten away with crimes that I suspect could be solved if we were able to determine exactly what had happened to the body."

"Such as the effect of poison?"

"Indeed. I have been reading Orfila's book about detecting poison in the human body. If we can persuade the courts to accept such evidence, it promises to be very helpful in the future."

"Do you have a copy that I might borrow, Mr. Stanford?"

"Yes, I do." He smiled at her. "May I ask why you are so interested in such gruesome matters?"

Lucy hesitated. Major Kurland had already warned her not to discuss details of her suspicions with anyone, but she had a sensation that time was running out and that any help would be beneficial.

"I hope I can rely on your complete discretion, Mr. Stanford, but I am interested in what has been happening to the Broughton family."

Mr. Stanford sat back. "In what way?"

She met his interested gaze. "Don't you think it odd that the dowager countess and Oliver died so suddenly?"

"It is unusual, I grant you, but not unheard of. The dowager was an elderly lady and Oliver was known to be rather . . . unstable."

"But what if they were murdered?"

"Then someone would have to provide the evidence of such a crime and take it to the coroner and the local magistrate."

"And what if that evidence was difficult to obtain?"

"Does this fall into the category we just touched upon? Poison?"

"Yes, I believe it does."

Lucy told Mr. Stanford the whole story and he listened intently, only interrupting to ask sensible questions, which made Lucy approve of him even more.

"It certainly is a tangle," Mr. Stanford said. "But here is one thing to think on. Putting poison in the orgeat at Almack's was a terribly risky venture. If the dosage had been high enough, the murderer could have killed more than just the dowager countess."

"I agree." Lucy shuddered. "I was about to drink a glass myself, but someone hit my elbow and I spilled everything over my dress." She paused. "I wonder if someone did that deliberately."

"Can you remember whom you were standing by?"

She hesitated. "It might have been Oliver."

The clock on the mantelpiece chimed six times. Mr. Stanford glanced over at it and rose to his feet.

"Good Lord, it's getting late and I'm in court tomorrow. I'll send that book to you right away, Miss Harrington." He bowed over her hand and then turned to Sophia. "Always a pleasure, Mrs. Giffin."

Sophia smiled up at him. "Are you sure you don't want to stay for dinner?"

He kissed her fingers. "Thank you for the invitation, but I regret I must leave. I have some rather interesting research to do."

Lucy let Sophia walk Mr. Stanford to the top of the stairs while she considered what had happened during the long and stressful day. When Sophia returned, they decided to forgo a more formal meal in the dining room and eat their dinners from a tray in their respective rooms.

Just as Lucy finished eating, a knock on her door heralded the arrival of Orfila's book from Mr. Stanford. With a contented sigh, she settled down to read it again. Perhaps using the scientific method might help her more than she had imagined and finally sort out the intricacies of the case.

Chapter 15

Broughton, I believe I'll return to Fenton's today."

Broughton looked up from his substantial breakfast at Robert, who sat opposite him. He wore his uniform with a black armband around his sleeve. His face looked drawn and worry lines creased his forehead.

"I understand. It hasn't been much fun for you here, has it?" His mouth twisted. "I hardly expected to be mourning two family members at once."

"It must be very hard for you. If you need anything, please don't hesitate to contact me at the hotel. I will always stand your friend."

"I appreciate that, Kurland. There is a lot to do here, so you will probably be more comfortable in a hotel. My mother's taken to her bed and I don't blame her. One good thing is that my father is definitely on his way home from India. We received a letter from him with the name of the ship he's traveling on, and the anticipated date of arrival at Southampton."

"Well, that at least is good news." Robert finished his coffee. "I need to speak to Foley and make sure he knows what to pack. I believe after my soaking in the lake, he borrowed a couple of military items from your wardrobe. I'll make sure to return them."

"That's not necessary. I'll hardly be wearing them myself, will I?" Broughton forced a smile. "I can't imagine how I'm going to tell my father that Oliver is dead when I can't quite believe it myself." He suddenly buried his face in his hands. "God, what a disaster."

Robert stood up and after collecting his cane came around the table to take Broughton's shoulder in a hard grasp.

"I won't disturb your mother when I leave, but please give her my thanks."

Broughton didn't reply, and Robert went out into the hallway where the butler awaited him.

"Good morning, Major Kurland. A note was just delivered for you."

"Thank you." Robert took the sealed note and

went up the stairs into his bedchamber, where Foley was already packing his bags. Ignoring Foley's chatter, he opened the note and read the contents before throwing the paper on the fire. Miss Harrington wanted to see him at his earliest convenience. The last three words were heavily underlined. He wondered what on earth she had involved herself in now. Or had the note simply been a reminder for him to complete the task that she had set him?

On that thought, he turned to Foley.

"Is Lieutenant Broughton expected to go out today?"

"Indeed he is, sir. He's due at his solicitor's this morning, and then he plans to go to his club on Portland Street."

Robert was always impressed at Foley's ability to know what was going on in a household. "I've got some items I need to return to the lieutenant, so let me know when he's left the house."

"I'll do that, sir."

Robert went down the stairs and out through the library into the large back garden. A few flowers were emerging from the beds and the grass was greening up nicely. As he inhaled the London smoke that seemed to hover constantly an inch over his head in the leaden skies, Robert wondered how his fields at the manor were looking. Had his potential new land agent started work, or was he waiting for a more formal agreement between them? He should write and engage Mr. Fairfax's services immediately. He hadn't heard back from the Prince Regent's secretary as to a date for his more formal investiture and he wanted to go home. . . .

Unfortunately, he was subject to the whims of his monarch. And, to be honest, he *would* rather like to find out exactly what was going on at the Broughtons'. With that thought firmly in mind, he walked down the main path and took the branch that led off to the dowager's stillroom. Making sure that there was no one observing him from the house, Robert found the key where Miss Harrington had told him it would be, unlocked the door, and let himself in.

The dowager's herbal lay on the table. It looked a lot larger and heavier than he remembered. But it was a relatively simple matter to tuck it under his arm, cover it with his military coat, and return to the house. He kept walking until he reached his room and deposited the book on the bed beside the bag Foley was packing.

"Has the lieutenant left the house yet?"

"Yes, sir. He exited just after you went into the garden."

"Good."

"Do you want me to find his valet and give him the cufflinks and the silver polish we borrowed?"

Robert held out his hand. "If you give them to me, I'll get out of your way and take them back myself. Don't bother to call for Broughton's valet. I can leave them on his dressing table."

Miss Harrington wasn't the only one who could make suggestions as to how he should proceed. If he was leaving Broughton House, it would be his last chance to survey the more private places of the great house. He wasn't sure quite what he was looking for in Broughton's bed-chamber, but it seemed too good an opportunity to waste.

He knocked on Broughton's door, but there was no sign of his valet or any other member of the household. After depositing the cufflinks, spare silver buttons, and polish on the walnut shaving stand, Robert took stock of his surroundings and whistled in surprise. Most military men of his acquaintance were neat in their habits, but this seemed not to be the case with Broughton. A large desk was pushed up against the window. The surface was stacked high with books and note-books and other scholarly items that continued in a pile on the floor.

Robert approached the desk and discovered the drawers were so stuffed full of papers that they wouldn't shut. Broughton was obviously very serious about transforming his life and pursuing his new interests. He went even closer. It appeared that not all the papers were of a scientific nature. Amongst the scholarly texts and scribbled notes there were several demands for payment of large bills and other twists of paper that looked like copies of vouchers for gambling debts. Broughton had never struck him as a gambler. Perhaps he was attempting to deal with Oliver's debts so that he could report the totals to his father on his return?

After considering the mess for another second or two, Robert turned on his heel and made his way back to his room, one of the larger gambling debts folded into a neat square in his hand.

"I'm going out to see Miss Harrington and her sister, Foley. I'll be back shortly. Send a note around to Fenton's and tell them to expect us this afternoon."

Lucy glanced approvingly at the clock as Major Kurland was announced by the butler and came through the door. After depositing the dowager's herbal on the table beside her, he bowed and stopped short when he spotted Mr. Stanford.

"Have I come at a bad time? I thought you wanted to see me immediately, Miss Harrington."

"I did, Major Kurland. Thank you for being so prompt." She smiled at him. "I also invited Mr. Stanford."

The look he cast her was eloquent with disapproval, but he did at least sit down. "I assume you went against my advice and asked for his help in this matter as well?"

She held up the book she had on her lap. "He

had a copy of Orfila's treatise on the effects of poison in the human body."

"Oh, well, that explains it."

Lucy ignored his attempt at levity and turned to Mr. Stanford. "I wonder if you might clarify a point for me, sir. In the book, Orfila suggests that natural poisons are more difficult to detect in the body than industrially produced ones."

"So I understand."

"And natural versions of a poison are slower acting."

"Yes."

"So if someone wished to kill the dowager at precisely that moment in Almack's, the poison administered would have to have been a more manufactured and concentrated powdered form?"

"Why?" Major Kurland asked. "Poison is poison, isn't it?"

"Well, no," Mr. Stanford said. "As I understand it, it depends on several factors as to how fast it works. Drinking a diluted or more natural form of a poison is much slower to act because it has to travel down into the stomach and then onto the organs it wishes to affect."

Lucy nodded. "That's correct, Mr. Stanford. Also, the strength of a natural remedy can vary depending on the quality of the plants used, the time they are harvested, and other mitigating factors."

"So you're saying that if the dowager swallowed

poisoned orgeat made from a natural remedy at Almack's, she wouldn't necessarily have dropped dead on the spot?"

"Exactly."

Major Kurland raised his head. "But we know that Broughton ingested the poison, too. I saw him. He wasn't faking his condition."

"But he didn't die."

"Which means either the dowager got a more concentrated dose than he did, or that he didn't react to it in the same way." Mr. Stanford shrugged.

"What if a manufactured poison like rat poison was put into the orgeat?" Sophia asked.

"It would definitely be more powerful."

"And it wasn't that long between them drinking the orgeat and the dowager taking ill," Lucy murmured half to herself. "This doesn't really help us at all, does it?"

"Why not?" Major Kurland asked.

"Because if it had been manufactured rat poison, then according to Orfila, it might have shown up in the dowager's body."

"It depends on what Dr. Redmond found when he investigated that body."

"If he's in league with the Broughton family in some way or is, in fact, the murderer, he's hardly likely to share that information with us, now is he?"

"Ah, but there are other ways of finding out

those results." Mr. Stanford smiled. "I'm a member of Fletchers. In fact, I'm the current secretary of the club."

"Broughton is a member, too," Major Kurland added. "I had dinner with him there."

"Dr. Redmond is also a member. If he has been writing any scholarly articles about the dowager, then I might be able to find out about them."

"He's hardly going to write everything down, is he?" Lucy said.

"You'd be surprised what a keen scientific observer will keep notes on, Miss Harrington. Some of our members keep detailed records of the most intimate nature."

Major Kurland produced a familiar black bottle out of his pocket. "And while you're doing that, Stanford, perhaps you might care to find out exactly what's in this?"

"Where did you get it?"

"Be careful," Major Kurland warned. "I suspect it's the last thing Oliver Broughton ever drank."

Mr. Stanford examined the handwritten label. "But it's supposed to be an elixir for coughing and fever."

"And that might be all it is, but it doesn't hurt to be careful. I'd also recommend you don't let Dr. Redmond or Broughton know what you are doing."

"You suspect that Dr. Redmond is trying to poison off the whole Broughton family?" Mr. Stanford demanded.

"I'm not sure." Major Kurland's gaze rested on Lucy for a moment. "But, as Miss Harrington always reminds me, we have to consider all the possibilities. There is one more thing." He dug into his pocket and brought out a folded piece of paper. "Is there a way I can find out whose debt this is?"

Mr. Stanford held out his hand and took the paper. "It's from Tattersalls demanding settlement of a thousand guineas." He looked up at Major Kurland. "We can go and look up the original wager in their betting book."

Lucy managed to take the paper from Mr. Stanford before he passed it back to the major, and she put on her spectacles to study it.

"Where did you find this, sir?"

Major Kurland avoided her gaze. "I happened to find it in Broughton's bedchamber while I was returning some cufflinks. I thought it might be important. I wonder if Broughton needs money from the estate to pay off Oliver's debts?"

Lucy gazed at him with new respect. "What an excellent idea, Major. I've often found that money, or the lack of it, is at the core of many disputes in Kurland St. Mary."

He gestured at the herbal. "Not to hurry you along, Miss Harrington, but I would prefer to get that book back to the Broughtons as soon as possible. I locked the door of the stillroom and pocketed the key, but I'm fairly sure there are duplicate keys available for the staff."

Mr. Stanford rose. "Then why don't you and I pay a visit to Tattersalls, Robert, and let the ladies investigate the herbal? Then, when we return, we can tell them what we've found and you can take the book back to its rightful place."

"What an excellent suggestion, Mr. Stanford," Sophia exclaimed.

After a swift glance at Major Kurland, Lucy spoke up. "If Major Kurland wishes to stay here and review the book with me instead, I would be grateful for his assistance."

"I suspect I'd be far more use at Tattersalls, Miss Harrington."

Her attempt to help him having been met with nothing more than a raised eyebrow and a mask of stoicism made her want to shake him.

"As you wish, Major." She smiled sweetly at him.

After the gentlemen left, Lucy put her spectacles back on and turned her attention to the herbal, Sophia at her side.

"There's one thing we should remember amongst all this confusion."

"And what is that?"

"That no one associated with the Broughton family is above suspicion."

Sophia smiled. "Does that include Major Kurland?"

"Well, I doubt he murdered anyone, but he might be reluctant to believe that a fellow officer like Broughton is *involved* in murder." She sighed. "I just can't see Dr. Redmond acting without an accomplice, can you?"

"Not unless he is insane. He might be a bit of a prosy bore for such a young man, but overall he seems quite sensible to me."

Lucy opened the herbal at one of the pages the dowager had marked and scanned the writing. "Did Mr. Stanford leave the bottle that Major Kurland gave him behind?"

"Yes, it's here." Sophia rose and brought back the carefully wrapped bottle.

Lucy exposed the handwritten label and peered intently at the writing. "I don't think that is the dowager's hand."

"Well, how could it be if Dr. Redmond prescribed the medicine for Oliver?"

"But I don't think it's the doctor's writing either." She showed Sophia the page she was studying. "Lieutenant Broughton told me that he and Hester made a fresh batch of the rose-hip cough syrup together. So, the writing on the label must belong to either Hester or the lieutenant." She pointed at one of the other scripts on the page. "See? The label is written in the same hand as this entry."

"And whose writing is that?" Sophia asked. "And even if we work that out, we still don't know what's in the medicine, or if Dr. Redmond added something to it at a later date."

"That's true, but it does mean the dowager didn't create this particular bottle of cough syrup."

"She still could've brewed the poison and someone later added it to the original."

Lucy turned to another page. "Your logic does you credit, Sophia, but I do wish it weren't so complicated. I'm beginning to believe that the dowager did not intend to poison anyone."

"Is Hester still employed by the Broughtons?"

"I believe so. Major Kurland talked to her quite recently."

"Then I wonder if she would help us further?"

"Major Kurland said that she seemed genuinely fond of the dowager, so perhaps she'd be willing to help us to discover a murderer."

"We can but ask." Lucy traced a finger over the dowager's handwriting. "I don't think Oliver died in the same way as the dowager. From what Major Kurland said, he was suffering from a high fever and seemed delusional."

"Then perhaps it is quite simple after all," Sophia said gently. "Maybe his guilt over poisoning his own brother and grandmother caused his fever and in an act of remorse, he chose to kill himself."

"But what about Lady Bentley? She drowned while Oliver was in his sickbed."

"Perhaps that is a separate issue entirely."

Lucy frowned down at the herbal. "I can't

accept that." She raised her head to meet Sophia's sympathetic gaze. "I know in my soul that all these things are connected, I just don't see *how.*"

Sophia smiled. "Then let us hope Major Kurland and Mr. Stanford are successful in their quest as well."

Robert stepped out of the hackney cab and, keeping his eyes firmly on Andrew Stanford's back, followed him into the hallowed ground of Tattersalls. If one wished to buy or sell prime bloodstock or bet on any horse racing, this was the place to do it. The smell of horse sweat and dung made Robert feel quite ill. He moved quickly to one side as a horse was brought through the crowded colonnaded passageways and turned out into the ring. A spirited round of bidding got under way immediately, and within seconds the horse was sold and being led out the other side of the quadrangle.

Another horse was brought in and a crowd of gentlemen of all ages stood around smoking and commenting on the stallion as it was led around by one of the stable hands. The horse constantly fought against the constraints of the halter, his nose flecked with foam, and his back legs attempting to buck and lash out at the railings with each lethal kick of his metal shoes.

"That's a fine-looking horse," Andrew commented. "Do you mind if we take a closer look?" He strode off toward the viewing area.

With a silent groan, Robert followed him, aware that he was flinching at every slight noise like a novice drummer boy under cannon fire.

"Do you need anything new for your stables down at Kurland St. Mary, Robert?"

Robert cleared his throat. "I haven't really thought about it. I've been focusing on clearing up the mess left by my last agent and investing in the farming side of the business."

"Farming, you?" Andrew chuckled. "The dashing hussar?"

"Hardly that anymore." Robert stared bleakly at the horse.

His friend turned to look at him. "It's just occurred to me that I haven't seen you astride a horse at all. Is everything all right?"

Robert focused his attention on the bidding and pretended he hadn't heard the question. "Shall we proceed inside? It looks like it might rain and it's the devil on my leg."

"Of course." Andrew hesitated. "I wouldn't give up hope, Robert. After such a terrible injury I'm sure it will take quite a while for you to ride properly again."

"I am aware of that, but thank you for your concern."

Robert turned toward the main building and made his way carefully over the treacherous cobblestones. The problem was that he didn't believe he'd ever have the nerve to get up on a horse and test that theory. But he also understood that his friend was attempting to be kind and didn't deserve to be snapped at.

The betting book at Tattersalls occupied pride of place in the hallway, and had its usual cluster of eager gentlemen standing around it. With his winning smile and a few deft words, Andrew managed to engineer his way through the crowd to get to the book and Robert followed him. Bringing out the receipt for the gaming bet, Robert flipped back through the closely written pages to the date mentioned on the paper and ran a finger down the long column.

"Broughton," Andrew murmured in his ear. "No Christian name, so one must assume it means the debt belongs to the first-born son." He whistled softly. "From the look of things, the debt is accumulating interest. That's not the first time Pike has pressed him for payment either."

"Damn," Robert said, and put the paper back in his pocket. "Do you know Mr. Pike?"

"Oh yes, he's usually around here somewhere. He fancies himself as something of an expert on the horses. His father is an impoverished Irish peer. Pike gambles well enough to live off his income in style."

They moved away from the betting book into a slightly quieter area of the room.

"Should we speak to him to make sure?" Robert asked.

"I don't see why not. He's a reasonable enough fellow if you pay your debts on time."

Andrew continued to walk through Tattersalls, greeting acquaintances and asking after Mr. Pike. Robert followed him and gradually forced himself to relax and even pay attention when a comment was directly addressed to him.

"There he is."

Mr. Pike was chatting to one of the jockeys, who despite their lowly station in life were often lionized by a certain section of the *ton* who considered riding abilities akin to godliness. Pike looked up as Andrew approached him and smiled, displaying a gap between his front teeth. Robert judged him to be Oliver Broughton's age.

"Mr. Stanford, have you come to place a wager with me?"

He had a soft Irish accent with a decided lilt that reminded Robert of many of the men in his regiment.

"Not this time, Mr. Pike." Andrew turned to Robert. "Have you met Major Robert Kurland of the Tenth Hussars?"

"A hussar, eh? Obviously a man who recognizes good horseflesh. Are you looking for some stock, Major? I could help you with that. I have an excellent eye."

"I'm sure you do. Every Irishman in my

regiment was something of a magician with the horses. I'm not looking to make any purchases at the moment, thank you." Robert shook Mr. Pike's proffered hand. "It's a pleasure to meet you, Mr. Pike."

Andrew put his hand on Mr. Pike's shoulder. "We were wondering if we might have a quiet word with you about a rather delicate matter."

"Of course, gentlemen. Shall we adjourn to the coffee house on the corner?"

When the butler announced his and Andrew's return to the Hathaway house, they first had to join the ladies for lunch. Restraining his impatience with great difficulty, Robert took his seat and realized that he was quite hungry. The ordeal of visiting Tattersalls had proved to be bittersweet. He'd managed to conduct himself like a gentleman in the crowds and around the horses, which was a definite improvement.

When he returned to Kurland Manor he might even take his head groom into his confidence and try and find some old nag to ride to regain his lost abilities. He missed riding greatly. It had always been his way to escape the world. Now that it was denied him, he felt he moved on the land like a caught fish choking for breath and out of his element.

"Major Kurland?"

He looked up to see that everyone had finished

eating, and that the servants were waiting to clear the table. He wiped his mouth with his napkin and stood up.

"Miss Harrington."

They returned to the cozy morning room where sunlight streamed through the window and there was a warm fire in the grate. Miss Harrington placed the herbal beside him.

"We discovered that the label on the bottle of Oliver's medicine must have been written by either Hester or Lieutenant Broughton." She pointed out the different sets of handwriting and compared them to the one on the bottle. "But we also have to consider the possibility that Dr. Redmond tampered with the contents."

"Are you certain Broughton was involved in making the elixir? He told me he despised his grandmother's herbal learning and only had faith in the new science."

"When I deliberately asked the countess to help me find a remedy for Anna's cough, she referred me to the lieutenant. He told me himself that he and Hester had made up a new batch of the rose-hip cough syrup."

"Why did he become involved in dosing the household?"

"Because, apparently, the dowager's concoctions had become unreliable. Lieutenant Broughton actually checked the bottle himself before he would allow me to take it for Anna."

"That was good of him," Robert said.

Miss Harrington didn't look convinced. "Sophia and I also considered whether Hester, the dowager's maid, was involved in this. You spoke to her, didn't you, Major?"

"I did. Despite her loyalty to the Broughton family she appeared to be as afraid of her mistress as everyone else."

"Would it be possible for me to speak to her?" Miss Harrington inquired. "She is still at the Broughtons', isn't she?"

"As far as I am aware, she is." Robert hesitated. "I'm leaving the house today. I'll try and speak to her before I go, and ask if she will see you."

"Thank you." Miss Harrington closed the herbal. "Now, what did you and Mr. Stanford discover at Tattersalls?"

Robert withdrew the folded note and spread it out on his knee. "The debt isn't Oliver's. It's Broughton's, and that isn't the worst of it." He sighed. "We spoke to the holder of this note, a Mr. Pike. He said that Broughton owes him in excess of ten thousand guineas."

"Ten *thousand?* That's a fortune."

"Which might explain why the dowager had to die," Robert said grimly. "Perhaps with his father away in India, Broughton thought to access the family finances and repay his debts from the dowager's coffers."

"Oh my goodness." Miss Harrington sat back.

"He *must* be in league with Dr. Redmond."

"I wish I could think of another explanation, but I can't." Robert stared into the fire. "There are still too many things that I don't understand. Why was it necessary for Dr. Redmond to poison Broughton?"

"We don't even know if Dr. Redmond was at Almack's that night, Major."

"Then we need to find out." Robert started walking up and down the room. "And why kill Lady Bentley and Oliver?"

"Well, one might hazard a guess that Oliver makes an excellent scapegoat. For all intents and purposes, all Broughton has to do now is quietly allow it to be known that his poor brother Oliver killed himself out of guilt for poisoning his grandmother and the matter will soon be forgotten. No one considers Lady Bentley's death as anything more than a separate tragedy." Miss Harrington shook her head. "I should imagine Broughton thought he could take control of the dowager's finances, pay off his debts, and have everything straightened out before his father returned from India."

"I suspect you might be correct, Miss Harrington," Andrew agreed. "Is it possible that Lady Bentley's drowning was an accident?"

"No." For once Robert and Miss Harrington spoke in unison.

Robert carried on speaking. "Broughton's boat

was involved in that crash. I suspect that when the hotheaded Mr. Bentley came after him, Broughton decided to play the victim and took revenge on poor Lady Bentley when they were both under the water."

"All he would need to do is hold on to her skirts and stop her reaching the surface." Mrs. Giffin shuddered.

"And Anna told me that Lieutenant Broughton seemed unable to avoid the other boat coming too close to him. She thought he was merely overtired and shouldn't have been out on the lake in the first place."

"I'm trying to recall his conversation with Mr. Bentley," Robert muttered. "It *has* to have something to do with those damn rubies."

"Maybe Lieutenant Broughton knew what really happened to them and didn't want the Bentleys creating a public nuisance of themselves." Miss Harrington looked up at Robert. "With his current financial difficulties, is it possible that he had already sold them and encouraged the dowager to imagine they had been stolen?"

"I suspect she would've leapt to that conclusion all by herself," Robert murmured.

"I wonder if we can find out if Broughton did sell or pawn them?"

"Unless you have a bill of sale, or a ticket from a money lender, that might prove difficult." Robert paused. "Wait a minute. Mr. Bentley said he had evidence that the jewelry belonged to his family estate. Broughton wasn't expecting to hear that, I remember how angry he was."

"Then we need to speak to Mr. Bentley. Either he has the original bill of sale or . . . Lady Bentley didn't want her son to speak to Broughton, did she?"

"So you said at the time."

"Why not?" Miss Harrington asked.

"Have you considered that you are complicating things unnecessarily, Miss Harrington?"

She raised her chin at him. "I'll speak to Mr. Bentley first and find out if I am *complicating* things or not."

Andrew chuckled and Robert turned to find him and Sophia Giffin smiling at them.

"This is almost entertaining, Robert. You and Miss Harrington would make an excellent pair of dueling lawyers in a courtroom." His expression sobered. "But as a man of law, I have to tell you that everything we *think* we have discovered is pure speculation until we can prove it. And even then, getting a prosecution might be difficult. The Broughton family is very influential in certain circles."

"I understand that." Robert looked around at the other three faces. "Then how *can* we prove it?"

Miss Harrington rose and went to the desk, returning with a piece of paper and her pen and ink. "Perhaps we should start by making a list."

Chapter 16

As Robert stepped over the threshold and shook the rain from his cloak onto the marble-floored hall, the Broughton House butler appeared and bowed.

"May I take your hat, Major?"

"No, thank you. I'll take it up with me." He glanced down at his bedraggled headgear. "It got rather wet in the rain. Foley has a special way of reviving the feathers. Is he in my room?"

"I believe he is finishing up your packing, sir." The butler cleared his throat. "We shall be sorry to lose you and Mr. Foley."

"Thank you, but I don't wish to further inconvenience Lady Broughton at this difficult time." Robert paused on the bottom step. "Is Lieutenant Broughton home?"

"Not yet, sir, although I believe he is expected shortly. Her ladyship is still in her bedchamber and not to be disturbed."

"I'll write her a note before I leave. If the lieutenant does come in, will you let me know?"

"Certainly, Major."

Robert continued up the stairs, his hat tucked in the crook of his arm. Foley was in his bedchamber, busy counting the bags stacked by the door.

"There you are, sir. Do you wish me to go ahead to Fenton's and start unpacking?"

"Yes, why don't you do that, Foley." Robert hesitated by the door. "There is one more thing you could do for me before you leave."

Foley clucked his tongue as he came forward to relieve Robert of his hat. "I'll certainly do my best to dry this out, sir, but the damage might be permanent."

"That's very good of you, but I need your help with another matter."

"Anything, sir."

"Without drawing attention to yourself, will you give Miss Hester Macleod the address of the Hathaway house on Dalton Street and ask her to attend Miss Harrington there as a matter of urgency?"

Foley frowned as he confiscated Robert's hat and stroked the bedraggled feathers. "What am I to say if she asks me why?"

"Tell her that it concerns the dowager countess's death."

"You haven't got yourself involved in something dangerous again now, Major, have you? Don't you remember what happened last time?"

"I don't have time to explain the intricacies of the situation to you right now, Foley. Just obey my orders and give Miss Hester the message."

"Yes, sir." With an obvious huffing noise, Foley turned on his heel and left the room, shutting the door very firmly, but precisely behind him.

Robert stood in front of the fire and warmed his hands. All his instincts urged him to find Broughton and confront him with his suspicions, but what good would it do? Broughton would either get angry and challenge him to a duel, or laugh in his face. In either scenario, Broughton stood to gain valuable information that might convict him if they played their cards carefully.

He needed firm evidence. And what better place to start looking than the untidy desk in Broughton's bedchamber?

Robert walked down to Broughton's rooms and knocked on the door. There was no answer, so he went in. Nothing had changed since his previous visit. The room was still untidy and the desk even more so. Edging closer, Robert began to read the scattered pieces of paper and mentally tallied up the demands for payment they represented. He slid the bill he'd borrowed from Tattersalls into one of the piles.

If Broughton was defaulting on paying the two pound and ten shilling coal bill, how much debt was he in, and how long had he been accruing it? They were only two years away from Waterloo when Robert had served alongside Broughton throughout the last desperate campaign to prevent Napoleon's return to power.

"Kurland? Were you looking for me?"

Robert turned slowly to face the door where

Broughton now stood. "Indeed, I was. I'm intending to leave for Fenton's shortly. I wanted to make sure that I said good-bye."

Broughton continued to lounge in the doorway, blocking Robert's line of retreat.

"My butler said he told you I wasn't in."

"He did." Robert moved casually away from the cluttered desk and toward the shaving stand. "Foley said he'd taken the cufflinks and silver buttons I borrowed from you and brought them back here. I distinctly remembered you saying you didn't need them and decided to come and retrieve them myself."

He pointed at the shaving stand. "Ah, there they are. Seeing as I have to attend a ball sponsored by the Prince Regent this Saturday, I thought I might be needing those rather modish cufflinks again." He paused. "I hope you don't mind. It seems rather extravagant to send a messenger all the way to Kurland St. Mary just to collect a pair of regimental cufflinks."

Broughton's expression relaxed. "Indeed, especially if you won't be needing them much longer yourself."

"Exactly." Robert put them in his coat pocket and held out his hand. "Thank you for inviting me to stay with your family."

"It's hardly been a pleasurable visit, has it?" Broughton half-smiled as he came forward to shake Robert's hand. "Next time you come up to London I hope things will take a better turn."

"I certainly hope so." Robert paused. "Have you fixed a date for Oliver's funeral? I would like to attend."

"I'm considering waiting for my father's return so that we can take both the bodies down to our country estate and bury them more privately." Broughton grimaced. "I suspect our local parson might be the only man willing to allow Oliver to be laid to rest in the family vault on consecrated ground."

"But surely Oliver didn't mean to kill himself? I assumed his mind was disturbed by his illness and he was unaware of what he was doing?"

"That's what the coroner agreed to say, but you and I know better, don't we?"

"I'm not sure I understand you."

Broughton took a deep breath. "It's obvious, isn't it? You were there. Oliver killed himself because of what he'd done to his grandmother. He was always an emotional, *unnatural* boy. I suspect his guilty conscience allowed him no rest."

Robert forced himself to maintain steady eye contact with Broughton. "I hadn't thought of that, but I suppose it makes sense."

Broughton gripped his upper arm. "And I know I can depend on you to keep that to yourself? They are both dead now. No one gains anything from exposing our family shame to the masses."

"Your stance does you great credit, Broughton. I give you my word of honor that I will never malign Oliver to *anyone*." Robert saluted and stepped back. "I wish your family nothing but good fortune in the future."

"Thank you."

Before he could betray himself, Robert left, but not before he'd seen Broughton's slight smile. At least now he had no doubt that his erstwhile friend was involved in several murders. It would give him great pleasure to bring the man to justice.

"Anna sent me a note this morning asking if we were both well," Sophia said. "She sounded rather worried."

Lucy sighed. "I'll have to talk to her about Broughton soon. I must admit that I keep putting it off. She seems rather infatuated with him. I cannot imagine why."

"Men in uniform, my dear." Sophia held her arm as they alighted from the carriage in front of the Bentley residence. "They have the strangest effect on a woman. Look how fast I fell in love with Charlie." She pinched Lucy's gloved wrist. "Look at your Major Kurland."

"He's certainly not mine, Sophia. But I have to admit that he does look rather dashing in his uniform. I can only imagine how he might appear astride a horse brandishing his sword."

Sophia turned to her at the bottom of the steps that led up to the black painted front door. "Do you know, I don't think I've seen him astride a horse in uniform or out of it since he recovered from his wounds. Isn't that odd?"

Lucy fixed her attention on the front door where the brass knocker was tied with a black ribbon and picked up her skirts. "Come along, Sophia. It's too cold to be standing around out here in the rain."

Sophia wouldn't be the first person to notice the major's peculiar aversion to riding a horse, or the last. His chances of going out in public in London and keeping that secret worsened by the day. Lucy only hoped he had a plan to overcome his fear, but suspected he would be too proud to take her advice on the matter. Men's pride was a peculiar, prickly thing. And he wasn't really her concern after all.

"May I help you?"

Lucy smiled at the butler and handed over her card. "We'd like to see Mr. Bentley. Is he at home?"

The butler bowed. "If you will come into the hall, ma'am, I'll inquire."

Eventually, they were ushered into a drawing room dominated by a large oil painting of a young Lady Bentley with a little boy sitting on her lap gazing up at her adoringly.

"Mrs. Giffin? Miss Harrington? I understand that you wish to speak to me about my mother?"

Lucy turned to see Mr. Bentley coming into the room and caught her breath. He looked as if the loss of his mother had made him lose himself, too. She impulsively went forward and took his hand.

"Oh, my dear sir. I am so *sorry* for your loss."

He patted her gloved hand and then released it, the sheen of tears in his eyes. He wore black and seemed to have aged a thousand years. "Thank you. Please sit down. Would you like some tea?"

"No, thank you, Mr. Bentley." Lucy waited until he sent the butler away and took the seat opposite him. "May I be blunt with you, sir? Just before she died your mother confided in me about her issues with the Broughton family. I wanted to ask you about the circumstances surrounding her death, and whether you have had any further thoughts about the matter."

"I can't stop thinking about it." He looked even more wretched. "I will never forgive myself for causing the death of the woman I loved most in the world."

"But what if you weren't entirely responsible for her death?"

He raised his troubled gaze to hers. "Whatever do you mean?"

"You and your mother were taking the Broughton family to court to regain jewelry you believed the dowager countess had stolen from you."

"That was the original plan, yes. But what does this have to do with my mother's death?"

"If I might continue, sir. I believe you told Lieutenant Broughton that you had evidence to support your claim."

"So my mother told me."

"Might I be so bold as to ask what that was?" He hesitated and she continued. "I'm not asking out of vulgar curiosity, sir. I'm simply trying to right a terrible wrong and bring you some peace."

He sighed. "It's rather complicated. I assumed my mother meant that she had letters or inventories from the Bentley estate that showed the provenance of the jewels, but actually she had something rather different."

"And what was that?"

"You have to understand, Miss Harrington, that my mother had obsessed about the return of those rubies for decades. In her quest for justice she kept in touch with a network of London jewelers and money lenders who were paid to alert her if any rubies came into their hands. Within the last year, one of the jewelers did."

"Which explains why she decided to raise the matter with the dowager countess again."

"Indeed. In truth, I was unaware of the full nature of her plan to discredit the Broughtons until the day of the boating party."

"What did she intend to do?"

"She ascertained that the rubies were the ones

she considered part of the Bentley estate and bought them back. One might think that having achieved such a coup she would be satisfied, but she decided to pursue a lawsuit to make the dowager's life as difficult as possible. She wanted to see her exposed as a liar and a thief."

"Quite understandable, Mr. Bentley, if she thought the dowager had deliberately pawned her rubies and was still busy trying to ruin her socially. I assume that when you went directly to Broughton at the boating party, she became worried about you becoming involved in her plans and told you the truth?"

"Exactly. My beloved mother didn't want me involved in a lawsuit that was for her own private amusement. I don't think she ever meant to go through with it. She said she was hoping the dowager would come crawling back to tell her the rubies had been sold, and then she would've been able to pull them out of her drawer and crow over her rival." He grimaced. "Not a very pretty picture, but the dowager countess was something of a shrew."

Lucy drew a slow breath. "I don't suppose your mother kept the receipt from the jeweler for the rubies, did she?"

Mr. Bentley stared at her. "On the contrary, I'm quite sure that she did. I doubt she would've neglected any opportunity to wave a piece of evidence like that directly in the dowager's face."

He rose to his feet. "Would you like to come and see my mother's bedchamber? Her dresser is currently sorting out her possessions. We might find something useful there."

By the time Lucy and Sophia returned home, it was getting dark, and they had both almost fallen asleep in the carriage. Lucy's mind was whirling with ideas and conjectures and . . . she wished Major Kurland were there to talk to. He had a unique ability to take her ideas and somehow make sense of them. She didn't always agree with his conclusions, or appreciate his somewhat acerbic manner, but having another opinion was always helpful.

She ran through the rain into the hallway followed by Sophia and smiled at the butler. "Has Mrs. Hathaway been wondering where we've been? We haven't missed dinner, have we?"

"No, Miss Harrington. Mrs. Hathaway is in the drawing room, and dinner will be served in half an hour."

"Thank you. We have time to change and warm up a little." She blew a kiss to Sophia as they separated on the first landing and headed to their respective bedchambers. "We'd better hurry!"

When she rejoined the Hathaways in the drawing room, she had put on one of her older and warmer dresses from her Kurland St. Mary wardrobe and dressed her hair in a simpler style.

She felt far more like herself. Her sister, Anna, jumped up out of her seat and came toward her.

"Lucy, where on earth have you *been?* We've all been so worried."

She embraced Anna tightly and they sat down, their hands still interlinked. "I'm very well, Anna. I've just been rather busy."

"Too busy to see your own sister?"

"I'm sorry, love." She held her sister's indignant gaze. "I never meant to worry you."

"But you're still not going to tell me what you've been up to, are you? Does it concern Major Kurland?"

"Why would you think that?" Behind her she heard Sophia snort.

"Because he seems determined to fix his interest with you."

"He does *not.*"

Anna blinked at her. "Then I shall be speaking to him myself. If his intentions are not honorable, he has no business singling you out!"

She glanced back at Sophia and Mrs. Hathaway, who were making no attempt to hide the fact that they were both listening. "Do you think I have time to speak to Anna privately before dinner, ma'am?"

"Of course." Mrs. Hathaway smiled at them both. "It's only family this evening, so no one will mind if you are a few minutes late to the table."

Taking Anna's hand, Lucy went back to her bedchamber and waited until her sister sat on the side of the bed with her arms crossed.

"Well?"

The stubborn expression on Anna's face should be a warning to all the men who imagined her to be beautiful and manageable.

"I have been spending some time with Major Kurland, Anna, but only because of a matter that concerns the Broughton family."

"And what would that be?"

Lucy gathered her resolve. "Murder."

"What?"

"I know that you have conceived a *tendre* for Lieutenant Broughton, but I fear your affection may be misplaced."

Anna stared at her for a long time. "You and Major Kurland think that Lieutenant Broughton is a murderer?"

"Quite possibly." Lucy looked squarely into Anna's blue eyes. "You might not believe me, but—"

"Oh, I believe you." Anna shuddered. "I fell out of love with him when he described his sickening experiments on those poor animals."

"Then you aren't angry with me?"

"Not at all." Anna raised her eyebrows. "Apart from the fact that you excluded me from your confidence again."

"I thought I was protecting you."

"I understand, but I'm no longer a child, Lucy. I can take care of myself. I worry about you more than I worry about myself. Are you aware that Major Kurland's particular attention toward you has meant that other men who might have been considering you as a potential wife will have drawn away?"

"That's very sweet of you, but no one has really looked at me twice." Lucy forced a smile. "I don't think I'm suited to a life in London. I really want to go home."

"Home to Major Kurland?"

"No, just *home.*" Lucy sat next to Anna on the bed. "Looking after Father, helping in the parish, dealing with Kurland Manor . . . perhaps that is what I am meant to be doing after all. I like being my own mistress."

"Oh, Lucy . . ." Anna kissed her cheek. "I cannot allow you to think so poorly of yourself that you believe caring for others is your station in life. You deserve so much more."

"But I am a rather managing female, even you can't deny that." Lucy smiled. "Perhaps Father's new curate will be young and handsome."

"And malleable."

Lucy smiled. "Exactly."

"I don't want you to end up alone, Lucy," Anna whispered.

"How could that happen? If I don't find a husband, I'm hoping I'll be welcome in your home or in any other of my siblings' houses who choose to invite me." Lucy swallowed back a ridiculous urge to cry and rose to her feet. "Perhaps we should go down to dinner? I don't know about you, but I'm rather hungry."

Chapter 17

They'd agreed to convene in one of the private parlors at Fenton's the next morning and Robert was impatiently awaiting his guests. The relief of being out of Broughton House had been immeasurable, particularly after Broughton's unsubtle attempt to direct Robert's thoughts into believing Oliver was a murderer. Every time he pictured Oliver's panicked expression as Dr. Redmond and Broughton had arrived home that night he wanted to flay Broughton alive.

A knock on the door drew his attention back to the present as one of the maids brought in a tray of coffee and other victuals and placed them on the table. Her exit was swiftly followed by the arrival of Andrew, Mrs. Giffin, and Miss Harrington, who brought the snap of the cold easterly wind with them in their pink cheeks and disheveled locks.

It didn't take long for bonnets to be discarded, cloaks to be set aside, and for the four of them to be seated around the table. Miss Harrington produced a stub of pencil and a piece of paper that was already covered in writing.

"Well, where shall we start?" she asked.

Andrew Stanford raised his hand. "I went to Almack's and checked the subscriptions book for the ball the night the dowager died. Dr. Redmond was present."

"Damn," Robert said. "So we still can't discount him."

He turned back to Miss Harrington. "Tell us what happened with Mr. Bentley."

Miss Harrington talked, and Sophia Giffin added her impressions, building a picture of the events leading up to the disaster on the boating lake that made a terrible kind of sense.

"Mr. Bentley entrusted me with the rubies." Miss Harrington laid a flat green velvet jewelry box on the table and opened it to display a sumptuous ruby and gold necklace that shone even in the shadows of the room. "And even more importantly, with these." She placed two pieces of paper on the table. "One is the original bill of purchase from the jeweler to Lieutenant Broughton. The other is Lady Bentley's receipt from the jeweler for the same rubies."

Andrew Stanford whistled. "That's pretty damning, although there is still no direct evidence to convict Broughton of murdering Lady Bentley or anyone else."

"I know." Miss Harrington sighed. "Mr. Bentley

also asked us to convey his apologies to you, Major. He said that he misjudged you and appreciated your effort to save his mother's life. When he first approached the scene, he thought you were strangling her."

"Now I come to think of it, her neck was rather red," Robert admitted. "I assumed that was because we'd had to drag her out of the lake. But maybe Broughton wanted to make absolutely sure that she wouldn't rise to the surface and be saved. . . ." He shook his head. "Not that it matters. For all intents and purposes she was dead once Broughton realized she might know what had really happened to the jewelry."

"But why couldn't he leave the matter alone? With the dowager dead, surely the whole thing would've been quickly forgotten?" Miss Harrington asked. "Lady Bentley had her jewels and the satisfaction of knowing she'd won in the end."

"Not if Mr. Bentley insisted on carrying out his threat to bring the matter to court. Everything would've come out in public. Broughton couldn't afford for any suspicion as to his need for money to be revealed, or all his creditors would've been dunning him."

"But Lady Bentley had already decided to tell her son the truth, hadn't she?"

"Yes, but Broughton didn't know that or even exactly what evidence the Bentleys had. I suppose he decided to err on the side of caution."

"And took advantage of the collision on the lake."

"I asked Anna about that again last night. She said that Mr. Bentley was originally making right for them, but seemed to think better of it and eased back. It was *her* boat that collided with the Phillips boat, which became entangled with the Bentleys and tipped everyone overboard."

"So Broughton might have managed that, too."

"Yes." Miss Harrington sat back. "I also spoke to Hester Macleod and she gave me a sample of her handwriting. She *did* write the labels, but she insisted it was Lieutenant Broughton who made up the elixir. Of course, if it comes down to it, Broughton can claim to have no knowledge of this particular bottle of medicine because it looks like Hester made it and one would assume it was given with Dr. Redmond's approval."

"So, again we can prove nothing," Robert said. "And if Broughton's story about Oliver's culpability is accepted, then he will get away with murder."

"We still don't know that he murdered anyone, Robert." Andrew tapped the list. "All we know is that he is desperately in debt and we assume he needed to gain control of his grandmother's finances before his father returned to see what a mess he'd made of everything."

"Which gives him all the motive in the world."

"To prove that he poisoned anyone, we'd need evidence from the body. And finding *that* despite Orfila's and others' work is still a dark art."

Robert rubbed an impatient hand over his jaw. "Do we know what was in that bottle by Oliver's bedside yet?"

"Not yet. I have someone from Fletchers analyzing it for us. He's very discreet."

"Then the only thing I can think of to do now is have an honest conversation with Dr. Redmond." Robert looked around the table. "Does everyone agree?"

"I wonder if Broughton intends to cast the doctor as the other villain of the piece?" Miss Harrington asked. "One has to suspect that if anyone doesn't believe that Oliver was responsible, Broughton might need to produce another likely culprit."

"And Dr. Redmond is the Broughton family physician. I've found out some interesting information about him," Andrew said. "Did you know that he attended Eton and knew Oliver *rather well* before he met the lieutenant?"

"Are you suggesting . . . ?" Robert didn't want to discuss Oliver's personal proclivities in front of the ladies, but Andrew simply nodded.

"One has to wonder about that, doesn't one?"

"About what?" Miss Harrington demanded, her attention swiveling between Robert and Andrew. "Why would Dr. Redmond countenance the murder of someone he was friends with? Do you think he expected Broughton to pay him, too?"

Robert stood up. "Perhaps we should go and alert Dr. Redmond to his peril. Where might we find him at this hour of the day?"

"I believe he has an office on Harley Street; we can visit him there," Andrew said. "I'll escort the ladies home, and then I'll come back and pick you up."

Miss Harrington made a huffing sound and stared pointedly at Robert. "You must promise to tell us what transpires with Dr. Redmond."

"Naturally, Miss Harrington. I wouldn't dream of doing anything else."

Andrew paused at the door. "If you would prefer it, Miss Harrington, I could escort Mrs. Giffin home and you could go with Robert to visit Dr. Redmond?"

"But she wouldn't be chaperoned," Sophia Giffin said.

The sudden fall in Miss Harrington's hopeful expression stopped Robert's instant denial of her claim to be present at the crucial interview.

"I'm sure one of the maids here at the hotel could accompany us."

"Then that's settled." Andrew winked at Mrs. Giffin. "You can take my carriage, Robert, and Mrs. Giffin and I will quite happily walk back to the Hathaways' house."

• • •

"To what do I owe this honor, Major Kurland, Miss Harrington?"

Robert took the seat offered to him in Dr. Redmond's study and waited until Miss Harrington settled beside him. Despite his relatively young age, the physician occupied a respectable set of consulting rooms on one of the best streets in London and appeared very at ease in them.

"We wish to talk to you about the recent deaths in the Broughton family."

"Such a tragedy." Dr. Redmond shook his head. "The dowager countess was an elderly lady who tended to ignore my advice and insisted on medicating herself. I confess that I wasn't terribly surprised when she succumbed to heart failure, although the timing of her death was rather unfortunate."

"In what way?"

Dr. Redmond's eyebrows rose. "I simply meant that dying at a subscription ball at the most exclusive club in London was bound to create just the sort of publicity a well-to-do family strives to avoid."

"Ah, I see, how *vulgar* of her."

"Is something wrong, Major Kurland?"

"There might be. If the dowager's death was *understandable,* what do you make of Oliver Broughton's decision to throw himself off a window ledge?"

Dr. Redmond flinched and dropped his gaze to his desk where he began to rearrange his notepads. "I . . . regret Oliver's death more than I can say."

"Do you feel responsible for what happened?"

"Of course I do." He shoved a hand through his hair. "I don't understand why he wasn't getting better. I tried everything—"

"May I ask," Miss Harrington interrupted him. "What exactly did you imagine was wrong with Oliver in the first place?"

"I assumed he'd merely suffered from the same gastrointestinal complaint Broughton had, and I treated him accordingly, but he also seemed . . ." His voice trailed off. "Why are you asking me all these things? Do you have Broughton's permission to question me and interfere in the private affairs of his family?"

Robert crossed one booted foot over the other. "We don't have his permission, because we suspect he wouldn't give it to us. Are you aware that Lieutenant Broughton is seriously in debt, doctor?"

"I beg your pardon?"

"Are you also aware that he is quietly telling people that Oliver poisoned his grandmother in a fit of jealous rage and then killed himself because of his 'unnatural leanings' and his guilt over taking a life?"

All the color bled from the doctor's face. "That can't be true, Broughton wouldn't—"

"I hate to disappoint you, Doctor, but that's exactly what he's doing. He'll blame Oliver for everything, and bury him and the dowager in the countryside where no one will ever think of them again. Is that what you want?" He paused. "I understand you knew Oliver from Eton. Will you forget him as easily as his brother will?"

"No," Dr. Redmond whispered. "How could I?"

"Which brings me to my next question. Was Lieutenant Broughton really ill after Almack's?"

"Yes, of course he was. Why do you ask?"

"Dr. Redmond, let me be blunt. You were at Almack's that night. Did you conspire with Lieutenant Broughton to poison his grandmother?"

With a stifled groan Dr. Redmond covered his face with his hands. "*Conspire?* I'd hardly call it that. Coerced might be a better word, or even blackmailed."

"Are you suggesting Broughton *forced* you to help him? Why would he do that?"

"Because of Oliver. Because he knew—" Dr. Redmond's breath shuddered out. "A year or so ago Broughton sought me out and made me believe he was interested in my scientific studies. I must admit that I was flattered by his attention and I needed a patron to introduce me to the right people. He also introduced me to Oliver, not realizing, I assumed, that we already knew each other from Eton. I did my best to keep away from him. Eventually Broughton told me that he knew what I'd done and that if I didn't help him he'd expose me to my colleagues as a . . ." Dr. Redmond glanced at Miss Harrington and stopped speaking.

Robert nodded. "I understand. So you agreed to help him dispose of the dowager."

"Yes, the dowager countess was extremely frail anyway. Broughton suggested that a slight increase in her self-administered heart medicine might hasten her end. He didn't mention anything about needing money and, having met the dowager on several occasions, I could see how one might grow to hate her."

"How did you intend to accomplish your goal?"

"As I said, the dowager was already brewing a tea made of foxglove seeds and leaves to aid the regularity of her heart. I did speak to her about the dangers of such a concoction, but she wouldn't listen to me. William Withering had already made a study of foxglove, or digitalis as it was more formally known in 1785, which advocated its scientific use as a modern therapeutic, so I considered it marginally acceptable."

Robert nodded impatiently. "Yes, yes, but what exactly did you change in the medication?"

"I made the tea more concentrated. That's all."

"And what effect would that have?"

Dr. Redmond shrugged. "As I said, it increased the likelihood of the dowager having a heart attack."

"In fact, you were shortening her life."

"Yes."

"So what happened at Almack's? Did you misjudge the dose?"

"I don't know."

"What do you mean?" Miss Harrington sat forward, her gloved hands clutched tightly together in her lap.

"Broughton asked me to make him a new vial of the concentrated digitalis, as he was running out. I gave it to him at Almack's that night. I ended up leaving earlier than I intended because I saw Oliver storm out in a rage and I tried to talk to him." He sighed. "I believe I just made things worse. By the time we'd finished arguing, the dowager must've been dead. I suspect I was meant to be available at Almack's to confirm the dowager's death from natural causes, but in my haste to confront Oliver, I wasn't there."

"So it's possible Broughton chose to administer the poison himself?"

"I really don't know," Dr. Redmond said slowly. "It was only when I saw the dowager's body that I realized something was wrong. Not only was her heart badly damaged, but she bore additional signs of arsenic poisoning."

"And did you mention that to Broughton?"

"Yes, he suggested that I keep my mouth shut. When I protested that it was against my principles to lie about such matters, he showed me the bottle of digitalis with my handwriting on it. He said that if I didn't keep quiet, he'd make sure he 'found' the bottle and would have no hesitation in denouncing me as his grandmother's murderer."

"Clever."

"Yes." Dr. Redmond cleared his throat. "So I agreed to keep quiet."

"Because you were implicated in her death."

"You don't understand. I thought helping him shorten the dowager's life would stop him blackening my name and reputation, and that he'd leave me alone. I thought it would make Oliver's life easier, too, if the old harridan wasn't there to bully him. But, of course, I was wrong."

"With all due respect, Dr. Redmond, you didn't simply 'shorten' the dowager's life, you *ended* it by giving Broughton the poison *you* brewed," Robert snapped. "I hardly think this matter reflects well on you at all. If Broughton is ever challenged about these convenient deaths, I suspect he'll inform on you just as easily as he implicated Oliver."

"God, *no.*" Dr. Redmond shook his head.

Robert made no effort to reassure the man. As far as he was concerned, he was almost as bad as Broughton. "I presume you thought the matter would be over when Oliver regained his health, as you expected him to do so."

"But poor Oliver became worse." Miss Harrington sounded far too sympathetic for

305

Robert's liking, but the doctor turned gratefully toward her.

"Yes, he became very weak and confused and was unable to keep most foods down. He also kept insisting he could see ghosts in the corners of his room. Broughton believed his mind was disturbed."

"He would." Robert couldn't keep the sarcasm out of his voice. "Did you know Lieutenant Broughton has been conducting some scientific experiments of his own?"

"I was aware of his interest in such matters, yes. He's been exterminating vermin using the scientific method to record and evaluate his findings."

"Using what type of poison?"

"White arsenic, I believe. Why?"

"I'm not sure. Did you prescribe Oliver some of the dowager's rose-hip cough medicine as well?"

"I knew Oliver was taking it, but Broughton assured me that Hester Macleod had made the last batch, so there was no fear of the dowager having made a mistake."

"I saw Oliver just before he died. His nurse had just given him the rose-hip syrup."

"How do you know that for sure?"

"I spoke to her just before she was dismissed for incompetence, and I confiscated the bottle of medicine."

Dr. Redmond half-stretched out his hand. "Do you have it with you?"

"It's already being tested."

Horror dawned on the doctor's already ashen features. "You think Broughton killed Oliver, don't you?"

Robert smiled. "Well, if you didn't, who else could it be?"

Lucy glanced up at Major Kurland as he handed the maid onto the outside seat of the carriage and then helped her inside.

"You were very harsh with poor Dr. Redmond."

"My dear Miss Harrington, he willingly conspired with Broughton to shorten the dowager's life! In my book that makes him almost as guilty as Broughton. Does that not offend you?"

"Yes, but he certainly didn't aid Broughton *willingly*. He did it out of fear for his reputation."

The major's expression remained stern. "And self-interest. What about his Hippocratic oath to do no harm to his patients?" Major Kurland snorted. "He only remembered *that* when he saw the dowager's body and realized he might be implicated in a murder."

"He obviously panicked." Lucy smoothed down the gray skirt of her pelisse. "You have no concept of how it must be to make your own way in the world like Dr. Redmond had to do."

"I've made my own way, Miss Harrington."

"To a certain extent I suppose you have. Although, as far as I understand it, you need money to purchase a commission in a decent regiment and your family always had ample funds."

"Only in this generation. My grandfather was a common laborer before he built his own mills and became a wealthy man. I've had to overcome my fair share of aristocratic prejudice."

"And Dr. Redmond is the fourth son of an earl with no income to speak of, and from what I gathered at our meeting, a somewhat spotty reputation."

"Ah, you picked up on that, did you?"

"That he was in love with Oliver?" She sighed. "Yes, it's rather sad, isn't it?"

"Not according to the teachings of the church."

She studied his shadowed face. "You don't seem to share Lieutenant Broughton's horror at such a thing."

"I don't. I've spent most of my life in the company of men, and I know what goes on between some of them. In my experience, as long as they were willing to fight to the death, where they chose to lay their pack at night made no difference to me. In fact, some of the men fought harder to ensure the safety of those they loved who were standing right beside them."

"What a highly unorthodox opinion, Major."

His smile flashed out, surprising her. "I don't

notice you being shocked either, Miss Harrington."

"Because it makes sense of everything, doesn't it? Broughton killed for financial gain, and Dr. Redmond helped him out of fear and love."

"And we still can't prove a single thing."

"I know. I wonder why the dowager showed signs of arsenic poisoning?"

"Perhaps Broughton decided the digitalis wasn't enough and made sure of her end with some arsenic he just happened to have with him in his pocket."

"And it appears that came as a surprise to Dr. Redmond, too." She wrinkled her nose. "It also complicates matters even further. How did he manage to get concentrated digitalis *and* arsenic in her orgeat?"

"I have no idea."

The major sounded rather short. It must be hard for him to face the fact that his friend was a murderer. Lucy looked out of the window and decided to change the subject. "Are you intending to return to Kurland St. Mary in the near future, Major?"

"It depends on the Prince Regent. I'm awaiting my summons to the royal presence for the formal presentation of my baronetcy. If I don't hear from the prince's secretary this week, I'm going to write to him and explain that I'll be going home for a few days and he can reach me there. I haven't spent a single moment with my potential new land agent yet, and I wish to hear his plans for my estate." He paused. "Why, is there something I can do for you in Kurland St. Mary?"

"I have a letter for my father, Major. I thought if you were going back I would entrust it to your care."

"Of course, I'll take it." He paused. "Is there anything wrong at home?"

"No, I write to him every week. He enjoys hearing about our adventures."

"I'm sure he does. Has London lived up to your expectations, Miss Harrington?"

She regarded him warily. "In some ways I've enjoyed it very much, but as an unmarried lady, my sphere of influence is obviously very limited. My aunt has some charities that she favors, but she doesn't do more than offer them money and make a yearly visit, whereas I would *insist* on being more involved in what was going on. There is such huge wealth in this city and yet so many people are starving."

"As in any city. Even you would struggle to find a way to feed them all."

"If someone would offer me the chance, I'd dearly love to try." She shook her head. "You will think me foolish."

He nodded. "Idealistic maybe, but scarcely foolish, Miss Harrington. Unfortunately, you'd need to marry a prince of the realm, a nabob, or a real Indian prince to have such a fortune at your disposal. Has Miss Anna met a man worthy of her yet?"

"I'm not sure. I do know that she has received two proposals of marriage."

"Hopefully not one from Lieutenant Broughton."

She shuddered. "No, she told me that she'd fallen out of love with him when he showed us his gruesome experiments in his laboratory."

"Thank goodness for that." He half-smiled. "At one point I imagined she would marry him, and you would be off with Stanford, but of course that isn't likely to happen now, is it?"

"Why not?"

He blinked at her. "You still believe Stanford might make you an offer?"

"You find the notion that someone might wish to marry me so preposterous? Not everyone sees me as some sort of convenience, Major."

"That's not what I meant at all, it's simply that—"

She turned her head away before he could see that he had upset her and gazed unseeingly out into the street. She had almost confided to him that she planned to tell her father she was coming home early and that she was leaving Anna in excellent hands with the Clavelly family. But if she said that to him now, he'd probably either remind her that he'd told her so, or even worse, laugh.

"Miss Harrington . . ."

She bit down on her lip and refused to respond to him. As the carriage drew to a stop, he leaned across her to open the door. She didn't wait for his help to step down, but managed by herself. She reached the top step and reached for the doorknocker.

"Miss *Harrington*."

Schooling her features into a bland mask, she slowly looked down into his all-too-familiar face.

"Yes, Major?"

He studied her for such a long moment that she forgot to breathe.

"I offended you." His dark blue gaze searched hers. "Worse, I upset you."

"It's of no matter."

"I didn't mean to suggest that you weren't having a successful Season."

"Oh yes, I'm positively *surrounded* by potential suitors. As you mentioned before I embarked on this pointless exercise, I am obviously not what any *gentleman* wishes for in a wife." She banged the knocker hard. He carried on speaking behind her.

"If there was any justice in this world, they would be fighting over you, Miss Harrington," he said gently. "They are obviously all fools."

Lucy briefly closed her eyes and started to turn back to Major Kurland. The door swung open and the Clavelly butler cleared his throat.

"Good evening, Miss Harrington, Major Kurland."

Major Kurland saluted from the flagstone path. "Good evening, I've brought Miss Harrington and her maid to see her sister."

It took another gentle prompt from the polite butler before she remembered to step into the warmth of the hall so that he could shut the door. She walked up to the drawing room in a daze only to find that Anna was still dressing. After avoiding yet another quizzing from her aunt about Major Kurland, she escaped up the stairs.

She could hear someone coughing as she approached the bedroom door and opened it to find Anna and her maid in deep conversation.

"Oh, Lucy, I was just telling Edith how good that cough medicine the Broughtons gave me was." She held the bottle up to the light. "There is a little bit left in there that you can take, Edith."

Lucy stared at the dark brown glass of the bottle as an outrageous idea flowered in her head. "By all means let Edith finish the bottle, but make sure you keep it so that we can return it to Lieutenant Broughton."

"Thank you, Miss." Edith allowed Anna to give her two spoonfuls of the rose-hip syrup. "Ooh, miss, I can feel it warming the back of my throat already."

Chapter 18

T hat's a ridiculous suggestion," Major Kurland said.

Lucy refused to lower her gaze. "Why? If we can't find a way to implicate Lieutenant Broughton in any of these murders, why can't we trick him into revealing himself?"

"Because it's highly unethical."

"And when have such niceties ever bothered Lieutenant Broughton?"

Major Kurland maintained his stance in front of the fire in the center of the hearthrug, a position that reminded Lucy strongly of her father. Before the rest of the Hathaway household had awoken, she'd taken a maid and gone to see him at Fenton's. She and her maid had been ushered into the same parlor as on her last visit and had time to kick up her heels while the major was presumably woken up, shaved, and dressed by his butler.

"But what if he doesn't take the bait?"

"Then we've lost nothing, have we?"

He frowned down at her. "I'd have to ask Dr. Redmond to help. I cannot guarantee that he'll cooperate."

"He doesn't need to know what is afoot. In fact, it would be better if he didn't and was thus able to play his part more convincingly."

"I suppose that's true."

"I wonder what he thought about Oliver's remains? Orfila says that it is possible to detect and identify some types of poison in the human body."

"I don't imagine Dr. Redmond has the stomach to dissect Oliver, do you?"

"Then perhaps someone else should."

"What do you hope to achieve by such an act?"

"We know that Oliver and Broughton fell ill at about the same time as the dowager."

"Agreed."

"The dowager died, Broughton was ill, but recovered, and Oliver got worse and then killed himself while his mind was disturbed."

"Yes."

"We are assuming that all three of them received different doses of the same things."

"It is the simplest way to proceed."

"But from what Dr. Redmond told you, the dowager was given an increased dose of digitalis. Neither Broughton nor Oliver showed symptoms of heart failure, did they? They were both beset with digestive problems, which suggests they ingested something different—if Broughton was truly ill."

Major Kurland finally abandoned his commanding perch on the rug and sat down. "He certainly looked ill when I saw him. I doubt he would've been able to fake that."

"And you saw Oliver, too, didn't you? Did he complain of heart problems?"

"Not really. He looked rather like Broughton did on that first night, but he soon got worse and other symptoms appeared."

"So either Dr. Redmond intends to do away with the whole Broughton family, which we now know is patently ridiculous, or Broughton decided to play his own hand. I sincerely doubt that they worked together."

"And I sincerely doubt that Dr. Redmond would attempt to do away with Oliver."

"Then it *has* to be Broughton, and this might be the only way we can make him confess."

He looked up at her. "I wonder if Dr. Redmond has actually seen Oliver's body?"

"As you said, he probably wouldn't want to."

"But if it proved that Broughton had been poisoning his brother, he might be more willing to help us expose his killer." He frowned. "Now how can we find out where Oliver's remains are being held?"

"Oh, I already know that. Lady Broughton said that both the bodies were being held in the crypt of a church the Broughton family help fund in the city. I believe it is one of the guild churches, St. Mary in the Wall."

"I know it." Major Kurland nodded decisively. "It's set into the side of the old Roman wall that enclosed the city of London. I'll persuade Dr.

Redmond to visit the church crypt with me while you ascertain if Broughton and his mother will allow us to visit him at home to pay our respects."

"Then you've decided to go along with my plan?"

He was already at the door, but he looked over his shoulder at her. "It might be fantastical, Miss Harrington, but at this point it is the only option we have."

Lucy felt rather like a general marshaling her troops for battle as she surveyed all the people who had insisted on being present to witness Broughton's downfall. He was a very intelligent man and he might still come about. Anna had written a note to Broughton asking if they might visit, and he had replied with alacrity. Sophia had insisted that she had to accompany Anna and Lucy to chaperone them. Major Kurland had sent her a note to tell her that he was bringing Dr. Redmond along.

She could only hope that the countess wouldn't object to such a large party descending upon her home, or that Lieutenant Broughton wouldn't become wary. According to Major Kurland, he seemed to believe he was above suspicion, which worried her. Would her amateur efforts to trap him fail? And if they did, how would he react?

"Lucy? Are you coming in?"

Anna's voice recalled her to her surroundings,

and she followed her sister and Sophia up the stairs and into the now-familiar drawing room of Broughton House. The countess looked even frailer than when Lucy had last seen her. Fresh indignation hardened her resolve against the countess's eldest son.

After saying all that was necessary, the countess rang the bell and asked the butler to find the lieutenant. When he returned to say that Broughton was entertaining guests in his laboratory and had asked not to be disturbed, Lucy immediately rose to her feet.

"We are quite willing to go down and see what fascinating experiments he is engaged in, aren't we, Anna?" She patted the countess's pale hand. "You don't need to accompany us, my lady, we know the way."

Lucy led the way down the stairs and out into the garden. The stillroom was dark, but a faint light shone through the window of Broughton's laboratory. Gathering her resolve, Lucy fixed on a smile and went in. Lieutenant Broughton, Major Kurland, and Mr. Stanford were gathered around one of the worktables with their backs to the door. There was no sign of Dr. Redmond.

Major Kurland was the first to look up as Sophia firmly shut the outside door. "Good afternoon, Mrs. Giffin, Miss Harrington, Miss Anna."

Lieutenant Broughton swung around, too.

"Good Lord, I became so engrossed in my conversation that I forgot that you were all coming to see my mother. Please forgive me." He placed a bloodied knife on the table. "Excuse me while I wash my hands."

He moved away, revealing what looked like the remains of a frog pinned out on a wooden board. Lucy swallowed convulsively and Sophia resorted to pressing her handkerchief to her nose.

After a swift glance at the ladies, Mr. Stanford picked up the board. "Shall I bring this over to you as well, Broughton? I don't think our companions will enjoy viewing this as much as Major Kurland and I did."

"Of course! How remiss of me." Broughton chuckled as he washed his hands. "I forget how delicate the female of the species can be."

"And the male," Major Kurland murmured as he moved away to look out of the window. To Lucy's surprise, his complexion held a hint of green. "I've seen far too much of the insides of living beings in my life already to want to see any more."

Anna stepped forward with a determined smile and wandered back toward the cages at the end of the room, coughing as she walked.

"Do you still have the white rat, Lieutenant Broughton?"

"No, Miss Anna."

"Did you set him free?"

Broughton smiled indulgently at her. "I don't think my mother would have appreciated me setting a rat free in her house, do you? The rat helped me prove a very significant point in my latest theory."

"Oh." Anna coughed again and covered her mouth with her gloved hand. "The poor little thing."

The door opened and Dr. Redmond appeared, his medical bag in one hand and a leather-bound journal in the other.

"Lieutenant Broughton, your mother said I would find you all out here. I'm sorry to interrupt, but I wanted you to have the latest edition of the *Fletchers Scientific Journal*. They published that article you wrote."

"They published it?" An incredulous smile broke out on Broughton's face. "That's the first time anything I've written has been accepted."

Anna coughed again. "Congratulations, sir."

"Thank you. It might seem a small matter to you all, but it will help me convince my father that there is a future career available for me that does not involve the military."

Lucy rushed over to Anna. "That is indeed good news, Lieutenant, but might I trouble you for a glass of water for my sister? She seems unable to get rid of this worrying cough."

"Of course, Miss Harrington." Broughton hurried to do Lucy's bidding while Anna continued to cough. When he returned, he studied Anna intently.

"Did the medicine I gave you ease the cough at all?"

"Indeed, it did," Anna replied. "In truth, we were hoping you might give us another bottle as ours is all gone."

"Of course, Miss Anna. I'll fetch one from the stillroom for you myself."

"That would be very kind of you, Lieutenant." Lucy smiled at him. "A dose of that excellent rose-hip medicine would be most appreciated."

"Then I'll go and get you a bottle right now."

"There's no need." Dr. Redmond joined the conversation. "I happen to have a bottle of that here in my bag. I meant to return it to you last time I was here."

He produced a brown bottle from his bag and shook it before pouring a dose into a silver measuring cup and holding it out to Anna. As she slowly brought it to her lips, Dr. Redmond continued talking.

"I found this bottle beside Oliver's bedside. I'm fairly certain it came from the same batch Hester Macleod made."

"No!" The lieutenant moved so quickly that Lucy gasped as he dashed the cup out of Anna's hand. The dark red liquid splashed over her blue muslin skirt, staining the fabric like blood. "Don't drink that!"

Major Kurland stepped in front of Anna. "Whatever has come over you? Why shouldn't she drink it, Broughton?"

"Because . . ."

Robert picked up the bottle and examined it. "Please continue, Broughton. We're all very interested in hearing what you have to say."

"It might have spoiled. It's better to give Miss Anna a new bottle."

"Spoiled?" Robert brought the open bottle to his nose and slowly inhaled. "It smells perfectly fine to me." He paused, holding Broughton's gaze. "If you don't want Miss Anna to endanger herself tasting it, how about me?"

"I'd rather take that risk myself." Broughton held out his hand. "Give it to me. My grandmother's potions are not always safe."

"Your grandmother didn't make this one." Robert checked the label. "You and Hester Macleod did; however, I agree that it's probably not fit to drink."

Broughton lowered his hand. "Whatever do you mean?"

"I think you know."

"You'll have to be more specific, Kurland."

Robert withdrew a piece of paper from his pocket and squinted down at the cramped handwriting. "According to the man who studied it for me, it does indeed contain rose hip, honey, and other palliatives that one usually finds in a syrup of this kind. Unfortunately, it also contains something else."

Broughton rounded on Dr. Redmond. "What did you do?"

"I did nothing, I merely—"

"Don't lie to me!" He turned back to Robert and the ladies. "I had hoped to keep this a secret, but Dr. Redmond has gone beyond the pale! I have in my possession a bottle of digitalis I retrieved from my grandmother's reticule that he gave her that caused her heart failure!"

Robert leaned back against the table. "If that is truly the case, Broughton, why didn't you take your findings to the coroner and the magistrate at Bow Street?"

"Because Dr. Redmond didn't work alone." His features twisted. "He led my poor brother astray. He and Oliver were involved in a sinful relationship. I suspect that when Oliver asked him for his help to dispose of his grandmother and myself, Dr. Redmond was too weak to disagree."

"That's not true! I—"

Robert held up his hand and Dr. Redmond fell silent.

"And what if I say I don't believe that for a minute?"

Broughton went still. "I beg your pardon?"

"I said I don't believe you. Even if Dr. Redmond was involved in the dowager's death, I doubt he had anything to do with Oliver's."

"But he took the innocent bottle of medicine that I made with my own loving hands for my brother and put arsenic in it!"

"I don't think he did. You are the first person to mention arsenic, Broughton." Robert put the bottle back on the table beside him. "And you're the one who uses industrial white arsenic powder to dispose of vermin, aren't you? Did you give it to the dowager, too?"

"Don't be ridiculous, Kurland, why would I do that when Dr. Redmond had already planned to kill her?"

"To make sure she died at Almack's? I also understand from Mr. Stanford that a new test has recently been developed by a Mr. James Marsh that can specifically detect arsenic poisoning in a body."

"That's not correct," Broughton snapped. "No such test exists."

"But it does. Mr. Stanford has the research papers with him if you care to take a look. The test performed on the dowager's body was quite conclusive. Did you dissolve the powder in the orgeat as well as the digitalis?"

Broughton raised an eyebrow. "One might imagine that you injured more than your leg at Waterloo, Kurland. Your mind appears to be quite unhinged."

"I almost wish that were true, Broughton, but the fact is that you poisoned your grandmother in order to gain access to her finances, and science can prove it."

"It can prove she had arsenic in her body. It can't prove that I put it there."

"I have a suggestion of how he *did* put it there." Miss Harrington stepped forward. "The dowager countess took snuff. She took a large pinch just before she drank the orgeat and died."

The slightly smug look of satisfaction on Broughton's face confirmed to Robert that Miss Harrington's suspicion might be correct.

"Is that snuffbox listed amongst the dowager's possessions, Miss Harrington?"

"I believe it went missing."

Robert studied Broughton's face. "One wonders if it ended up somewhere in here. Perhaps the magistrate can check. From what Oliver told me, you considered him to be vermin as well."

"He had unnatural appetites. No man of worth can accept that. He was inherently weak."

"What do you mean?"

"I'm not some emotional fool, Kurland. I made sure I studied my brother's abnormalities in the same scientific manner as I endeavor to solve every problem."

"And what exactly did that entail?"

"You systematically poisoned him!" Dr. Redmond shouted. "I've seen his body, Broughton. He has all the symptoms of chronic arsenic use, white lines on his nails, scaly skin, and—"

"And what, Doctor? He was *weak*. I proved it."

"I don't understand," Robert said slowly. "You used your brother in a scientific experiment?"

Broughton exhaled. "I suppose I might as well reveal the whole to you. I conceived of a way to determine if Oliver's *weaknesses* affected his strength as a man. By giving him small regular doses of arsenic, I was able to note the progression of his ailments and compare him to my test subject—me."

"You're saying that you took arsenic, too?"

"Yes." Broughton looked impatient. "For the study to work, I needed to have data from a normal man such as myself."

"But you're still alive," Miss Harrington said.

"Exactly, which proved my theory. I must admit I've suffered some ill effects of ingesting the poison, but unlike Oliver I *survived,* proving he was too morally and physically weak to endure the poison."

Before Robert could even begin to frame a reply, Dr. Redmond pushed past him and stood in front of Broughton.

"And you were intending to publish these so-called results, were you?" His voice was shaking and his hands were clenched into fists. Robert readied himself to intervene.

"Of course not. They were merely for my own satisfaction."

"Even though your logic is flawed and your results are laughable?"

"That is an illogical conclusion fueled by your own innate weaknesses, Doctor."

"It is damn well not. You forgot to take one thing into account in your so-called fair and even trial. Oliver was a slight, slender man and you are probably double his weight. Of *course* the poison affected him more quickly than it did you!"

"I—" Broughton shook his head. "Damnation, you're *right*. I didn't think of that, and there is no way I can go back and reconfigure my results."

Dr. Redmond lunged at him and it took both Robert and Andrew to pull him away. "Oliver is dead, you bastard, and all you care about is your ridiculous experiment!"

Robert patted Dr. Redmond on the shoulder. "Don't worry, we'll find justice for Oliver in the courts."

"I doubt it." Broughton brushed down his disarranged coat and cravat. "Who is going to take me to court? In order to prosecute me, a member of my own family has to place evidence against me at the Bow Street Magistrate's Court. Neither my mother nor my father will want to do that. In truth, they might even be grateful to me. I've disposed of a tyrant *and* a pervert and cleansed our family name."

Robert glanced over at Andrew, who nodded.

"Unfortunately, he is correct. By law, only the

family of the deceased can decide to take the matter further."

Broughton smiled. "Then perhaps we might all agree to put this unfortunate matter behind us? The dowager and Oliver will be received into the family tomb at our country church, and no one will be any the wiser."

With great difficulty, Robert restrained himself from planting Broughton a facer.

"I think you're forgetting something."

"What would that be?"

"Lady Bentley."

Irritation flickered behind Broughton's brown gaze. "What about her?"

"Mr. Bentley intends to prosecute you for selling a set of rubies that didn't belong to you and for murdering his mother."

"You can't be serious."

"Oh, but I am. He has evidence to prove both, and even if his case doesn't succeed, it will draw attention to you and your family and the current state of your finances." Robert paused. "I've already told Mr. Bentley that I will stand as a witness for him. And I cannot guarantee that under oath I won't reveal the reasons why I believe you killed your own brother and grandmother as well."

"You—"

Broughton leaped at Robert and brought him crashing down to the ground, his hands wrapped around Robert's neck. Even as he fought to get free, Robert was aware of Broughton's superior strength and his own frightening inability to throw the man off.

"Let him go!"

Just as he recognized Miss Harrington's voice there was a crack and Broughton slumped over him, dousing Robert in the vilest tasting liquid he had ever imagined. By the time someone rolled Broughton off him, Robert lay in a puddle of rodent parts, broken glass, and embalming fluid.

"Are you all right, Major?"

Miss Harrington knelt beside Major Kurland and considered his dazed expression.

He gingerly sat up and clutched his head. "Was that completely necessary?"

"I thought you were going to die. I picked up the heaviest thing I could find and hit the lieutenant on the head with it."

"Thank you."

"You are most welcome." She glanced to the side and bit her lip. "Lieutenant Broughton is still unconscious. Mr. Stanford has sent for the magistrate."

"Let's hope Mr. Bentley did his part and gave his information to Bow Street in time."

"We can but hope." She handed him her dainty handkerchief. "You might wish to wipe your face." She shuddered. "There are *things* on it."

This time he accepted her assistance to get to

his feet and then sat down at one of the workbenches. He stretched out his injured leg and occasionally rubbed his thigh, but apart from the throb of his head, he didn't seem to be in too much pain.

He lowered his voice. "May I suggest that Dr. Redmond escort Miss Anna home?"

Lucy cast a distracted glance at her sister, who was talking animatedly to Mr. Stanford. "Perhaps we should all go."

"No, I need Stanford to stay. As a respected lawyer he'll be invaluable in convincing the magistrate that we have a case."

"Then Sophia could take Anna home."

"I doubt she'll leave without Stanford."

"I suppose you want me to leave as well."

"As you were the one who knocked Broughton out, I believe you should stay to protect my reputation, Miss Harrington."

"Then I'll try and persuade Anna and the doctor to depart before Lieutenant Broughton regains consciousness. I suspect Dr. Redmond might need to leave Town in rather a hurry."

"I don't like him getting away with this, but he does have some excuse."

She blinked at him. "That was my earlier contention, Major. I'm glad you have come around to my way of thinking."

"How could I not?" He smiled at her. She turned away in some confusion to find Anna, and send her and the doctor on their way. As she closed the door behind them, she considered what to do next. Should she return to the major's side, or join Sophia and Mr. Stanford, who were talking intently to each other?

Another slight motion caught her gaze and she turned to see Lieutenant Broughton reaching upward for the brown bottle of cough medicine that sat on the worktop.

"No!" she shouted, and ran toward him, but it was too late, he swallowed the contents of the bottle and let it smash on the floor beside him. Within seconds his smug expression disappeared, and he curled up into a ball and writhed on the floor screaming.

Lucy took a step backward and then another, her hands pressed to her mouth.

"Miss Harrington."

She turned blindly and threw herself against Major Kurland's chest. He wrapped one arm around her shoulders.

"Come away, it's all right. I have you safe, come away."

She closed her eyes tightly and let him draw her backward out of the building and into another. She only wished she could stop up her ears from hearing the lieutenant's continual screams as the poison tore through him.

The warmth and the scent of tropical flowers and damp earth made her aware that they were in the conservatory. She was also aware that Major Kurland continued to hold her within the circle of his arms. It was surprisingly comfortable. Her head fitted nicely under his chin and, beneath the embalming fluid, he smelled pleasantly of bay soap and a hint of cigarillo smoke.

She looked to her left and discovered that Mr. Stanford had gathered Sophia into his arms and was dropping little kisses over her hair and forehead.

"Oh," she whispered. "That's the way of it."

And that was what Major Kurland had meant when he'd suggested that Mr. Stanford wasn't for her. She watched for a moment longer, until Sophia lifted her head and kissed Mr. Stanford back. She'd been so caught up in solving the mysterious deaths with Major Kurland that she'd completely missed the growing romance between Sophia and Mr. Stanford.

Very carefully, she placed both her hands on Major Kurland's chest and pushed backward until she could look up into his dark blue gaze.

"You can release me now."

"As long as you are all right."

"I'm quite recovered. That was horrible."

"I know." He grimaced. "I should never have left that bottle out on the worktop."

"You couldn't have known he'd be prepared to do *that*. What an agonizing way to die." She shuddered and his arm tightened around her waist again. "He was quite mad, wasn't he?"

"I believe he was."

"Poor Lady Broughton. She's lost both her sons now."

"Indeed."

A commotion in the garden made her look toward the open door of the conservatory.

"I should imagine that's the magistrate."

"Yes."

She risked another look upward and found he was studying her intently.

"Major Kurland, shouldn't you be going to help them?"

"Yes, I suppose I should."

"Then—"

He slowly released her, his hands running down from her shoulders to her hands. "May I suggest you and Mrs. Giffin return to the main house? The magistrate will probably need to speak to you."

"Yes, Major." She hesitated. "Are you quite recovered from your fall? You look a little dazed."

"I'm fine." He shook himself down like a horse. "Please go into the house."

Lucy watched him walk away from her, his expression resolute. Mr. Stanford followed him, leaving her alone with Sophia.

"Lucy?"

"Yes, love?"

"Are you all right?"

"I believe I am." She let out a shaky breath. "Perhaps this is the best way for this to end."

"With everyone dead like in a Shakespearean tragedy? Although Andrew did say that securing a conviction against Lieutenant Broughton would still have been almost impossible."

"Then I suppose we should be glad that the lieutenant decided to take his own life." Lucy shuddered. "Although it is a *horrible* way to die."

Sophia came close enough to pat her on the shoulder. "More of a Greek tragedy, then?"

"I'm sure the gentlemen will see it like that." Lucy buttoned up her pelisse with hands that still shook. "I must write a note to Mr. Bentley and tell him what happened. I'm sure he will be relieved to hear that his mother's death was not his fault after all."

"*And* that he can drop his lawsuit and bury his mother in her rubies."

"That reminds me, I must return them to him before I leave London with the box tucked in my baggage."

"You're not leaving yet, are you?" Sophia held her at arm's length. "The Season has barely begun!"

"I appreciate everything that you and Mrs. Hathaway have done for me, Sophia, but I don't think I want a husband anymore. I just want to go home."

Sophia held her gaze. "This isn't because of Mr. Stanford, is it?"

"Not at all, why?"

"Because I would hate for him to come between

us." Sophia drew an unsteady breath. "I know this isn't a good time to tell you this, but Mr. Stanford just asked me to marry him."

Lucy smiled. "One would hope so, considering how he was behaving."

"Are you angry with me?"

"Why would I be angry? You are perfectly suited. I wish you nothing but happiness."

"I'm so glad that you said that. I've been feeling ridiculously guilty." She embraced Lucy.

"Then don't. If he hadn't been intending to propose to you after all that kissing, I would've thought him a rake."

Sophia smiled. "You saw that? Then perhaps I should be asking you the same question about Major Kurland."

"Whatever do you mean?"

"Mr. Stanford wasn't the only man behaving in such an intimate fashion."

Lucy went still. "Major Kurland was merely shielding me from the horrors of Lieutenant Broughton's death."

"I'm sure he was, but I did happen to notice that he wasn't averse to dropping a kiss on the top of your head." Sophia turned toward the door, leaving Lucy frozen to the spot. "Now perhaps we'd better do what Major Kurland suggested and return to the house. I'm sure Lady Broughton will need our support."

Chapter 19

Robert cleared his throat and attempted to ease the collar of his tightly buttoned-up uniform coat. He'd been "invited" to visit the Earl of Clavelly at home to discuss the matter of the Broughton murders, and more importantly, he suspected, to provide an explanation as to how the earl's nieces had become embroiled in the matter. The invitation had all the impact of a royal summons and had sent a reluctant Robert straight around to the Clavelly mansion. He was rather reminded of being hauled in front of his commanding officer for a severe dressing-down.

"I've spoken to the coroner and the magistrate at Bow Street, my lord. As the Countess of Broughton is too distraught to be asked if she wishes to pursue the case, the matter will remain private until the earl returns from India."

"Has the earl been informed of what has happened?" The Earl of Clavelly sat forward, his hands folded together on his desk. His resemblance to his younger brother, the rector of Kurland St. Mary, was far more noticeable when he wasn't smiling.

"I believe he knows about the dowager's death, but I doubt the countess has had the opportunity to write to tell him that both his sons have died." Robert sighed. "I can't believe that Broughton survived ten years of war, and then decided to do *this*."

"I understand he was in considerable debt."

"That's correct, my lord. From what I've been able to ascertain, he invested a lot of money in making the right impression on the scientific community, family money that wasn't actually his to use. When he ran out of ready cash, he chose to gamble with his grandmother's remaining capital and matters simply went from bad to worse."

In order to safeguard the Countess of Broughton from gossip, he and Andrew had decided not to mention the more bizarre aspects of Broughton's attempts at experimentation and focus instead on his need to gain control of his grandmother's fortune to pay his debts.

"Perhaps, as a family friend, you might write to the earl and deliver the bad news. I'm sure the countess would appreciate it."

"I'll certainly do that, my lord, but as the earl is currently at sea, I have no notion of where such a letter should be delivered to him. I assume I could have it sent to the shipping company and ask them to help." He paused. "I'm also not sure how much to reveal. Such news might be better delivered in person."

"I'd stick to the basic fact, Kurland, that two

men are dead. If his lordship wishes to learn the full story, I'm certain you'll make sure to be on hand to provide him with it."

"Yes, my lord."

The Earl of Clavelly drew in a breath and looked Robert right in the eye. "I do not appreciate my nieces' names being dragged into such a scandal. I would appreciate your assurance that if you must speak publicly on this matter, you will do everything in your power to refrain from mentioning that they were there when Lieutenant Broughton killed himself." The earl shuddered. "To allow such delicate females to witness such a thing was very poor form on your part, Kurland, very poor form indeed."

"I could hardly keep them away, sir, seeing as Miss Anna Harrington was integral to the success of unmasking Broughton, and Miss Harrington was the originator of the entire scheme."

The earl scowled. "Your explanation is unacceptable. You should've thought of another way to deal with the issue without involving my nieces."

Robert knew it was pointless to argue. The earl's view would be shared by everyone in polite society and could damage the Harringtons' marital prospects. In his opinion, that was ridiculous, but unfortunately it was also true.

"I understand your position, my lord, and I sincerely apologize for any distress the incident caused to Miss Harrington, Mrs. Giffin, or Miss

Anna Harrington. I will, of course, be offering them my apologies in person."

The earl looked down at the items on his desk and rearranged his pens in a straight line. "I believe you are to receive a title, Major Kurland."

"That is correct. I've been made a baronet."

"I wish to congratulate you on such an honor."

"Thank you, sir," Robert said cautiously.

"And I also wish you to know that having such a rank would make you an acceptable husband for the granddaughter of an earl."

"I beg your pardon?"

The earl sighed. "Let me be frank with you, Major Kurland. Your interest in my niece has not gone unnoticed either by our family or society."

"Which niece would that be, my lord?"

"Don't be coy, Major. You know I am referring to Lucy. I understand from my wife that she has been of great help to you in Kurland St. Mary in the past."

"Yes, but—"

"A man in your position should be thinking about marrying and setting up his nursery. Lucy would make you an admirable wife. You have an honorable name and, more importantly, a title to pass on now."

"That's true, but I'm scarcely in my dotage. I have plenty of time to make a decision of such magnitude."

The earl's eyebrows drew together. "Are you

suggesting you were merely *trifling* with my niece's affections?"

Robert sat up straight. "Good Lord, no, sir."

"Then one can assume that you will be setting your affairs in order and speaking to her father in the very near future." The earl sat back. "Unfortunately, Lucy isn't my daughter, or I'd be expecting an offer for her hand in marriage from you this very day."

"You would?" Robert asked.

He knew that he was being led through a maze constructed by society to trap a man into marriage. It had happened to him once before with Miss Chingford, and he'd be damned if he let it happen again. But how to extricate himself without hurting Miss Harrington's feelings? Good God, was she *expecting* a proposal of marriage from him? He remembered the feel of her in his arms, his sense that she fitted perfectly against him and that he didn't want to let her go. He'd been a fool to expect the *ton* to accept that he could just be friends with an unmarried woman.

Perhaps he'd even been fooling himself. . . .

He rose from his chair. "I'll think on this matter, my lord, and when I have reached a decision I will, of course, consult with Miss Harrington's father."

"I am very pleased to hear it." The earl looked up at him. "And, as you are proving so amenable, there is another favor I require of you. Mrs. Giffin and Lucy have decided to return to Kurland St. Mary. I understand that you are leaving, too. Are you going on horseback?"

"No, my lord. I intend to travel by carriage."

"Good, then you will be able to take them up with you, and offer them your protection on their journey."

Robert saluted and accepted his fate. "I would be delighted to be of assistance, my lord."

Lucy sat on Anna's bed, her hand clasped in her sister's.

"But I don't understand why you have to leave me here all alone, Lucy."

"You are scarcely alone, Anna. You have the Clavelly family to support you through the rest of the Season."

"But it isn't the same as having you here."

Lucy held her sister's gaze. "You said that you wanted to be independent. Here is a perfect opportunity for you to enjoy all the benefits of society without worrying about anyone but yourself."

"But it seems so *selfish*."

"Why? Because I prefer to go home?" Lucy sighed. "I don't enjoy it here. I'm bored pretending to be a young lady at home who isn't expected to have two thoughts in her head. I'm far too used to running a household, caring for the sick and poor, and generally managing people. I miss

Kurland St. Mary. I miss making a difference in people's lives."

"But if you persevered and found the right man—"

"I don't think I will, Anna. Not in London, anyway." Lucy smiled. "And I can be far more useful helping Sophia to arrange her wedding in the village while Mrs. Hathaway completes all the necessary tasks in London. Sophia and Mr. Stanford want to marry fairly quickly."

Anna squeezed her hand. "You are being very brave about Mr. Stanford."

"I do admit that at one point I imagined that Mr. Stanford would make me a good husband, but once I realized he spent his entire year in London, I found myself doubting my decision." She shrugged. "And he and Sophia are so openly in love that I can only wish them the best. I suspect they will be very happy together."

"While you waste away at the rectory doing Father's bidding."

"I'll hardly waste away. There is always so much to do there. At least I won't be bored. And, with Anthony and the twins away, I have more opportunities to visit our neighbors and reacquaint myself with the local gentry." She kissed Anna's cheek. "Don't worry about me, love. I'll be fine. I've gained a new appreciation for my unique position in the village and will not allow Father to stop me from making the best of it anymore. Just promise me that you will enjoy the rest of the Season and find a veritable prince to marry."

Anna held both Lucy's hands and looked apprehensively at her. "Are you quite sure about this?"

"Yes." Lucy smiled at her sister. "I am."

"Then you won't be too pleased by what is happening downstairs right now."

"What do you mean?"

"Uncle David asked Major Kurland to call on him this morning."

"To explain about the Broughton murders?"

"Yes, but also to quiz the major about his intentions toward you."

Lucy shot to her feet. "He wouldn't do that— would he?"

"From the discussion I accidentally overheard yesterday evening, it was very much on his mind even before Aunt Jane insisted he bring the matter up with the major today."

"Oh, no." Lucy groaned. "This is a disaster." She paced the hearthrug. "What if Major Kurland is forced into making an offer for my hand? He'll never forgive me."

"Why would he need to be *forced?* You must stop devaluing yourself, Lucy. He would be lucky to have you!"

"You don't understand. From what he's told me, he was pushed into offering for Miss Chingford by the machinations of her and her mother. I am quite certain he will never allow himself to be put in that position again. It makes everything so *awkward*. I wish my uncle hadn't interfered."

Anna gave an inelegant snort. "You were hoping Major Kurland would make you an offer all by himself?"

"I—" Lucy let out her breath. "No, not at all. I have never met a man less in the mood to be married than Major Kurland." She eyed the door. "Should I go down and try and intervene?"

"No," Anna said firmly. "If you believe Major Kurland will balk at being forced into marrying you, then let him fight his own battles."

"You are right. After his last experience, I doubt he'll be amenable to being coerced into matrimony again. And, as Uncle David is not our father, he can only bring the matter to Major Kurland's attention and not insist."

"Then you have nothing to worry about, do you, love?"

Lucy shook her head. "No, nothing at all."

Sophia Giffin glanced from Robert to Miss Harrington and smiled encouragingly.

"It was very good of Major Kurland to offer to escort us home, wasn't it, Lucy?"

"Indeed."

Miss Harrington continued to look out of the window as if she expected their carriage to be set upon and robbed by highwaymen at any moment. In the three hours they'd been traveling, she'd steadfastly ignored all of Robert's efforts to engage her in conversation. He was beginning to feel rather irritated.

"We'll stop for refreshments at Brentwood and change the horses and have dinner at the Queen's Head in Chelmsford. If the weather holds, we should be back in Kurland St. Mary before midnight," Robert said.

"Thank you, Major," Mrs. Giffin answered him. "I must confess that I am looking forward to seeing my home. My mother will close up our rented house and join me in a few days and then we will start planning the wedding."

"I am delighted to hear it, Mrs. Giffin. I have no doubt that you will make Andrew very happy." He smiled at her. "I have a new land agent *and* a new valet awaiting me at Kurland Hall and I'm equally glad to be returning home."

He glanced over at Miss Harrington, who had not contributed to the conversation. "Do you wish to stay with Mrs. Giffin at Hathaway Hall, Miss Harrington, or shall I leave you at the rectory?"

She didn't turn around. "My father won't be expecting me, so I'll stay with Sophia, thank you, Major."

"If you wish, Miss Harrington, I could stop at the rectory on my way home and let your father know your whereabouts."

She swiveled her head to look at him, her expression alarmed. "Please don't put yourself out on my behalf, Major. There is no need for you to speak to my father at *all*."

He frowned at that, but let the matter rest as the horses slowed to descend the hill that would bring them into Brentwood. When the carriage finally stopped and the steps were let down, he alighted and helped the ladies out.

"Please go ahead. I've engaged a private parlor and ordered a luncheon, Mrs. Giffin."

"How kind of you, Major."

The two ladies went in through the door of the inn and Robert followed, leaving his groom to take the horses around to the mews. The second carriage containing Foley, the baggage, and Mrs. Giffin's maid came through the archway into the stable yard. Robert spent a moment directing the staff around to the kitchens to secure themselves a hot meal. Then he went slowly into the inn, stretching his legs after the all-too-familiar discomfort of traveling on bad roads in a constricted space. He had to conquer his fear and ride again, or he'd end up never going anywhere.

After speaking briefly to the landlord, he made his way to the private room he'd asked for, and went inside to find Miss Harrington standing by the window staring out into the stable yard.

She had taken off her bonnet and was in the process of unbuttoning her pelisse. Her brown hair was braided into a severe coronet on the top of her head without a curl left free to soften her features. It was completely unlike the more fashionable style she'd adopted in London, but he preferred it. She jumped when she saw him and pressed her gloved hand to her bosom.

"Major Kurland, you startled me."

"So I see." He took off his hat and placed it on the table. "Where is Mrs. Giffin?"

"She went to find the innkeeper's wife. She'll be back in a moment."

Silence fell and she turned away from him and began to take off her gloves.

Robert took a deep breath. "Miss Harrington, have I offended you in some way?"

"Not at all, Major. Why would you think that?"

"Because you are behaving very oddly." She didn't reply and he soldiered on. "Did your uncle tell you that he spoke to me yesterday?"

"He did mention that you had called, yes."

"I didn't call, I was ordered to turn up and give an account of myself."

"I assume that he was concerned about Anna and me being exposed to such an unpleasant scene at the Broughtons'."

"He blamed me, and he had a right to do so."

She finally met his gaze. "It was my idea, Major. I told him that."

"I should not have agreed to carry out your plan."

347

"You didn't have to *agree,* Major. Anna and I were quite willing to go ahead and trap Lieutenant Broughton all by ourselves."

"You would not have been so foolish."

"That's hardly the point, is it? As I argued with my uncle, neither you nor Mr. Stanford was responsible for our actions. We aren't *children.*"

"But you are gently brought up young ladies of good family." He cleared his throat. "Which brings me to another matter. It has been brought to my attention, Miss Harrington, that my behavior toward you has given rise to general speculation that I should be asking you to marry me."

"Oh, really?"

"Apparently. So if you believe that I owe you an offer—"

"*Owe* me?"

Her voice had risen, but he was determined to continue. "Yes."

"You don't owe me anything, Major Kurland. I'm not like Miss Chingford. I would *never* marry a man who proposed to me just because he thought he had to."

Her eyes were suspiciously bright and there was a hint of trembling in her normally firm tone that made him take a hasty step toward her, hand outstretched.

"Miss Harrington—"

She gave him a brittle smile. "If you will excuse

me, Major Kurland, I must go and see what is keeping Sophia."

She swept past him, her head held high, and went out slamming the door with unnecessary force behind her.

With a groan, Robert sank into the nearest chair and stared down at his boots. What on earth had he said to put her in such a state? He'd offered to marry her, for God's sake, something he'd sworn never to be coerced into doing again. And he'd only offered because he'd destroyed her chances of meeting a decent man in London by monopolizing her time to investigate a murder. So why did he feel as if she'd slapped his face instead of merely slammed the door?

It made no sense.

He should be relieved.

The good thing was that he had hours of solitude ahead of him in the carriage to consider the error of his ways while Miss Harrington ignored him and Mrs. Giffin made brave, but ineffectual attempts to start conversation. He had a sense that the rest of his much-anticipated journey back to Kurland St. Mary was not going to be a pleasant experience after all.